Five for Silver

a John the Eunuch Mystery

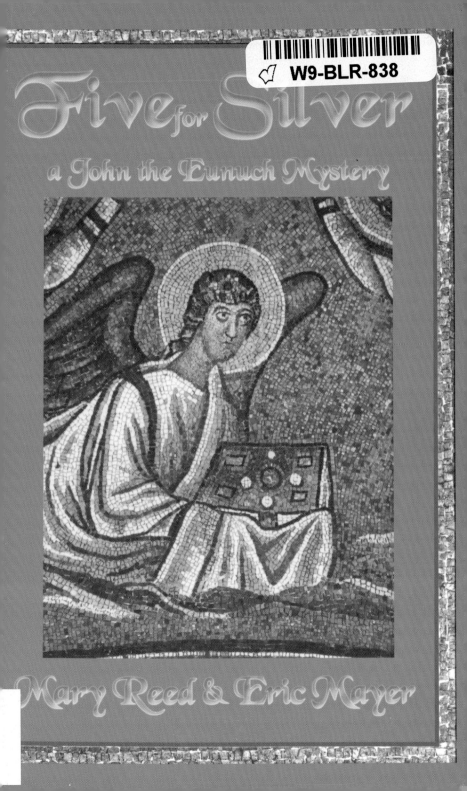

Mary Reed & Eric Mayer

Five for Silver

Five for Silver

Mary Reed & Eric Mayer

Poisoned Pen Press

Poisoned
Pen
Press

Copyright © 2004 by Mary Reed & Eric Mayer

First Trade Paperback Edition 2006

10 9 8 7 6 5 4 3 2 1

Library of Congress Catalog Card Number: 2003115435

ISBN: 1-59058-268-3 (978-1-59058-268-8) Trade Paperback

Poisoned Pen Press
6962 E. First Ave., Ste. 103
Scottsdale, AZ 85251
www.poisonedpenpress.com
info@poisonedpenpress.com

Printed in the United States of America

For our siblings

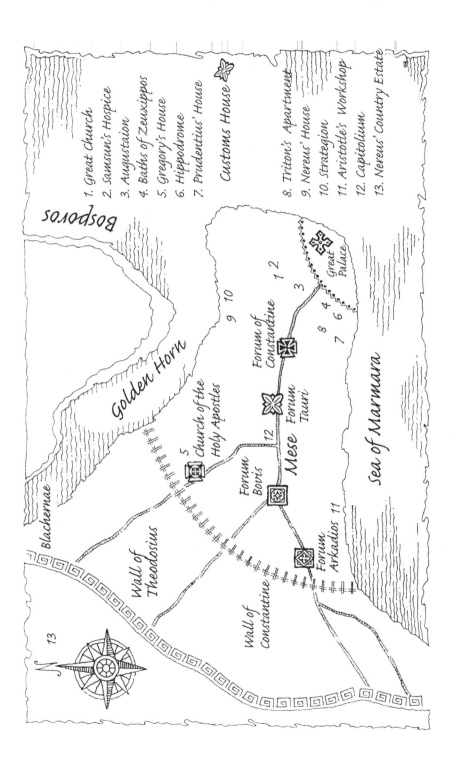

Bosporos

Golden Horn

Blachernae

Wall of Theodosius

Wall of Constantine

Church of the Holy Apostles

Forum Bovis

Forum Tauri

Forum of Constantine

Mese

Forum Arkadios

Great Palace

Sea of Marmara

1. Great Church
2. Samsun's Hospice
3. Augustaion
4. Baths of Zeuxippos
5. Gregory's House
6. Hippodrome
7. Prudentius' House

Customs House

8. Triton's Apartment
9. Nereus' House
10. Strategion
11. Aristotle's Workshop
12. Capitolium
13. Nereus' Country Estate

Prologue

The young man awoke in the embrace of a suffocating nightmare.

To darkness.

A monstrous heaviness bore in on him from above and all sides.

He tried to move. His foot came down on a surface which resisted for an instant, then gave way. Wetness trickled into his boot. The invisible mass pinning him shifted with a soughing noise and the weight of the world settled onto his chest. What felt like an elbow or knee dug into the small of his back.

His eyes were open, but he could see only those ghostly lights that drift beneath closed eyelids.

He couldn't breathe. He struggled to turn his head, to find air. His cheek was brushed by cold, stiff fingers.

Then he understood.

He was buried with the dead.

The miasma of death filled his nostrils, flooded his lungs. He tried to cry out for help, but could only manage to spit up a choking sob. In the blackness, his flailing hand encountered the rounded shape of a skull.

More than once as he had walked through the city he had stepped into the street, fastidiously distancing himself from a corpse sprawled beneath a colonnade or crumpled in a doorway. Here the dead pressed themselves against him with obscene intimacy, as if he were already one of them.

Perhaps he was.

From above, from the world of the living, came a muffled shout.

"Lies! More lies!"

A cascade of liquid trickled across his back. Blood?

No. Rivulets of fire, burning like hot coals. He must be alive. An incorporeal shade could never feel such blistering agony.

"Lye. More lye," the shouter somewhere beyond the darkness repeated.

The young man clenched his fists, arched his back, and began to fight his way up toward air. He scrabbled higher, pushing with his feet wherever he could find purchase on a head or shoulder blade, pulling himself up through the nightmare of tangled limbs.

His hands slid against liquescent flesh, boiled off bones by lye poured endlessly into the heaped corpses. Was he at the bottom of a pit, or in one of the towers that Justinian had ordered be filled with Constantinople's dead? Clutching at the darkness his hand fastened unexpectedly on a face.

He gagged convulsively.

For a heartbeat he lay still. The blazing fire inside his chest was as intense as that outside. Had he swallowed lye?

Ignoring the pain, he snaked one hand upwards and grabbed a cold, rigid arm. Once it might have been part of a prosperous merchant, a starving beggar, a Christian, a pagan.

To the young man, it was just another rung on the ladder back to life.

He forced himself on, pulling, slithering, pushing with feet and elbows.

A lifetime passed. Then, abruptly, he could see the vaguest wash of light, the merest suggestion of shapes.

He lunged upwards. A hand reached down. He grasped it.

Decayed flesh slid off the bone.

A final spasm propelled him into light. He saw then that he held a ragged strip of skin entangled with a silver ring, the gift of the pit.

"I'm alive!" he screamed as he looked up, just in time to receive a bucket of lye in the face.

Chapter One

John, Lord Chamberlain to Emperor Justinian, followed the physician Gaius through the crowded corridors of Samsun's Hospice.

John was there because his elderly servant Peter had experienced a vision.

Gaius, a stout, balding man, plowed ahead, more than once treading on outstretched limbs and sprawled bodies. John picked his way more carefully, but could not prevent the gold-embroidered hem of his heavy blue robe from brushing against the sick who overflowed from crowded rooms into the hallways.

It made him uneasy because it seemed disrespectful. Many of Gaius' patients were in their final hours; their surroundings were insult enough. For lack of sufficient pallets, the hospice corridors had simply been strewn with straw. The sooty plastered walls displayed crosses at frequent intervals.

John remarked on this to Gaius.

"Many take comfort from them," he replied. "Why anyone should find comfort in a depiction of suffering is beyond my learning. Perhaps it reminds them their ills could be even worse? Then too, some rely on charms and amulets for protection against the plague."

Such beliefs puzzled John as well. Like Gaius, he was a Mithran, among the few who clung to an ancient, pagan religion.

It was an allegiance which could never be spoken aloud in the court of the Christian emperor.

"Tell me about this vision, John," Gaius continued. "Why did Peter suppose it was anything more than a dream?"

"Because he was wide awake when the angel appeared."

"But an angel? Surely that proves it was a dream? And how did he know it was an angel? What does an angel look like?"

"A man, apparently, with a glowing visage and surrounded by radiance. Peter said he had already put out the lamp and shuttered the window, and yet, when the angel appeared at the foot of his bed, he could clearly see the night soil pot in the far corner."

"I'd be interested in a close look at an angel, but then I doubt a specimen will ever turn up in our mortuary." Gaius sounded wistful.

They turned down another corridor more congested with patients than the last. Most of the sufferers displayed the grotesque swellings and black, gangrenous carbuncles characteristic of plague.

John avoided staring at the sick, but he could not shut out the sounds of suffering that came from every direction. Soft whimpers and moans, wracking sobs and screams filled the air. Occasionally he could make out muttered prayers, hoarse curses. If one did not listen too attentively, the cacophony merged into an almost soothing susurration akin to waves breaking against a rocky shore.

"In what language do angels converse, John? Greek? Or are they Latin speakers like the emperor? Not to say that an angel might speak any language we would know. How many is it you command? Four? Or perhaps is it more a matter of which tongue they choose to use?"

"You'd be an excellent theologian, Gaius. However, according to Peter the angel did not use any particular language. Peter was so amazed, he mentioned that specifically more than once. As he described it, the words formed in his head without his strange visitor making a sound."

"And what words are sufficient to bring the Lord Chamberlain into a place full of the pestilence?"

"'Gregory. Murder. Justice.'"

"It sounds as if you believe this strange tale."

"What matters is that Peter believes it. I've rarely seen him so agitated."

Gaius' broad forehead wrinkled. He began to speak, then paused. "Do you know this Gregory?"

"Only by sight. Occasionally he came to meet Peter at my house, but he's never entered it so far as I know. They've been meeting every week since Peter's been in my employ and perhaps before then too. A few days ago, Gregory failed to appear at the Forum Constantine as they'd arranged."

"So he is an old friend of Peter's. Do you know anything else about the man?"

"I gather he and Peter served in the army together years ago. It's my belief that Gregory hasn't fared well since those days. I've noticed the evening before these visits, Peter always seems to find stale honey cakes or moldy bread unfit for a Lord Chamberlain to consume, as he puts it." A brief smile illuminated John's lean face. "He asks my permission to take these scraps with him to give to Gregory, rather than just throw them away. Naturally I always say yes."

Gaius laughed. "I wouldn't want your job, John, serving both an emperor and an elderly cook." He stopped at an half-open door at the end of the hallway. "We've turned the old cistern beneath the hospice into a mortuary."

John found himself studying his friend closer. When had Gaius gained so much in girth? The physician had always been stout. Now he looked obese, his stride laborious. He had obviously resumed his worship of Bacchus. Yet could anyone blame him, given the terrible scenes the man witnessed every hour spent at the hospice, ministering to patients who persisted in dying in horrible agonies, no matter how much Gaius and his colleagues labored to save them?

"You've been examining me ever since you arrived, John," Gaius said in an irritated tone. "Do you think I haven't noticed? Don't worry, I haven't caught the plague. There's no danger from working with my patients so far as I can tell. In fact, we don't even known how the illness is contracted. It seems entirely capricious. We see carters bringing the sick here day after day and they stay perfectly healthy, even though the rest of the time they're hauling the remains of cautious folks found rotting away behind locked doors and boarded windows. Mind the stairs, John. They're slippery."

Before they could step through the doorway, a dark-haired young man with a face the color of bread dough came running down the hall toward them, stepping at a dangerous speed in and out among the haphazardly arranged patients blocking his course. He came to an awkward, stumbling halt.

"Are you one of the new volunteers come to help us?" The young man waved frantically at nothing in particular and thrust his pasty face as close to John's as he could contrive, considering he was a head shorter. His hot breath smelled of wine. It was obvious he had over-indulged. John drew back slightly.

"Take care, Farvus!" Gaius said. "This man isn't here to help you burst pustules. This is John, Lord Chamberlain to Justinian."

"John! Of course! The friend you've spoken about. The one the gossips call John the Eunuch." The young man leaned toward John again. "Well, John, at least you don't have to worry about bringing children into this terrible world."

"You're impertinent! As a matter of fact, the Lord Chamberlain has a daughter. Go about your business immediately," Gaius barked at the young man, before turning toward John.

"Now you're examining me," John observed.

"Do you mind if I don't discipline the fellow? We need all the help we can get. Death tends to make people forget who holds authority or the proper manner in which to address them. I've even seen aristocrats begging slaves for a last cup of water."

John shrugged. "Shall we attend to our own business?"

They descended the steep, stone stairway into a cool atmosphere redolent of corruption underlain by a rich, unmentionable sweetness. John would have choked, had the smell of death not become so familiar in the past weeks. Resinous torch smoke massed beneath the vaulted roof.

"You could preserve fish down here with all this smoke," Gaius remarked. "It does mask the smell a little. They say Hippocrates drove the plague out of Athens with fire. Perhaps what we need is a riot. If the Blues and Greens put the torch to the city again, it might do some good for a change."

John did not reply, but glanced at the large club leaning against the wall at the foot of the stairway.

"Rats," Gaius explained.

His companion looked around the dimly lit vault. The dead, laid out in tidy rows between the columns holding up the roof of the disused cistern, were as silent as they were still.

The air, however, was murmurous.

John thought of the spring meadows alive with bees behind Plato's Academy, where he had studied as a young man. It reminded him of the ancient belief equating bees with souls. However, in the cistern of the dead it would not be bees which buzzed, John reminded himself as he slapped at a fly that hit his cheek like a fat raindrop. Perhaps flies were more likely vessels for souls than bees. They seemed to emerge from death as if from thin air.

Gaius led the way through flickering shadows. The recumbent forms they passed might have been statues, their eyes as blank as those of the marble philosophers and mythological figures decorating the city's public baths.

"These patients all died from the plague," Gaius noted. "However, there are still a few ingenious souls in Constantinople who manage to find other ways to depart. We've placed them together at the back in case the City Prefect's men show any interest. Which they haven't so far."

An archway, low enough to force John to bend his head, opened into a small chamber housing perhaps a score of bodies.

Gaius scanned them as if he were a shopkeeper surveying the stock on his shelves. "Here's someone who drowned. Probably not of interest? And this man died in a fall, although—"

"Never mind. Gaius. I've found Gregory."

John gazed down at an aged man with a sharp, beaked nose. Not hawk-like. More like a fallen sparrow, dusty, gray, and still. "How did he die?"

Gaius lumbered over to John's side. "Ah yes. This one was, in fact, murdered. A knife blade expertly inserted between the ribs and straight into the heart. I couldn't have done it more accurately. It was an easier death than the plague."

"Do you recall where he was found?"

"Not exactly. It was in one of those streets running off the Mese, I believe. I'll look it up in the records. But this isn't the man you're seeking, John. And just as well, if you ask me, because otherwise we would have to start believing in supernatural visitations."

"It's definitely Gregory."

Gaius shook his head. "From what you told me, that can't be. Let me show you something."

A long wooden table against the far wall held a number of baskets. Gaius rummaged in one and then another.

"It's astonishing," he remarked as he searched. "The dead are piling up so fast in the streets thieves don't have time to rob them all. I've been storing such items as came in with or on the departed although no one's claimed anything yet. There are even a couple of full coin pouches, if you can believe such a thing. Ah, here it is."

He flourished the scroll he had retrieved from the last basket investigated.

"I'm absolutely certain that is the man I saw come to my door to visit Peter from time to time," John said.

"Impossible." Gaius handed the scroll to John. It bore an official seal. "This was found on the murdered man. Your impression is that Peter's friend has endured hard times, but that can't be said of this fellow, judging from the documents he carried. Strangely enough, though, his name is also Gregory. However, I can guarantee he certainly wasn't the sort to make a habit of visiting servants, old friends or not, let alone taking charitable gifts of food from them. This particular Gregory was a high-ranking customs official and therefore a man of considerable means."

Chapter Two

"And you're certain he didn't suffer, master? That was surely heaven's mercy." Peter made the sign of his religion.

John paused, anticipating further questions about Gregory's death, but Peter said nothing. The only sound in the garden was the chuckling gurgle of water spilling into the pool from the mouth of an eroded and unidentifiable stone creature set in its center.

"You should rest, Peter," John continued. "Hypatia can prepare the evening meal."

"If you please, master, I would prefer to continue with my duties. Hypatia sometimes over-spices the food. Besides, she has enough to do here."

It was true. Since the young Egyptian woman had come to work for him a few years earlier, John had noticed many more herbs and flowers stealing in amidst bushes and shrubbery. Most of the new plantings were a mystery to the Lord Chamberlain, who could identify the workshop that created a silver chalice by its imperial stamp, but knew nothing of horticulture.

"Sit down, Peter."

John spoke quietly, but it was clearly an order rather than an invitation. Peter took a hobbling step over to the marble bench facing the pool and lowered himself stiffly. John sat down next to him. The clusters of white blossoms adorning the garden's single olive tree had begun to open, yet seemed to emit none of their familiar fragrance. The air held the only too familiar charnel smell, but faintly, as if it had drifted over the roof into this inner space or still clung to John's garments.

"The loss of an old friend is always deeply upsetting," John said. "I'm sorry I had to be the one to confirm your suspicions."

His elderly servant shook his head. "I've known Gregory was dead ever since the Lord's messenger told me so. I've already prayed for my friend's soul." Peter's army boot face, brown, mottled, and cracked, appeared calm although his eyes were glassy in a hint of tears not quite controlled.

John averted his gaze and instead stared at the cascading water sending ripples across the pool. "Are you certain Gregory didn't give you some indication he was in danger? Perhaps not in so many words? Some strange business he'd mentioned to you? Something that could pose a risk to him? Try to remember."

"It is merely as I explained, master. The angel appeared and—"

"Peter, consider how this must appear. You announce a man has been murdered, but have no idea who committed the deed or why. I look for this man and find someone has in fact thrust a blade into his heart. What am I to think? More importantly, what might others, who do not know you as well as I do, think?"

Peter sighed, but remained silent.

"Tell me about this angel again," John continued patiently. "You say he looked like a man?"

"Yes, but uncommonly tall and fair of face, and clothed in shining robes. There was a glow about him as bright as the setting sun and his eyes burned like the sacred lamps in the Great Church."

Grasping at wisps of straws, John asked if Peter had recognized the strange visitor.

"Only what he was, master."

John had questioned Hypatia, who had neither seen nor heard anything unusual the evening before. He had inspected the heavy, nail-studded main door for signs of forcible entry, checked all the windows overlooking the cobbled square the building faced, had even made a circuit around the inner garden, examining its soft earth to ascertain if someone might have entered by crossing the roof and dropping down into the shrubbery. Nothing untoward could be found.

It was obvious the heavenly intruder had got into the house by way of Peter's imagination.

Peter looked placid enough now, but he had been distraught and inconsolable when he related his tale that morning. John had gone out immediately to investigate the matter and thereby calm his servant's fears.

Instead he had confirmed them.

Further, Peter had made it clear he expected John to find the culprit. A nearly impossible task. Crimes committed in the street were typically solved when the perpetrator happened to be caught in the act by the City Prefect's men. However, John thought, Peter's peculiar foreknowledge of the murder indicated it could be more than a commonplace crime.

"I don't know much about this friend of yours, except that you've been meeting him now and again for years. Tell me about his history, Peter. There may be something in it that will help me find his murderer. For a start, what did Gregory do for a living?"

Peter looked away from John, toward the dark glass of the pool. "I can't say."

"He never told you in all the years you knew him?"

Peter confirmed it was the case. "We never spoke much about what we were doing now. As old friends do, we talked about past times. Our days in the army, mostly. Also the writings of the great church men. He had a wide knowledge of John Chrysostom. We've had some very lively discussions about his homilies."

John noted the catch in Peter's voice, caught the quick blink of his glistening eyes. Those theological discussions would be no more and the thought hung in the air as clearly as if it had been spoken aloud. "You never visited Gregory's house?"

"No, master. We usually arranged to meet at a specific place. In the Forum Constantine, outside the Great Church, or perhaps at the Church of the Holy Apostles. Sometimes we met in front of the house here."

"Never at his home?"

"He never said where he lived." Peter lowered his voice before he continued, although there was no one to overhear. "I think he was ashamed, master. When we were in the army I was a mere cook, not a soldier like him. Yet he befriended me anyway. After his discharge, I suspect he didn't prosper. Outside the army there's much more call for cooks than soldiers, especially ones who are older. The excubitors would never have accepted him, for example. His position wasn't as comfortable as mine, or so I guessed. I never questioned him. I wanted to spare his feelings, you see."

Yet, John thought, the document the dead man had been carrying suggested he was a prosperous customs official.

"Did you ever observe anything that might have given you an idea of his occupation? His clothing, ink under his fingernails, a wine stain on a sleeve, a particular expression he used?"

"Those are things you would doubtless have noticed, master, but I did not," Peter replied sorrowfully. "To me he was just an old friend. If he didn't want to tell me about his humble station in life, I was happy to accept that."

Would it be necessary for Peter to know about his friend's circumstances?

Not yet, John decided.

Besides, there might be some mistake, even though he was certain the man he had seen at the hospice was the same man who had met Peter on numerous occasions.

Instead he asked Peter when he had last seen Gregory.

"It was the day Anatolius visited you with that perfumed young versifier."

John suppressed a smile. "Crinagoras the poet, you mean?"

"I am sorry, master. My mind is calm enough, but I fear my tongue is not."

"Never mind, Peter. It is to be expected. Were you meeting Gregory before you came to work here?"

"Yes, for many years. After we left the army I did lose track of him, as so often happens. I never expected we'd meet again. Then one morning, during the time I served in Lady Anna's household, I saw him in the market by the Strategion."

Peter's voice strengthened as he recalled the event. "It was a raw day. I had been contemplating going to market, but when I woke up the rain was beating so hard at my window I decided to put it off a few hours. Then the sun showed itself. It was only a brief gleam, as if to remind me I shouldn't be neglecting my duties. If the clouds hadn't parted for just that instant, I might never have seen Gregory again. Or, for that matter, if Lady Anna had not instructed me to purchase leeks. It happened that only one vendor had leeks that morning and Gregory was seeking the very same vegetable. Imagine that, master. If he had been hungry for, say, figs, well…."

"If you think about it that way, Peter, all our lives are a quite improbable progression of circumstances."

"It was a miracle, master," Peter replied firmly. "Imagine the odds against two old friends meeting in that fashion in this teeming city. I believe if Lady Anna had wished me to buy figs, it was ordained Gregory would have had the same notion and so we would still have met again."

John wondered if Peter and Gregory had pondered this interesting question during one of their conversations. He thought the story revealed more about Peter than Gregory. "You mentioned you met Gregory during your army days. Where was that?"

"Isauria. We were both in our twenties. This was after Emperor Anastasius put down the rebellion. Our task was to clear the Isaurians out of the mountains where they'd retreated. It took years."

"I have heard it is a rugged country and breeds rugged men."

"Indeed it is and does, master. The mountains are made of what looks like bleached, crumbling stone. They don't look natural at all. Traversing them was like picking a way though a ruined fortress left by some vanished race of giants."

Peter fell silent. His eyes sparkled. He had returned to another country, more distant than the ends of the earth. His own youth.

"The fighting was brutal," he continued. "The Isaurians battled for every pass, every boulder. I was only a cook, but I learned soon enough a blade has other uses than slicing onions. Yet, hard as it was, not a day passed when I wasn't inspired by the knowledge I was treading the same dusty roads as the saintly Paul traveled on his missionary journeys."

Peter paused. "You can understand, then, that I thought a great deal about Paul," he went on. "I found it a comfort. If we stopped to rest beneath a stand of pines beside a clear cool spring, who is to say that Paul might not have found the place just as inviting and paused there to refresh himself too?"

John observed that it was certainly possible.

"Many must have passed that way through the years. Gregory and I once found a couple of old coins fallen into a crevice in a flat rock where we'd sat down to enjoy our ration of wine. The coins were dropped there by some traveler, no doubt. I saved one because its inscription showed it was from Derbe, one of the cities Paul visited. I always put the coin out the evening before I was to meet Gregory, to remind me of our appointment when I woke up the next morning."

Peter looked at his boots and blinked back tears. "I think I will just leave it out permanently now."

Chapter Three

John sat as stiffly as a bronze statue, trying not to rock the tiny boat. The muscles of his long legs, necessarily drawn up almost to his chin, tingled in protest at his cramped position.

Over the broad shoulder of the laboring oarsman, he could see the customs house rising from the water, close to the mouth of the Bosporos.

The official building was a tall structure, comprised of several unmatched, wooden stories stacked atop a stolid brick base. The edifice totally obscured the rocky outcropping to which it was anchored. It appeared to be rising straight out of the murky water or else attempting to stay afloat. Neither thought reassured John. He kept his gaze fixed on his destination, finding it preferable to looking down into the gentle swells of dark oblivion so near at hand.

"Don't worry, excellency," the oarsman said, catching his stare toward their destination. "We'll have you safe on dry land nigh as quick as a cleric out the back door of a whore house." The man—Gurgos, he had announced himself—let loose a rumbling laugh.

"We might not be the sort of fancy transport you're accustomed to, but we strive to do our best," he went on with a grin.

"It's far better than swimming, like Leander. Did you ever hear the story of Hero, Emperor Constantine's daughter? He had her locked up in a tower on the island where the customs house is now, to keep her pure, you see. Only that lusty lad had other ideas and swam over to visit her every night, until a tempest finished him off. A very sad tale, excellency."

John shifted his legs slightly, observing it was indeed a tragic story, but omitting to mention that Gurgos had got the details wrong.

"Sorry about the inconvenience, excellency," his irrepressible companion went on, looking not at all repentant. "The regular ferry men are all busy hauling the dead. Do you know how many corpses fit into even a small vessel like this? These days everyone with a boat is minting nomismata."

He rowed silently for a time. John stared at the tower and frowned in thought.

"Yes," Gurgos went on, "I sometimes ask myself what will be my final destination? The spacious pits across the Marmara, or perhaps one of the city wall's towers? They're filling up faster than the emperor's dungeons these days, so I hear. Then again, there are always a few berths left on those ships Justinian ordered requisitioned. The evenings are cool out on the water, I admit, but we'll be quite warm when the vessels are set afire and we're all cremated."

The boat dipped to one side.

Gurgos raised a dripping oar. "Sometimes folk just drop others off in the water." He used the oar to push a half-submerged form away from their prow. The corpse bobbed past, staring up at John without curiosity.

"Isn't this craft rather too small for you to be playing Charon?"

"I'm not complaining. Happy to take whatever comes my way. Fortuna smiled when I spotted this little boat lying against the sea wall. I thought to myself, well, the owner is nowhere in sight and is probably dead anyway, so I took it and set myself up in business."

The large man seemed determined to tell John his entire history.

"Always been a laborer, excellency," he continued jauntily. "It's hard work that pays nothing and gets harder to do as you get older. I admit, until now the closest I've been to navigating treacherous waters was making my way through the public latrine at night, but if you see your chance, you have to take it, don't you? I'm learning fast. It's been nearly a week since I last capsized, and the patches I put on the boat seem to be holding well!"

Gurgos emitted another laugh worthy of Neptune at his jolliest.

They rocked sickeningly on toward the customs house with all the grace of the three-legged cat John had seen in a particular city square more than once. He was painfully aware of each awkward oar-stroke. Their destination seemed to continually sidle away, but then Gurgos would grunt volcanically and adjust their course.

By the time they drew alongside the custom house dock, John was sweating and the coins he pressed into the giant hand were as wet as if they'd been plucked from the bowels of a drowned ship. "Wait for me, Gurgos. I won't be long."

The customs house appeared deserted except for a few gulls perched on window sills and along the ridge of its tiled roof. Several small vessels were clustered around the island. Their sails were furled, whereas they should have been shuttling officials to and from cargo ships waiting to unload grain or amphorae of wine or oil, or to depart with crates filled with the work of the city's finest artisans—delicately engraved silver goblets bringing a reminder of civilization to tables deep in the forests of Germania, or jewelry to decorate the neck of a wife or concubine in far off Egypt.

The heavy doors of the building opened into a perfunctory marble atrium. It was deserted.

John heard laughter.

Gurgos?

No. The sound was a giggle rather than a bellow.

John stepped between the columns framing an archway in one wall and entered a room as packed with crates and amphorae as the hold of a ship. Confiscated goods, no doubt.

He soon discovered that a portion of a wine shipment had been seized a second time, judging by the glassy-eyed looks of the young man and woman slouched at an ivory-inlaid desk in the center of the room, an open amphora at their feet.

The male sported a blotchy face and managed to project the look of a clerk, despite long hair hanging down over his back in the fashionable Hunnic style. He took another drink from a delicate, pale green exemplar of the glassmaker's craft that probably would have cost him many weeks of his salary had he decided to purchase it.

"We're not able to inspect your ship," he mumbled at John. "Everyone is at home. All sick."

The plump girl sitting beside him giggled again and tugged clumsily at her half-opened robe.

Her companion smirked. John took a step forward. The Lord Chamberlain realized he was not his normal picture of authority, being rather rumpled and not entirely steady on his feet thanks to the hellish boat ride he had just endured.

"Your name, young man?"

"Me? Why, I'm Emperor Justinian and my companion here's Empress Theodora. Can't you see who we are? Perhaps you ought to get out and about more often!"

"There is no-one else here?"

"I've already explained that everybody's busy dying of the plague, so the shipowners have apparently had their wish. Which is to say, the hand of heaven has descended on the tariff collectors. I, Caesar, have thus proclaimed a holiday in celebration." He lifted his wine over his head and gestured grandly, sloshing its contents on his companion.

"Do you know Gregory?"

The girl looked startled. "You mean the Patriarch? For such we call him. Rather too quick to quote the scriptures, if you ask me, considering he spends most of his time counting coins for the emperor."

"When was he last at work here?"

"Couple of days ago," the girl offered.

"Do you have any idea what business he had to attend to in the city that day?"

"The Patriarch tell us where he was going? Not likely!" The young man gave a snort. "Why are you questioning your emperor anyway? Be gone or I'll call my guards!"

John ignored the young man and addressed the girl instead. "Gregory's office is where?"

"Smaller of the two rooms on the top floor," she told him. "He was second in command. Or rather third, counting my emperor here."

John went quickly upstairs. Two flights of wide granite steps gave way to a much steeper wooden staircase that creaked and groaned under his boots. The wall lamps had been allowed to burn out and the only light available came in through window slits.

Gregory's office was brighter. It looked toward the Asian shore. The geometric shapes of distant scattered buildings were softened and obscured by mist, giving the view the look of a church mosaic glimpsed through smoky incense. The room smelled, not of incense, but of the sea.

John's gaze fell on the tortoiseshell-framed wax tablet sitting on Gregory's desk. It might have been left especially for him to find, since the wax still bore a list of names and addresses in Constantinople. Gregory's notes to himself? Why hadn't he taken the tablet with him on his rounds? Possibly he had returned to the customs house having made these calls and gone out again without erasing the list.

In any event, if these were indeed places Gregory had visited during his last hours, they would certainly be helpful in retracing his steps, to discover where he had been, to whom he had spoken, and what those people might know.

It was almost too fortunate a find.

Then again, John had never been indirectly asked by an angel to solve a murder. Perhaps he could expect heavenly assistance.

Lifting the tablet revealed a crinkled piece of parchment on which was inscribed what purported to be a poem, written in Greek:

See yon rock the unlearned call Leander's Tower?
They say fair Hero threw herself down
at the sight of Leander's lifeless form.
But who can say,
if customs then were as cruel as customs are today,
did Hero leap because she was bereft
or was she pushed by the emperor's tariff?

If the dreadful composition was Gregory's work, whatever other secrets the man's life might have held, he was not another Homer.

John made his way back downstairs, the prospect of the return boat journey slowing his step. As he crossed the atrium, the youthful clerk yelled at him from the store room.

"You're still here? What are you up to, scoundrel? I'll have you arrested!"

John strode in to confront the youngster. He had regained his authoritative bearing and after a swift glance, the girl tugged warningly at her friend's arm. The young man shook her hand off. "Who do you think you are! No closer! Unless you mean to kiss the emperor's feet, that is."

John produced the official document he habitually carried. "Perhaps Caesar has had too many libations?" he suggested. "Especially since you never imbibe wine. Don't you recognize your own Lord Chamberlain?"

The clerk fumbled through the document John handed him. No doubt he'd seen enough official papers during his employment to recognize the genuine article. "You stole this!" he sputtered.

"Ah," John said, his mouth drawing into a thin line, "and do you suppose your future would be much brighter if I am not in fact the Lord Chamberlain, but rather a man who has just murdered the Lord Chamberlain and relieved him of this document and his clothing?"

As the truth began to penetrate the clerk's alcoholic armor, his face became very pale.

The girl leapt up, threw herself to the floor, and grabbed the hem of John's robe. "Please, please, excellency," she wept. "We meant no harm. Don't send us to the dungeons. Not the red hot tongs and all them sharp knives…I'll do whatever you want…he'll do whatever you want…."

John pulled away. "That won't be necessary. Just curb your tongues in future, or you may find them removed."

***

Peter did not admit John to the house, having apparently put aside his duties for the day after all, as John had advised.

The sun was setting, but the atrium lamps were unlit. The quiet water in the impluvium reflected the dull, rose-tinted sky visible through the rectangular opening above.

John went upstairs. No fragrance of recent cooking emanated from the kitchen, only the dusty odor of last year's dried herbs. Hypatia was nowhere to be seen, although a scorpion-like clay creature, one of her numerous charms against the plague, squatted on the kitchen table.

Peter must have forgotten to instruct her to assume his culinary duties for the evening.

John took a jug of wine and his cracked cup into his study.

His servants were available only when ordered to be there. John preferred solitude. He did not like people hovering unbidden at his elbow and had never cultivated the aristocratic knack for regarding servants as little more than animated furniture. How could he, he who had once been a slave? Such unorthodox convictions caused him to traverse the streets and alleys of Constantinople alone and unguarded, a practice others considered unthinkably dangerous for a courtier of his high rank.

A Lord Chamberlain was powerful enough to do the unthinkable if he chose.

Besides which, he was no stranger to using a blade when necessary.

He sat at his desk and sipped raw Egyptian wine. Beyond the diamond-shaped panes of the window overlooking the palace grounds and the sea beyond, the sky was fast growing dark. Might one of the myriad distant lights beneath the emerging stars mark the customs house he had just visited?

He imagined Peter working in the study, cleaning the window perhaps, never knowing he was laboring within sight of the building where, at the same instant, the man he knew only as an impoverished former soldier was likely to be warning a wealthy shipowner that a cargo of silks could not be unloaded until the tariff was paid, even if the merchant considered the amount demanded to be larcenous.

Peter, John thought, would doubtless be singing, and tunelessly at that, one of the lugubrious hymns he favored, dismissing dust as Gregory dismissed the disgruntled merchant, who would stride angrily off, his retinue of bodyguards trailing behind.

He'd still have to pay the appropriate tariff.

Did Peter truly not realize the position his old friend had held, the power he wielded?

Should John reveal what he had learnt? Would Peter's new knowledge allow him to shed further light on Gregory's murder? Sometimes we know things that we recognize only when our perspective changes.

John turned his attention to the wall mosaic. In the shadowed room he could not distinguish details, but he knew by heart each of the pagan gods who populated the sky as well as the faces of the bucolic mortals working in the fields below. Most familiar was the one he had named Zoe, a young girl whose glass eyes seemed to hold an expression conveying she had glimpsed all the sorrows to which flesh is prey.

There was an unnerving naturalism about her, as if the image had been taken from life. John thought it possible she was the artist's daughter. The mosaic had been in place when he purchased the house, having been installed by the previous owner.

It was strange to think that if his surmise was correct, the model for Zoe could well still be alive. John might see her one day while inspecting some artisans' enclave, or she might appear in one of the hallways of an imperial residence, perhaps even be glimpsed moving down an alleyway off the Mese.

He was as likely to run into her as he was to see his own daughter again.

Would he recognize either of them?

He thought he heard someone moving about in the hall. Rising from his plain wooden chair, he looked out. A single lamp flickered at the far end, where narrow stairs led up to the mostly unoccupied servants' quarters. Nothing moved.

It hadn't been exactly a footstep. It was a softer sound, similar to heavy garments brushing against a wall. Birds often got into the house from the garden or through the compluvium, yet he couldn't help recalling Peter's imagined heavenly visitor.

Zoe stared solemnly at him as he sat down again.

"Peter doesn't like me talking to you, Zoe." John could not have said whether he spoke aloud or not.

There was a hint of sympathy in the girl's almond-shaped eyes.

"Strange to think, isn't it, that my servant possesses what I do not? That is to say, a past."

He brought the wine cup to his lips. It was a cup akin to the one he'd owned when he lived with Cornelia, the mother of his daughter. The vessel was a duplicate he had ordered made, down to the crack in the rim. It was all of the past he could bear to keep close to him. Of the man he had been before his capture and emasculation in Persia, there remained nothing.

As for the family and friends of the man he had been then, they had vanished as surely as if the emperor had ordered every one of them dragged off to the dungeons in the dead of night. Or as if his Lord Chamberlain had ordered it, for John could certainly wield such power if he ever chose to exercise it.

Still, he admitted, if only to Zoe, he missed hearing Cornelia's light breathing as she slept in the bed beside him, when the night was as silent as this one.

He lit the lamp on the desk and stared out of the window for a while. In the darkness there was no sign of the horror that stalked the city's streets. For that matter, it could be lurking within this very house. The plague could go wherever it chose.

John forced his mind back to his investigation. He had become a servant to his own servant, as Gaius had said. Yet Peter was part of John's household, and if it were possible, John intended to find out who had killed Gregory. Elderly men like Peter did not have much time left to outlive their sorrows and disappointments.

"He's already lost an old friend, but he at least has good memories of him. If I tell him the work Gregory did, will I murder those memories too? What do you think, Zoe?" John poured himself more wine.

Chapter Four

The bakery was deserted. Empty shelves in its front and cold brick ovens at the back confirmed what John had known as soon as he turned down the street and failed to smell freshly baked bread.

He crossed Eustathios the baker off the list on Gregory's wax tablet.

There were now no names left. The list had led John to a succession of closed shops and silent houses where knocks had gone unanswered, their residents having departed to the country—or forever—or were perhaps too ill or frightened to answer.

He wondered if the names had in fact been Gregory's itinerary.

That the bakery had been left open and unlocked indicated not only that Eustathios was dead, but that he had fallen prey to the most virulent variety of the plague, the type that took its victims within hours.

A muted thump caused John to turn quickly. Was there someone here after all?

He saw a cat, little more than an animated skeleton, stalking away from an empty grain bin. The cobwebs hanging off the animal's whiskers testified to the extent of its hunting efforts. No baker meant no grain to feed the rats and no rats to feed the cats.

The creature glared balefully at John, who had nothing to give it.

Only a few coins.

No use at all to a hungry cat.

John realized he was hungry too. It had been a long time since the chunk of bread that had formed his breakfast.

The sun, now high overhead, drove all shadow from the streets here, a lengthy walk from the Great Palace grounds. John had made his way along the northern ridge from which, between buildings crowded conspiratorially together, he could occasionally glimpse the scintillant waters of the Golden Horn. He had planned his route to avoid climbing and reclimbing the seven-hilled city's precipitous streets.

Now, however, he decided to walk down toward the docks.

When he reached a square facing the sea wall he was disappointed again. The seller of grilled fish, whose smoking brazier usually sat beside the marble statue of Emperor Anastasius, had gone. No sign of him remained except soot on the emperor's chin and a few discarded fish bones, picked clean by seagulls.

There were still a fair number of pedestrians. A traveler unaccustomed to the capital's jostling masses might not have noticed how relatively few they were or how most maintained careful courses, keeping a safe distance from strangers—rather like ships navigating the harbor, except that the ships in the harbor were not moving. There wasn't a sail to be seen, only a forest of bare masts.

John recalled what Peter had said about his visits with Gregory. Sometimes they met at the Great Church or the Church of the Holy Apostles. Both were certainly places of some interest to Christians, but the latter was a long walk from John's house. Was it was nearer to where Gregory lived? The thought occurred that there must be some record of where Gregory lived, either at the customs house or in the administrative warrens of the palace.

John turned away from the sea wall and started back up the steep thoroughfare. He often walked, since he found he thought better when his feet were moving. Thus he knew the alleys and byways of the city well. He crossed the top of the ridge, navigated a series of side streets not quite narrow enough to be called alleyways, passed under the Aqueduct of Valens, and eventually reached the Church of the Holy Apostles.

A motley assortment of associated ecclesiastical buildings all but hid the church. Not far beyond, the city's inner wall stood guard. Impregnable to men, the walls had provided no defense against the plague.

John looked up and down nearby streets until he found an establishment that appeared to be open. A pyramid chiseled above its entrance bore the admonition *The Wise Man is Prepared.* A plaque beside the door identified the establishment as belonging to one Paraskeve, Builder of Tombs of Distinction.

John found the owner in the courtyard behind the shop, surrounded by the equivalent of a warehouse's stock of marble, granite, and more exotic stones. Some were blank, awaiting the chisel, while others were in the midst of being carved into bas reliefs, cornices, or vine-entwined columns, or inscribed with appropriate verse.

Paraskeve hurried over to greet John, beaming. He had one of those round, snub-nosed faces that never age yet never look quite adult. Over his work tunic he wore an embroidered rectangular apron.

"How can I serve you, excellency?"

"I'm trying to find a man I believe may live in the area. Do you know a customs official named Gregory?"

"Yes, indeed I do." Paraskeve looked crushed.

"I shall naturally reimburse you for the information."

Paraskeve waved a stubby-fingered hand. "No. No, please, there is no need. I must apologize if my disappointment showed. The plague has all but carried my business off and I hoped you might wish to order…that is to say, for future use of course, not wishing any tragedy on your household, or in other words…." He floundered to a halt.

"I understand," John replied. "Although I would have imagined a tomb builder would be overwhelmed by work in the midst of so much death."

"The dead don't purchase tombs, excellency. My customers are dying before they can make appropriate preparations. Constructing a proper tomb can take years. It's not just hacking a few stones about, as some in the profession are wont to do."

"You've had business dealings with Gregory?"

"Not exactly, but I can tell you where to find him. You can't miss his house. Continue up the Mese from here and it's the house just before the obelisk the candlemaker erected in front of his emporium."

"You don't know Gregory personally?"

"No. He is, however, said to be a good Christian." Paraskeve's tone was abrupt.

John asked why people had formed this opinion.

"For one thing, he petitioned Justinian to renovate the Church of the Holy Apostles." Paraskeve didn't seem inclined to add a second thing.

"Emperor Constantine built that church to be his tomb, didn't he?"

Paraskeve's cherubic face brightened suddenly. "That's right. There's a fine example of forethought, excellency. It's one reason I set up my workshop as close as I could to the church."

John inspected a carved piece of black-veined marble leaning against a pile of sandstone blocks. As he bent to examine the partially completed inscription, heat from the sun-warmed stone touched his face. He read the half finished verse aloud. "'Do not believe you have twice five thousand years; death is close at hand, thus while—"

"—you breathe, while there is time, live in a fitting fashion,' Marcus Aurelius," Paraskeve finished the verse.

"You are quite a philosopher, I see."

"Not at all, excellency, but when you're in the business of constructing tombs you just can't avoid Marcus Aurelius. I think I must've engraved every word of his miserable Meditations at some time or other."

"You don't agree with his thoughts?"

"I'm an optimist! Tomorrow I might die, but as long as I know that it means I'm still alive, doesn't it? How could an emperor be so gloomy? Especially considering just about everyone's going to die without ever being emperor. I encourage my customers to choose contemporary verses, if verse they must have. Something specially composed. Not that I can afford to engage a decent epigrammist the way things are right now."

"So you think we should contemplate our deaths to the extent of commissioning our tombs?"

"Please, excellency! Clients who commission tombs, well, their deaths are the last things on their minds. No, not at all. I'll give you an example. Years ago a basket-maker came to me. At the time he was practically a youth. He had his tomb constructed in a secluded corner of a cemetery just outside the city wall. Was he contemplating his mortality? Hardly! He wanted to impress a young woman whose hand he sought. It worked too! A man of sufficient substance to finance such a project at such a young age and so responsible and practical as shown by the very act…well, excellency, women like men who have their tombs already built. Now he tells me he and his wife take a basket of food out there on sunny days and enjoy the country air."

John remarked that tomb construction sounded like a very interesting profession, but before he could turn the conversation back to Gregory, Paraskeve, seemingly happy to have someone to talk to for a time, had embarked on another story.

"So the bootmaker's tomb is no more than a hand's-breadth from the Via Egnatia, practically in sight of the city. Naturally it gets as dusty as the boots he sells," Paraskeve concluded. "Ah, but consider this! It's also readily seen by every footsore pilgrim. What a fine advertisement for his goods. Idle boasts read much better as epitaphs!"

John agreed there was some truth in the statement.

"Then there was a certain senator," the other rushed on. "You'd know his name immediately were it to pass my lips. His tomb overlooks the Marmara from a promontory on his estate.

He was so pleased with the edifice I built he hired me to add apartments to it where he could sit and meditate."

"I can't say I would want to spend more time than necessary in my own tomb," John observed.

"His wife apparently felt the same. She was horrified and refused to set foot near the place." Paraskeve laughed. "Ah, but then again, his mistress is not so squeamish and I understand is much given to meditation!"

"Did Gregory have a family?"

"A wife, but he refused to show her my design for their final resting place. It was a representation of the hold of a cargo ship. The tomb itself was in the shape of a crate, adorned with angels and set amidst monumental amphorae and crosses. They would be part of the heavenly ship's cargo, bound for some higher land, you see. Very appropriate for a high-ranking customs official. I still have the…but wait! Why are you asking me about Gregory? He's not been taken off too?"

John confirmed his suspicions, without elaboration.

Paraskeve's shoulders slumped. "I may as well throw those sketches away then. His wife won't commission anything like that, you can be certain of it. On the other hand, there are other customs officials who might be interested, aren't there? Yes. I shall save them, then. Now you, excellency. Have you made suitable arrangements, if I may be so bold?"

"I don't intend to have a tomb built."

"It's natural enough to be afraid of death, but it's no use pretending—"

John cut him off abruptly. "I don't fear death. What happens to my remains doesn't concern me in the least."

***

John rapped again at Gregory's door.

There was no reply.

He stepped back and looked up at the second story window. There was no movement behind the tiny panes.

While to passersby the house displayed only a plain brick facade, doubtless it was well appointed inside. At four stories, it looked out over the roofs of the surrounding buildings. From the top floor, Gregory would have had a magnificent view of the Sea of Marmara.

For years the customs official had met Peter, often not far from here. The pair might have walked right past this very house. What would Peter have thought if he knew his old army friend lived here, rather than in some dingy tenement? What if he were to find out?

John debated questioning Paraskeve further, but decided he had heard enough tales of the tomb builder's trade and started back. Better to go home to his evening meal and further thought on the knotty problem with which he was grappling.

As he drew level with the Church of the Holy Apostles the noise of a sudden uproar broke out, sounding somewhere between a fully fledged riot and a flock of angry seagulls. The church doors burst open and white-robed figures rushed into the street, shrieking in terror. Most were children.

Several boys raced frantically past John, their garments flapping around spindly legs. They were followed, at an increasing distance, by two lumbering middle-aged men, obviously unaccustomed to running. The men stopped, looking relieved, when John accosted them. Both had the soft, immaculate look of clerics.

"Thief," gasped one. "Did you see him?"

"Some crazed old man," added his companion, panting. "Yet spry on his feet all right!"

The other man took a few deep breaths and wiped his perspiring brow on his sleeve. "It was this holy fool everyone is talking about, sir. He tried to tie himself to the Column of Flagellation. Blasphemy of the highest order." His tone conveyed his horror at the recollection.

"Trying to steal it, you mean," his companion corrected him. "He was trying to tie it to his back to make off with it. The very instrument of our Lord's torture meant nothing to him but a few gold coins."

"Anyway, we chased the fool away. It's only a fragment of the column that we have, but even so, it's too heavy to carry, or so I'd have thought. The boys will follow him and find out where he's gone, then we'll alert the authorities and they can take care of the matter."

The clerics continued on after their vanished charges, limping rather than running.

John set his course for home. No matter the disaster, there was always someone ready to take advantage, he thought. The Christian church seemed to attract more frauds than might be expected. Perhaps it was because their god seemed less inclined to interfere with the mortal world, less likely to let loose thunderbolts than Zeus would have been.

He passed a street he'd visited earlier. Movement caught his eye as a thin shape slunk into an alley. The starving cat from the bakery, carrying something in its mouth.

John sighed. "I'm glad the day has brought someone good fortune, my feline friend."

***

Gaius perched his bulk uncomfortably on a stool in John's kitchen. Hypatia shifted a bronze pot to the back of the brazier, added water, and stirred the mixture in an attempt to tame the wildly bubbling concoction. Nose-stinging smoke hung in the air. Evidently some of the pot's contents had boiled over when Hypatia went downstairs to admit Gaius to the house.

"I'm sorry to have made you wait, sir. Peter's usually prompt to answer the door. He isn't himself right now."

"Of course. He will be mourning his friend. And what are you preparing, Hypatia?"

"This is a mixture to fortify the body against afflictions. It is commonly used in Egypt."

"What I could actually use to fortify myself is a cup of wine."

Hypatia set jug and cup on the table. Gaius emptied the cup at one gulp and poured himself a second libation.

Hypatia gave the pot another stir and pushed a strand of black hair away from her tawny forehead. She had very striking eyes, Gaius thought. He shifted and the stool creaked alarmingly under his weight. He needed to visit the gymnasium more often, he told himself, lifting the wine jug to pour again.

"Are there any potions I could prepare for you to use at the hospice, sir? If there was only some cure…."

Gaius shook his head. "The only cure seems to be good fortune. Do you happen to have a recipe for that?"

"No, but I've made a number of charms to protect us all." Hypatia waved her ladle toward the baked clay scorpion crouched on the table. "You can take that one with you if you wish, sir. The house is well guarded by others."

"What I need is more something with hands. Hands is what we're short of. To bathe the sick, calm the humors, administer pain-killing mixtures, that sort of thing."

"That's all you can do for your patients?"

"I've tried lancing the swellings. When they burst spontaneously the patients tend to live, but in those cases I've attempted it, I generally find carbuncles inside and they die anyway."

Hypatia wrinkled her nose. "Peter says it's judgment from heaven to punish the sinful."

"I couldn't tell you which among them are sinners. Sin doesn't seem to have symptoms. I do know most die with the name of their god on their lips." Gaius drained his cup for the third time. One would expect a Lord Chamberlain to own decent sized goblets, he thought irritably.

"You mentioned Peter's friend?"

Gaius stared thoughtfully into his cup. At least he hadn't been presented with that cracked specimen John insisted on using, a cup not fit for a beggar in his opinion.

"Yes," he finally said, "Gregory. I cannot stay too long, so I wish you to convey to your master that it occurred to me to do a complete examination of his body. There hadn't been any reason hitherto since the cause of his death was obvious enough. But seeing John's great interest in the man…well, anyway, tell your master my advice is not to waste any more time looking for his murderer. Gregory had swellings in the groin so it is more than likely he would've been dead in a few days anyway. Whatever scoundrel slid a blade between his ribs did him a favor."

Chapter Five

"If you ask me, Gaius was right. There must be hundreds in this city praying right now for the quick end Gregory had." Felix swirled the last of his wine, peering down into its dregs as if he were seeking information on his future. "You've had to put a mortally wounded comrade out of his misery on the battlefield more than once, I'll wager."

John scowled at the burly, bearded excubitor captain seated by the study window. "Once, yes. He begged me to do so. It was a merciful act. However, I must find the culprit for Peter's sake, not for Gregory's."

"These things happen all the time, John, like cart accidents or being struck by lightning, except a lot more frequently. From what you've told me I see no reason to think his death was anything more than the result of robbery."

"No, there's no logical reason to suppose otherwise," John admitted. "Only Peter's vision."

"The angel? Well, if his god went to the trouble of sending a heavenly messenger, why not reveal the name of the culprit as well? Why push the job on to you, an unbeliever?"

"You remind me of Anatolius in his wittier mode."

Felix tugged at his beard. "Yes, well…I suppose I shouldn't be so flippant. I'm about to depart the city for a while, which is what I came to tell you. I've been ordered to take some of my men and escort Justinian and Theodora to their Blachernae estate."

"I hadn't heard they were leaving the palace. Then again, it's been some days since Justinian summoned me and, thankfully, even longer since I was ordered to attend an audience with Theodora."

"A thousand people are dying every day and the bodies can't be cleared from the streets fast enough for the carts to get through. It's best for our emperor and his wife to be away from the contagion, if only a short distance. It suits me, too. I don't think Fortuna cares much for excubitors. We've been particularly hard hit, and for every guard who's fallen ill another has decided to flee the city. I have so few men left, we're keeping entrances locked rather than guarding them. I don't think the palace has ever been less secure."

Felix fell silent for a moment. "Still," he finally said, "the imperial couple being absent from the palace at a time of great crisis and Peter missing from his kitchen….Perhaps the end is truly at hand."

"Peter would agree with you on that. Still, I imagine the rest of the court will hasten to their own estates now Justinian and Theodora are leaving. As long as they remained at the palace nobody dared to suggest the possibility." John refilled his cup and passed the wine jug to Felix. "Before you ask, I'm staying here."

"I wasn't going to bother inquiring." Felix looked into the jug and frowned fiercely at its lowered level. "You know, John, I'm beginning to develop a taste for this foul Egyptian wine you persist in offering your guests."

A thin smile quirked John's lips. "You and Gaius both, according to what Hypatia tells me."

"Seeking treatment from the physician Bacchus again, is he? Not that I can blame him." Felix paused. "It's not just courtiers being freed from the confines of the palace, by the way. I've also received personal orders from Theodora to arrange transport for that bear she keeps in the imperial menagerie. She's taking it with her. I gather she's suddenly got the notion to set it free in a forest."

"Better than setting it free on the streets, which is more the sort of thing you'd expect from Theodora." John's tone was mild.

"True enough. Perhaps that explains my surprise. An act of kindness by her is more shocking than any villainy she might concoct."

"Possibly she still has a soft spot for bears, having been born a bearkeeper's daughter?"

Felix guffawed. "I don't think Theodora has any soft spots and I'm never going near enough to find out if I can help it. I was rather glad to get the task, to be honest. I don't worship the bear goddess as many in Germania still do, yet I will admit Theodora's is a magnificent specimen. And that reminds me, the last time I saw the bear a rather curious thing happened. Hektor was there."

"The court page? What was he doing?"

"Tormenting the poor beast, of course, and I suspect not for the first time. I've patrolled past the menagerie numerous times and noticed the bear had a bloody muzzle more than once. Anyhow, there was Hektor in his usual finery. Green robes this time, no less, and fine blue boots, although he seemed to have lost that ridiculous hat with the peacock feather. He was pitchforking dirty straw out of the bear's cage, but not being too careful where the tines went while he was doing it."

Felix's broad features darkened as he continued with his story. "When he saw me, Hektor gave that unpleasant laugh of his. His breath absolutely reeked of wine. He gave a low bow that was an insult in itself and then informed me that he called the bear Felix."

John inquired if Hektor had revealed his reason.

"Indeed he did. 'Because it's fat, hairy, and smelly, just like you!' was what the insolent fellow said. Naturally, I laid him flat on the straw before he'd finished smirking at his own joke. Didn't look so cocky then, especially as the filth positively ruined his finery. Not to mention I rubbed his face in the dung."

Felix roared with laughter, good humor restored, at the memory. "You'd think he would have found some old rags to wear for a job like that. Perhaps he thought one of the ladies of the court would stroll along to visit while he worked. Now I find myself wondering why he was ordered to perform such labor in the first place."

"Knowing that young man, it was doubtless punishment for some misdeed or other. Whoever ordered it would have plenty to choose from. It's only a couple of months since he was caught stealing from the Master of the Offices, and he's been picked up from the gutter intoxicated to a state of unconsciousness several times as well. That's dangerous behavior for a man at court."

"Even more dangerous for someone like Hektor. He's at a perilous age for a court page, being now more use to the ladies than to the lecherous old aristocrats his livelihood depends upon. Perhaps he was attempting to blot out the shame of his misdeeds by blistering those dainty hands with some hard work. What with the hand of God descending on sinners, as I've heard many warn, people are starting to watch their behavior. You don't think that's why Theodora's decided to release the bear, do you? At any rate, Hektor's been avoiding me ever since. I haven't had a glimpse of him for days."

Felix stood. "Speaking of beasts," he continued, "I have an appointment with the Master of the Offices. He's arranging transportation for the bear. Carts are hard to find right now, so he's lending me an old imperial carriage."

***

John did not accompany Felix to the door. He didn't care for good-byes at any time. At the moment any departure might tempt Fortuna.

When he judged his friend had gone, John decided to go out to walk. To his annoyance, he had barely left his doorway when Anatolius intercepted him.

"John! Thank Mithra I caught you! I've just had a terrible shock."

The younger man's smooth features, those of a classical Greek statue, were flushed. Black ringlets of hair clung damply to his forehead, as if he'd been running.

"Why is that?"

"Senator Balbinus is ill!"

"The plague?"

Anatolius nodded grimly. "I heard talk of it, so I went to his house to see if I could do anything to help."

"You saw Balbinus?"

"No. He's taken to his bed. Lucretia told me."

"She received you?"

"Certainly. Well, after I made it clear I wouldn't leave until we had spoken."

John sighed and invited Anatolius to accompany him on his walk, although he would have preferred to be solitary. His long stride forcing the younger man to labor to keep pace, they began traversing the palace gardens.

They soon passed under a vine-covered archway and down a flight of flagstone steps to a grassy terrace planted with exotic shrubs and flowers. Squat administrative buildings were barely visible on the slope above them, all but concealed by poplar trees whose leaves fluttered like so many tiny hands waving good-bye. Dark groves of cedars lined retaining walls from which an occasional artificial waterfall gurgled down into a marble basin on the next level. Below them, more green terraces dotted with buildings, flower beds, and trees descended toward the sparkling Marmara. The peaceful view was marred by the sight of a burning ship sitting beneath a column of greasy black smoke some way offshore, one of Justinian's waterborne crematoriums.

"You are well aware you should not be visiting Lucretia under any circumstances."

Anatolius licked his lips nervously. "I know. I know. But that's all past, John. How many years has it been since she and Balbinus were married? Mithra! I haven't even set eyes on her except from a distance for almost a year."

"Your memory fails you. You mentioned you saw her coming out of the Great Church several days ago. A week or so before that you noticed her purchasing perfume from—"

His companion smiled ruefully. "Well, that's true. Despite the time that's passed since we, well, she looks just the same as she did…."

"That shows she must be very happy with Senator Balbinus."

A cloud passed over Anatolius' face, as dark as the smoke rising from the blazing vessel. "I suppose you're right. She'll always be beautiful to me, however careworn she looks. She only just stepped into the atrium for a brief word. I think she was afraid to talk to me in case it should bring back memories."

"Or perhaps she did not wish to speak to you? It was foolish to go there, my friend. When Balbinus recovers, you'll certainly hear about it."

Anatolius stopped walking and stared out to sea. It was impossible to say whether he was contemplating the ship, the soaring gulls, the far shore half hidden by a blue heat haze, or something not of this world. His eyes held a feverish gleam. "What are the chances, do you think? Some recover. Many die. The knucklebones have been thrown. How long before they rattle to a stop?"

"I hope you haven't made a wager you can ill afford on the outcome."

"What do you mean? I'm concerned about Lucretia. That doddering old blowhard is her husband, after all."

"You believe she would be better off without him," John corrected him sharply. "Are you only thinking of yourself?"

"John, I—"

"The plague has turned everything upside down, but eventually it will depart. For those of us who remain, the world will right itself again. Remember that. Don't do or say anything you will have cause to regret when things return to normal."

"You're right. I won't."

They resumed walking. Sunlight played brightly across an ornamental pond like liquid fire. A fragrant stand of pines offered cool shadow.

Anatolius picked up a cone and hurled it toward the Marmara. The sea looked much nearer than it actually was. The cone vanished into a huge rhododendron on the next terrace down. "When I heard about Balbinus, I first came to you to ask if you knew anything about it. Then, since you were out, I went to his house. Not that I'm blaming you for not being home," he concluded hastily.

John explained he had been investigating the background of a friend of Peter's and then related how Gregory had died and Peter's vision.

"Felix and Gaius are both certain it was nothing more than street violence, and I've found nothing that would indicate otherwise," he continued. "However, Peter has got it into his head that the murderer can be found. Frankly, I'm at a loss about where to go next, angels or no angels."

Anatolius looked thoughtful. "'Gregory. Murder. Justice.' Not a very eloquent message, coming from an angel. Still, we live in strange times. It's almost enough to make one believe in miracles. Do you remember when I visited you with Crinagoras not long ago?"

"How could anyone easily forget his recitation of his Ode to a Granary?"

"I'm sorry about that," Anatolius grinned. "The sight of Hypatia in the garden set him off. His poetry inevitably flows as soon as he glimpses a pretty woman. Well, I can understand that, but what I forgot to tell you is that as we were leaving we ran into Peter and his friend Gregory returning from one of these weekly visits you've just told me about. It was right outside the excubitor barracks opposite your house, as a matter of fact."

"Indeed?"

"Yes. Gregory was taking his leave of Peter because he had a call to make. I had to return to my office, but since Gregory's business was in a street right on Crinagoras' way, he volunteered to accompany the old fellow. The streets are more dangerous than ever and Gregory was happy to accept the offer of an escort.

He did keep saying he didn't want to cause any trouble, but if Crinagoras would see him to the door, that would be helpful."

"Do you know where was he going?"

Anatolius beamed. "To visit a shipper by the name of Nereus. Crinagoras told me all about it when I saw him next day. He was beside himself with excitement. Apparently Nereus was on his deathbed and frantic to make an oral will, so Crinagoras and Gregory were both recruited as witnesses! The experience was new to Crinagoras…and perhaps deserves an Ode."

Chapter Six

Empress Theodora stepped out of her silk tunica and pushed it away across the tiled floor of the Great Palace baths with a deft flick of her bare foot.

Naked, she was a short, middle-aged woman with thick ankles and slightly fleshy arms, hardly the glamorous subject for sculptors as she was when clothed in imperial regalia. She did, however, still possess the shapely calves and thighs of the dancer, one of the professions she had followed in her youth.

This afternoon her audience consisted of her ladies-in-waiting and two aristocratic matrons, standing nearly up to their chests in the steaming circular pool, plus the startled bathers' two servants.

Theodora's ladies-in-waiting carefully folded the layers of glinting, gem-patterned robes she'd just shed and gathered up several pieces of jewelry. The empress glanced down over herself, performing the ritual examination that had become common for the city's inhabitants. "Do you see any of the signs?"

The attendant she'd addressed, trained never to stare at her mistress, timidly directed her gaze toward the empress. Finally she shook her head and quickly turned away, bending to retrieve the discarded tunica.

Would anyone dare tell her if they did note some indication of the plague, Theodora wondered.

She padded over to the steps leading down into the water. The baths she had chosen occupied a semicircular room, reminding her of the apse of a church. Steam from the pool coiled upwards through a shaft of light descending from the circular aperture in the large room's domed ceiling. Benches and tables sat against the walls. A monumental Diana, hunting gear strewn around her chiseled feet, stood nearby, looking ready to place a bare marble foot into the pool.

"My private bath is well appointed, ladies, but it gets lonely, bathing with only echoes for companions," Theodora observed to the room at large.

One of the bathers, chubby and pink, began to execute a low bow, became suddenly aware that her pendulous breasts were, perhaps, not an appropriate display of respect, and clamped her arms down over them. Her companion, a pallid, angular woman with sunken cheeks and chest, stepped backwards in the water, wincing as her spine came up against the sharp snout of a fancifully carved, water-spewing fish.

"There is no need for formalities, Priscilla," Theodora addressed the plump bather. "Just think, now you'll be able to tell everyone you've bathed with the empress. That stable boy you've been trysting with in the palace gardens will be most impressed, not to mention your husband the senator."

Priscilla was suddenly much less pink despite the hot water.

"As for you, Galla," Theodora observed to the other woman, "I expect you don't have anyone to tell your secrets. But you don't have to run away. I won't bite." She narrowed her eyes. "You're not a devotee of Sappho, are you? Might it be I will not be safe with you in there?"

"Oh, no, excellency. Never. That is to say...."

Theodora giggled. "This is so much more pleasant than my solitary ablutions. I know, let's play." She splashed a handful of water into Galla's face.

The woman sputtered and coughed.

Theodora splashed her again. "Come now, fight back. It's no fun otherwise. You too, Priscilla. Hurry up!" She sent a spray in the direction of the plump woman. "What? Afraid to splash the empress? Just pretend I'm someone else. Pretend I'm your stable boy." Her tone sharpened. "I might as well be bathing with the Patriarch. Play!"

Priscilla bent slightly, cradling her bosom with one hand, dipped her fingers into the water, and shook them in Theodora's direction.

The empress gasped. Her hands flew up to her eyes. "What did you do?" she wailed. "I can't see!"

Her ladies-in-waiting rushed to the edge of the pool.

Priscilla gaped in horror.

"Don't stand there! Help me!" Theodora cried.

Priscilla stumbled forward clumsily. The empress executed a well practiced dance step, swung her foot, and cut her fellow bather's legs out from under her. Priscilla disappeared below the water, sending a wave up over the rim of the pool, soaking the ladies-in-waiting.

Theodora laughed with delight.

As Priscilla surfaced, choking and spitting, Theodora gleefully prepared to dunk her playmate's head beneath the water.

Before she could do so, a shadow passed over the pool.

Something was blocking the light from the aperture in the dome.

Theodora looked up.

A dark shape almost filled the opening.

A great, black bird.

It dropped, dark wings spreading, and hit the center of the pool in an explosion of water.

What bobbed to the surface almost immediately wasn't a bird, however, but a man whose leathery face was half hidden by a sodden hood. In one claw-like hand he clutched a sack from which emanated a hideous, demonic cackling.

The matrons and attendants shrieked in unison.

"Silence!" Theodora commanded. "All of you! If I'm not mistaken, we have a holy visitor."

The hooded man shook the dripping sack, which cackled even more frantically. "What do you mean, highness? Can't you see, I'm Death! Just thought I'd drop in unexpectedly, like I always do!"

"You're the holy fool we've all been hearing about," Theodora told him with a scimitar of a smile.

"Am I? Well, you're the empress, I suppose, so if you say so, I must be." He lurched toward Galla, his cloak floating on the surface of the water. Galla covered her chest with her hands and cringed away, but was pinned against the carved fish head.

"Don't you want to hear my riddle?" asked the intruder. "Why is the empress like Rome?"

Galla's only reply was to tremble with horror and embarrassment.

"Because…because…she's the symbol of all that's great?" offered Priscilla in a quavering tone.

The man now sidled in Priscilla's direction. "You should be trying to flatter me, not her, don't you think? After all, I might be carrying a knife. As far as I can see, the empress isn't armed."

"Tell us why the empress is like Rome," Theodora demanded.

"Why, because Justinian will do anything to have her, even though she's already been well plundered by strangers!"

He scrambled nimbly up the bath stairs, scattering the ladies-in-waiting, and squatted toad-like, dripping water, on the tiles.

Theodora followed and hunkered down next to him, careless of her nudity. "Tell me, fool, how did you get in here? There are guards everywhere outside."

"It was a miracle, highness."

"It will be an even greater miracle if you can get out…still attached to your head, that is."

"Of course, for I have seen too much." The man leered. "Well, if the Lord wills it, so be it. But, first, allow me to entertain you."

He opened the soggy sack, tipped out an extremely agitated chicken, and then scooped two handfuls of wet grain from the depths of the sack.

The bathers couldn't stifle their gasps. From one of the cowering attendants came a nervous, uncontrolled titter.

The fool turned his hooded, shadowed visage toward Theodora. "Ah. You're smiling, I see, highness. You know how this works, then?"

"Do you think I don't know half the population of Constantinople claims to have watched chickens peck corn from my groin in the days when I was working in the theater?"

"I've heard that on one occasion a certain high-ranking foreign official paid good silver to play the chicken," the man informed her.

"Now that's a slander that hasn't reached my ears before now!" Theodora leaned toward the fool until her face nearly touched his. His eyes glinted within his hood. His shabby cloak appeared encrusted with grease, but the only smell about him was that of desiccated papyrus. "Sitting here with you like this reminds me of my past. People are amazed that a bearkeeper's daughter can command senators to prostrate themselves at her feet. But, you know, senators have been prostrating themselves at my feet since I was…well…a child…."

The fool had taken hold of the chicken and was stroking its feathers idly. "The Lord will forgive your sins, if only you will ask."

"Sins? It is I who was sinned against, fool." She lowered her voice to a whisper. "I remember the first occasion my sister brought a man to me. Some high official or other he was, he claimed. A fat, nasty man. When my sister explained what he wanted to do, I didn't know whether to laugh at how silly it sounded or cry with disgust at what he required. I couldn't imagine why he would desire such a thing, but I'd learned to add up coins before I could read, so I knew immediately why I would allow him to…well…."

One of the attendants burst into noisy sobs, but was quelled by one look from Theodora.

"When my sister left, the old fellow began to paw me," Theodora went on. "I pretended to cry. 'Oh, sir,' I whimpered most convincingly. 'I want to obey you, but I'm so frightened. Perhaps if you pretended to be a little purring kitten I would not be so terribly afraid.' Yes, I've always been an excellent actress…."

The fool grinned. "Indeed. And you have made a practice of humiliating rich and powerful men ever since those far off days. Isn't that so, highness? Why, that's a homily worthy of Chrysostom."

A wet strand of hair had snaked over Theodora's shoulder, trickling water down between her breasts. "How do you intend to entertain me? Be quick, fool, before I call the guards."

Keeping the restless chicken grasped firmly in one hand, the man set the wet grain into two small piles. "I shall answer your questions. Or rather, my oracle here will. When I place this sagacious fowl between the piles of food, highness, ask it something, and then see toward which pile it heads to eat. The grain at my right hand means Yes, that to my left indicates No."

***

Felix put his shoulder to the door of the imperial carriage standing in a small clearing, turned its latch, and heard it click into place.

From inside the conveyance came a thunderous growl, then the noise of claws rattling and scrabbling. The carriage rocked slightly. A few in the bedraggled group of excubitors surrounding it cursed bears in general, and this one in particular. Although it was now safely contained, there was more than a little blood to give evidence of their struggle to get it into the carriage.

"Lucky for us our big friend here didn't escape from the grounds," Felix rumbled, sounding decidedly ursine himself. "Someone, and I suspect it would have been me, would have had to pay for the mistake then."

"It wasn't my fault," protested a young guard armed with a broken lance. "I didn't make that cursed weak net…."

"You're right. Still—"

"Captain, what are we, animal keepers?" protested another. "I didn't join the excubitors to haul the empress' pets around. It's not supposed to be part of our duties, pulling imperial carriages occupied by bears!"

"Now you know very well that the empress has such a kind heart she ordered three of you harnessed to the carriage so that none of the imperial horses would be terrified by the smell of its occupant. Need I remind you that your job is to do whatever she orders, and do it fast and without complaint?" Felix retorted.

The excubitors immediately began to detail orders they'd prefer to take from the empress.

"Those are wishes not likely to be granted," Felix grunted with a grin.

"Perhaps, but sometimes Fortuna surprises us." The speaker was staring open-mouthed down the path leading into the clearing.

Hardly had he spoken when two naked women raced past them.

"Murder…at the baths," shrieked one.

***

The hallway in the women's wing of the imperial baths swarmed with aristocratic ladies in various states of panic and undress, the more panicked among them the least clothed.

"Mithra!" said the young man with the broken lance. "And I thought having to stand guard at banquets and smell all that food was hard duty."

A decently dressed woman, an attendant no doubt, trotted by, glancing back over her shoulder.

Felix stopped her. "What's going on?" he demanded.

"It's Satan, sir. Satan's flying from one pool to another, shouting all manner of blasphemies and obscenities. Flying about like a horrible black bird. Everybody in the baths ran away, naked or not. The shame of it, sir, to be seen naked in public…but it was a question of garments or souls and not both, so it was." She looked down at the blue silk tunic in her hands. "Now I must find my mistress and get her decently clothed, sir."

As she ran out of the building, a familiar figure raced down the hallway toward them.

No, Felix realized, the figure wasn't familiar. It was its clothing, which was instantly recognizable. Its elaborate embroidered panels depicting the temptation in the Garden of Eden identified it as a garment he had seen the empress wearing.

It was not actually being worn, but rather was wrapped around the running figure. Whoever it was suddenly flung the robe off, straight into Felix' face, and bolted outside.

Felix knocked the garment aside. He saw the back of the black-cloaked figure that had worn it and set out in hasty pursuit.

His boots slid on wet tiles and he fell heavily, taking two excubitors with him. For a short space, the hallway was a confusion of sprawled, armored guards, bare flesh, swords, and silks.

Felix found himself pinned beneath the not inconsiderable weight of a plump, pink-faced, matronly woman.

He gently lifted her off and scrambled to his feet, trying not to look at her. "Priscilla, my apologies. Please give my regards to your husband the senator."

He contained his choice string of lurid curses until he was outside the baths.

"This way!" an excubitor shouted, gesturing toward the clearing down the path as his colleagues poured outside, heads swiveling back and forth, gaping after fleeing women.

"Look at me, men," bellowed Felix. "Pretend I'm a pretty sight! Keep your eyes on your captain! Now, follow! He can't outrun us!"

He was right. The leading excubitors burst into the clearing only a few paces behind their quarry.

Unfortunately, those few paces also marked the distance between the edge of the open space and the imperial carriage.

Without saying a word, the strange intruder grasped the carriage door and flung it open.

The furious bear erupted from its prison. In an instant it was on the excubitors like a storm howling in off the sea.

By the time they'd saved themselves their quarry was long gone.

Felix had just sent a number of his men with the tattered net after the bear when the empress made her appearance, properly dressed, albeit in someone else's fine silks, and accompanied by her ladies-in-waiting.

"Captain Felix! You and the rest of your men escort us to our residence immediately! I must tell the emperor what the chicken had to say."

Chapter Seven

Nereus' house looked deserted.

John stood at the foot of a wide street leading off the Strategion. The steeply roofed dwelling on the opposite corner showed no signs of life. Its shuttered windows gave the impression that the entire household was dead, fast asleep, or had sensibly decamped to less dangerous surroundings.

He glanced up the sloping thoroughfare. Not even a stray beggar was visible for its entire length. Yet behind him, one or two of the vegetable sellers who had long been fixtures of the Strategion market hoarsely cried their wares at the foraging seagulls.

On his way through the square, John had noticed goods were sparse. Here a pale man with a racking cough displayed bundles of limp leeks and shriveled radishes allegedly fresh from the country, while there a plump woman shouted praise for her fine chickens. John had a notion Peter would have sniffed in disdain over both the scrawny fowls offered and the outrageous price demanded. The customary noise and the smell of loam and leafage, recalling a country morning, rising above a chattering, colorful crowd, had gone.

Lack of business was not unexpected. Work and food were both increasingly hard to obtain, and many of the desperate broke into deserted homes seeking edibles or the means to buy them, a thought that directed his attention back to the household he had come to visit.

Stepping quickly across the street, he briskly rapped on Nereus' door. Muted echoes died away in the atrium. Given the futility of his investigations so far, John half expected no answer, but as he began to turn away there came a shouted reply from within informing him he would be attended upon shortly.

Soon the stout door swung open to reveal a stocky, red-faced man dressed in a short, grass-stained tunic and grasping a large pitchfork. He looked like a farmer just in from the fields, an impression reinforced by stray straws caught in his hair.

"May I be of assistance, sir?" the man inquired civilly, his politeness at odds with the implied threat of the sharp implement he carried.

John introduced himself and the other stepped back with a low bow, holding the door wide open.

"Please to enter the house. I fear that I, Sylvanus, am the only person here. All the other servants have gone to the late master's estate. He is to be buried there."

"I regret the death of your master, Sylvanus. However, it may be that you can provide—"

A loud bellow from the inner garden interrupted John's words.

Sylvanus glanced hastily over his shoulder. "Could I answer your questions in the garden, sir? Apis is agitated. The master would not have liked that."

"Nereus kept a bull in his town house?" John followed the bucolic servant across the atrium, noting the man had tracked dirt across the lively sea scene depicted by the floor tiles.

"Indeed he did. Apis was his most prized oracle!"

As they emerged into sunlight, John's first impression was of a miniature farm. Several large fish stirred the water of a shallow pool, an iron grate barring their escape into a channel leading to the bull's enclosure. A quartet of brass plates hung in the tree shadowing the animal's pen. Beyond that, chickens in a large cage scratched contentedly in the dust.

Trees and tall shrubs had been planted around the garden's perimeter, all but concealing the peristyles. It would have been easy to gaze up into the blue square of sky and imagine oneself in a secluded country setting.

Apis, standing at the fence of his pen, angrily tossed his head and emitted another bellow. It was a prime specimen of the animal sacred to Mithra, John thought. A long chain attached to a ring circling one of the bull's legs ran back to another ring set in a sturdy granite post. Nereus had apparently taken precautions to ensure his house wasn't invaded by the bull, sacred or not.

Sylvanus began to fork straw into Apis' enclosure. "Well, sir, I know many have wondered why Nereus would keep such odd company in his town house. The fact of the matter is" —he paused to wipe his brow—"he set great store by Apis and the other oracles, and his visitors were always fascinated as well."

"I see," said John. "Nereus' oracles were for the purpose of entertainment?"

Sylvanus shook his head. "To some extent, yes, but chiefly because he was a man of business. His business was shipping and that's an enterprise more prone to the whims of Fortuna than most."

John agreed it was so.

"Yes," the other went on with some pride. "I've cared for a number of different prophetic beasts over the years. You'll have noticed the fish—the very same species were consulted in one of Apollo's temples. Their swimming to and fro predict what's in store for the inquirer."

John suggested that if such oracles foretold the future as accurately as the ancients claimed, the knowledge provided would indeed have been most useful to Nereus.

"That's right, sir!" Sylvanus set aside his pitchfork. "Now it's true that occasionally the Dodona oracles—" he pointed to the four thin brass plates jingling gently in the breeze "—kept us awake on tempestuous nights, but the master would not hear of them being taken down. Set great store by them, he did, although we never knew how he found out the way to interpret the sound the leather strips make slapping against the plates. He often used to say the Dodona oracles can foretell the future, but who can foretell the wind?"

"An interesting thought," John observed, not entirely certain how to interpret Nereus' comment.

"These are not the actual Dodona oracle, needless to say. But of the same vintage, or so he was assured. Not that cost ever deterred him. He was about to receive a new oracle and was very excited about it. An antique statue of Hermes, inspired by the one at Pharae. He told me seekers after knowledge made an offering, asked the statue their question, and then covered their ears until they left its presence. The first words they heard when they uncovered them were said to answer their question."

Evidently, John thought, an auricular oracle.

"It wasn't just statues and animals, though, sir," Sylvanus continued with a fond smile. "Our cook complained more than once he had to keep a secret store of eggs and poppy seeds since the master would occasionally take them for purposes of divination, although neither of us know how they could possibly be used to foretell the future. You've perhaps noted the laurel bushes are a bit bare? The master would sometimes burn their leaves for the same purpose."

Sylvanus sighed. "Only last week the house steward mentioned one of the master's dinner guests had spilt wine and the master immediately prophesized the future from the shape the puddle made."

"Was he correct?"

"I can't say. However, no one can deny that Nereus thrived in his business affairs. No matter the weather, he spent an hour in the garden with me every morning consulting the oracles. He often said he had never known them to be wrong. Apis here was a particular favorite. The master paid handsomely for him. Bought him as a calf and happy to do it, since Apis is an exact copy of the bull oracle of old, what with being black and marked with a white square on his forehead."

He paused to contemplate Apis, who was now quietly chewing at fresh hay. A massive hillock of an animal, the bull flicked its tail slowly back and forth, barely disturbing a twinkling cloud of buzzing flies.

"Do you think oracles really can tell us the future, sir? Apis here, he hasn't eaten hardly a thing since the master died and usually he has a hearty appetite. Very strange, as I said to Cador only this morning. Cador's the house steward's assistant, gone to the country with the others. I shall be joining them as soon as they send a cart back to transfer the animals out there."

A look of distress clouded Sylvanus' face.

John commiserated, observing it must be difficult for a man of the soil to find himself stranded alone in a city.

"It's not that, sir. It's just that I'd much rather stay in Constantinople. Born here, so I was. I've worked in aristocrats' gardens all my life and, despite my name, I've hardly set foot outside the city walls. It's the thought of all that open space around me that I find disturbing. Fields and fields, with nothing beyond them but more fields, or perhaps a forest. There's bears in forests, you know."

"Perhaps you could arrange to stay here as caretaker of the house while various legal affairs are settled, and meantime you could seek another master?"

A look of gratitude spread across Sylvanus' face as he contemplated the suggestion.

"How does this bull indicate the future?" John asked, quickly, as much to divert the other as from a thirst for arcane knowledge.

"Ah!" Sylvanus' brown face furrowed into a grin. "It's very easy. No need for purification rites or anything like that! No, a person wishing to consult Apis on a course of action merely puts the question and offers food. If Apis eats, it means a fortunate outcome to the intended enterprise." A thoughtful look entered his eyes. "Since Apis found his appetite again just after you arrived, it may well mean you will find whatever it is you seek."

"I hope so. However, I would like to consult you rather than these oracles. I believe a customs official named Gregory recently visited your master?"

"Gregory? He visited quite often on matters of business, I believe. The master showed him around the garden a few times. He did not seem very impressed."

The gardener appeared reluctant to say more. John assured him he had nothing to do with customs duties or taxation for that matter. "Gregory was here the day Nereus died?"

Sylvanus looked dubious. "I truly can't say. I rarely venture into the house when the master has visitors. I wouldn't want to be tracking mud everywhere, for one thing. There were quite a number of people there that day, from the sound of it. A real commotion. I find it of some comfort, sir, to recall that the master did not die alone."

"You wouldn't know, then, who might also have been present to witness Nereus' will?"

Sylvanus shook his head. "That was none of my business, sir. My business is looking after the master's oracles."

"You mentioned Nereus showed them to Gregory, and to other visitors too. His lawyer, for instance?"

"I'm afraid I don't know who his lawyer might be. I don't think he's visited the garden, though, since being a lawyer he would surely have started arguing with the oracles."

"What about you, Sylvanus? Do you have any notion why Nereus decided to make a new will?"

Sylvanus patted the bull's flank and looked down into the pond, staring gloomily at the ghostly forms of the fish moving restlessly below its surface. "Everyone in the household knew why. It was on account of his son."

"An only child?"

Sylvanus nodded. "There is no other family left. Nereus named the boy Triton after the sea god. The master liked to say his own fate was embedded in the name his parents gave him and that because of it he was destined to make his fortune from the sea. Alas, while the mythological Nereus had fifty daughters, the master had only the one son, a lad who contrived to bring him more sorrow than fifty daughters ever could." The oracle keeper ran his hand through his hair, extracted a straw, and tossed it onto the surface of the pool. Eager fish rose, rippling the water.

"Has Triton followed in his father's footsteps and entered the shipping trade?"

"Hardly, although that is what Nereus intended. Excuse me, sir. I should not speak ill of his flesh and blood, but we all agreed Triton had finally gone too far. None of us were at all surprised when the master finally carried out his threat to disinherit him."

***

Hypatia looked up from chopping dill as Peter shuffled into the kitchen. Night had begun to darken the window panes and, having lit the house lamps, Peter carefully set the last one on the kitchen table. Its orange light danced across smoke-stained ceiling and walls, adding to the ruddy glow from the brazier.

"Isn't it strange how a good lamp and a warm fire make us feel much safer?" Hypatia remarked, emptying a plate of chopped herbs into the pot steaming atop the brazier.

"Unless the lamp gets knocked over and sets fire to the house." Peter peered into the pot. "You added too much water for that amount of bacon and not enough dill."

"You heard the master's order, Peter! I am to cook for the time being. And just as well, since obviously lighting the lamps has tired you out. As for lack of dill, I've added all we had."

"Make sure you slice the rind off that chunk of bacon before you serve it as well. The master has the old soldier's habit of eating everything placed before him without complaining, and bacon rind is bad for the digestion." Peter lowered himself on to the kitchen stool. "There is something else I wish attended to, Hypatia."

The young woman raised inquiring eyebrows.

"When I was lighting the lamps, I almost fell over one of your clay scorpions. It was sitting beside the master's desk. It's fortunate for you I saw it before he did. He would not have been pleased." Peter's tone made it clear that he was not happy about it either.

Hypatia frowned. "I realize you call my charms superstitious nonsense, Peter, but surely you understand I'm using them to protect the house and all who dwell here?"

"Them? There are more?"

"Yes, there are." She began to launch into a sharp retort, but sensed an unusual anger in the elderly servant's suddenly flushed face and instead lowered her voice. "I placed one at every entrance and each corner of the house, but I couldn't get up on the roof to—"

Peter interrupted with the comment that a woman seen clambering about on the Lord Chamberlain's roof would certainly have been fine grist for every palace gossip who happened to be passing by at the time.

"I know these scorpions come from a good heart," he went on kindly. "However, you need to conceal them. Remember that the master serves a Christian emperor and, in addition, may well have visitors who would not look kindly on such decorations. Besides, it's my understanding that the scorpion has some significance for Mithrans. The master most certainly does not want his beliefs placed on view, even by accident."

He sighed heavily. "I am confiding in this fashion because it may well fall to you to remember all these things one day."

"Gaius says there is no cure for the plague. If that's so, we can only try to scare it away."

"You would do better to put your faith in the Lord than in creatures of clay, Hypatia."

The young woman gave the pot a final stir and then stepped over to the window. Each pane held a wavering image of the flame from the lamp on the table. She leaned closer to the glass. "How can you put your faith in a god who visits such punishment as this pestilence upon his creatures?"

Peter quickly made the sign of his religion. "This world may be full of horror, but it is only this world. Who can say what lies beyond? We might well convince ourselves there is nothing outside this kitchen, but lean close enough to that dark glass, look through the reflections from our small lamp, and you'll see countless lights blazing forth beyond."

"For an old army cook you preach very well, Peter," Hypatia replied softly. "In fact, better than some prelates."

"We must remain humble! After all, there may well be prelates who are better cooks than I am." Peter began to smile, but then his face darkened. "Gregory and I had been discussing this world and the next for some time."

"And those words were composed for his ears?"

"Yes." Peter bowed his head.

Hypatia rubbed away condensation on the window panes. In the quiet kitchen, her finger made a faint squeaking sound against the glass. Boiling water murmured busily in the pot. Now the smell of bacon joined the odor of dill. "I might believe in your god if he sent a messenger to me, Peter, as he did to you. Yet why would you receive a message about your friend when so many are dying?"

Peter observed the ways of heaven were beyond understanding.

"They're certainly beyond mine. Those clay scorpions you scorn are more much straightforward. Besides, do you think I haven't noticed your lucky coin?"

Peter gave her a questioning look.

"The coin you keep in your room. I've seen it now and then when I'm cleaning."

Peter related how he had found the coin in Isauria. "And consider this, Hypatia. Paul himself might have held that very coin!"

"It could have magickal powers then," the young woman suggested slyly.

"You make it sound like one of those…." Peter hesitated, choosing his words with care. "…foreign talismans."

"This sort of foreign talisman, Peter?"

Hypatia took off a small pendant suspended on a thin, leather thong and handed it to him for inspection. "It's an udjat. They're very highly thought of in Egypt."

The green faience piece was a stylized representation of a large eye, with a trailing, curved tail descending from its left side.

"That's an Eye of Horus," Hypatia went on. "It protects its wearers against evil and ill health. Everyone in this city should be wearing one, if you ask me."

"What an odd thing," Peter observed. "And without intending blasphemy, it reminds me of the all-seeing eyes of the Lord."

"Why don't you put your coin on a chain and wear it, Peter? Then you'd be protected wherever you go."

"But why are you convinced it is lucky?"

Hypatia beamed. "Why, because it bears the likeness of Fortuna, of course."

Chapter Eight

Triton had not moved a great distance from his father's dwelling, but he had fallen a long way from its comfortable surroundings.

The address to which Sylvanus had directed John lay not far from the silversmiths' quarter, across the street from a squat edifice completely occupied, according to the plaque beside its entrance, by furriers. Chunks of the plaster facing of the apartment building where Triton lived had fallen off, revealing rough brickwork beneath. Many of its grubby windows displayed shattered panes or shutters hanging drunkenly from broken hinges.

Just inside a low archway leading to the building's inner courtyard, two chipped columns, which looked as though they'd been recently scavenged from a refuse pit, called attention to a splintered door.

John knocked and waited. Looking back across the street, he could see a formless brown heap against the wall of the building opposite. Presumably furriers' discarded wares. The malodorous smell wafting from that direction suggested rather a dead donkey.

A lock snicked and the door cracked open to reveal a tiny woman with the creased yellow skin of a quince and an expression almost as sour. Despite the warm weather, she was swathed in layers of black wool.

"What is it?" She firmly clutched the edge of her door, obviously prepared to slam it shut if necessary.

"Are you the owner of this building?"

"Yes. My name's Glykeria. How can I assist you?" She inclined her head to one side to look up at John. Her eyes had a glassy, vacant look.

John realized she was actually turning an ear toward him.

The woman was blind.

He told her he sought a man named Triton.

"Do I know where he is? Indeed I do," Glykeria replied. "Burning in the eternal fires, that's where. That young villain will be roasting long after the empire is dust and that's just for the rent he never paid. So whatever he owes you, I'm afraid you'll just have to be content with considering that he'll burn for that as well."

The sightless eyes gleamed as if reflecting the flames she contemplated.

John sighed. He'd never undertaken an investigation where death seemed to be not only the crime, but also the murderer's accomplice. Nonetheless he forged ahead, explaining he wasn't a bill collector but rather a palace official.

The woman glowered at him. "Of course not. You're a good friend and just want a word. He had so many good friends wanting a word. Never met anyone so popular, I must say. I could tell by my nose just who he'd robbed. The perfumer visited more than once. for a start. At the end he couldn't even pay the cheesemaker's bill. All good friends, so they said, although none of them claimed to be from the palace before now."

John assured her he was, in fact, from the palace. She gave no indication that she had heard him, or believed him if she had.

"When did Triton die?" he asked.

"Only yesterday. Or possibly it was the day before. Not long ago." She flapped a claw-like hand vaguely.

"Do you know anything about his family or friends? Perhaps some of these visitors you mentioned—"

"His father won't be settling Triton's debts, so you're out of luck there. I can assure you, the rogue had long since cut himself off from whatever family he had, or they cut themselves off from him. Little wonder, really. If he hadn't died, I would've evicted him at the end of the week."

"Triton was a troublesome tenant?"

"Named for a pagan god and had the morals of one."

Something in the woman's tone told John he would have to tread around the subject of Triton carefully. He asked to see Triton's room.

Glykeria's head inclined further to the side. "I see I misunderstood your intentions."

Suddenly she grabbed a fold of John's robe.

A toothless smile added another crease to the woman's face. "I can feel from this fine cloth you can afford my rooms. For an instant I thought I'd have to direct you to a tenement. If you would wait…."

She banged the door shut and emerged not long afterwards grasping a bundle of keys.

"This way," she said as she scuttled out. Despite her lack of sight, Glykeria crossed the paved courtyard without hesitation and vanished into an entranceway. John followed her to the top of a gloomy flight of stairs.

"I'm not proposing to become a tenant," he said, wondering how she had formed the misconception. "I only wish to see where Triton lived. I'm curious, though. How did you initially suppose I couldn't afford one of your rooms?"

"Excuse me, sir, but it was because you carry the smell of the most vulgar of wines."

Glykeria led him to the second floor. If any lamps were provided in the windowless stairwell, they weren't lit. The hallway was nearly as dark. Glykeria's key grated in a lock, a battered plank door swung open, and they stepped into a room whose furnishings consisted entirely of dust.

"Spacious, as I'm sure you'll agree. If you'd care to look out the window and direct your gaze between the building over the way and the warehouse next to it and then over the top of the distant granary, there's a fine view of the sea, or so I'm told."

John walked over to the window. Whoever had described the view to Glykeria possessed either eyes or a tongue that couldn't be trusted.

"A most pleasant view," she went on. "But then to me any view would be pleasant." She emitted a brief cackle.

Ignoring his recent statement that he did not wish to take a room, she continued. "I must caution you, sir, there's already been some interest in this fine place. Several well-spoken young men came by just yesterday. Come to think of it, that proves Triton must have been dead then. Unless it was this morning when I showed them the room. They looked around for the longest time. They wanted to meditate on the decision by themselves, so I left them. I suspect they were praying for advice. In the end, they did not take it. Perhaps it was heaven's plan the room should still be here for you, sir. They gave me a nummus for my trouble. Very pious young men, they were."

Not to mention strong, since the courteous thieves had apparently stolen everything in the room. Not that there had been much furniture to begin with, judging from the dust-free markings on the floorboards.

Glykeria secured Triton's former lodgings behind them. Having taken several uncannily sure steps down the hallway, motioning John to follow, she rapped a staccato summons on a door at the far end.

After some time a muffled screech came from within. "I told you, my husband's sick, you old crow. We'll pay the rent as soon as he's up and around and can get back to work."

"I'll have what's due, or you'll answer to the City Prefect!"

"Why not bring the Patriarch along with the Prefect while you're at it?" came the shouted reply. "Or how about Justinian? I am sure the emperor is as anxious about your rent as you are! Go away and stop bothering a sick man!"

"I've got someone here prepared to take you away now," Glykeria claimed. "If you don't believe me, look out and see."

The door opened briefly and shut again with a loud click. Not long afterwards the door opened a second time and several coins clattered onto the floor near Glykeria's shoes. She bent nimbly, her fingers explored the boards, found the money, and scooped it up in an instant. "Thank you for your assistance, sir. I'll be happy to give you a discount on that room."

"Perhaps you might have waited until your tenant resumed working?" John suggested as they clattered back downstairs.

Glykeria snorted in derision. "The fellow won't see sunrise tomorrow."

"What makes you think so?"

They were halfway across the courtyard. Glykeria stopped and turning toward John tapped her nose. "I can smell it, sir. Take the clerk on the second floor. He's afraid it's the plague, but he'll be back to his accounts next week. He just ate something that had spoilt, that's all. However, the potter next door to him will be clay before he touches his wheel again."

"How do you know this, Glykeria?" He almost expected to hear that she kept an oracle in her kitchen.

"I smell it on them."

"Ah, I understand." It was becoming obvious that Glykeria's blindness was less an impediment to her than her mental faculties. Which perhaps explained how she had transformed John so quickly from one of Tritons' creditors to prospective tenant.

She must have sensed the doubt in his tone. "Let me prove it, sir." She wrinkled her nose and sniffed. "What a strange thing. You have been to a farm recently. A gentleman like you in the midst of the capital, I agree it seems unlikely and yet it is unmistakable. Let me advise you, bulls can be dangerous beasts."

John remarked that she had an amazing gift.

"Gift? You call this a gift? Can you imagine what it is like to live by one's nose since the plague arrived? Be glad you don't possess my sensitivities, sir. Now, about the matter of Triton's old room…."

John explained yet again that he did not intend to rent anything. He pressed a coin into her hand, stifling her vague murmurs of disappointment. "For your help, Glykeria. Is there anything else you can tell me about Triton before I go?"

"I didn't know him as well as some, I admit. However, I make my daily rounds, to collect rents, to clean, to make certain all is in order. I noticed things from time to time. He imbibed heavily, for a start. He was often sick from too much wine."

Her face crinkled with displeasure at the recollection. "His father visited once. They argued. Such blasphemous language. I've rarely heard the like! It's no wonder Triton died horribly. Many of my tenants have left this life since the plague arrived and it's always a dreadful death, but his was the most terrible of all. I could hear him at the end, bellowing with pain, even down here in the courtyard. Heaven is just, sir, if not always kind."

She tilted her head toward the courtyard which they had just left, as if the paving stones still vibrated with echoes of Triton's last agonies.

John asked what Triton and Nereus had argued about.

"A woman, of course. What else? She insisted on calling herself Sappho. She thought I didn't notice, but I always knew when she sneaked in and out of the building. She smelled of cheap wine, expensive perfume, and garlic. A very stupid and low girl."

Glykeria leaned forward confidentially. "One day she brought in a piece of fox-fur one of the furriers over the way had discarded. I had a tenant who sewed, and I allowed her to conduct business in her room for a small weekly consideration. Apparently Sappho imagined she would look quite the aristocrat, with this nasty scrap of fur sewn along the bottom of her tunic. Still, the job provided my tenant a extra nummus or two, so she could pay her rent on time for a change, until the plague claimed her."

She pursed her lips. "My tenant described the woman to me in great detail. Sappho always wore saffron-colored garments, of a most indecent style I may add, and boasted endlessly about how she would one day wear golden silk. Well, to cut a long story short, she eventually moved in, but when she left him she took the nasty thing with her. I mean the fox-trimmed tunic, not Triton."

John asked, without harboring much hope, if Glykeria could remember the date of the woman's departure. Unfortunately, she could not. Nor could she say where this particular girl had come from. She'd really been no different from the others who stayed with Triton occasionally, except she'd stayed longer than the rest.

"But then what do you expect? She was an actress, sir, and very flighty in her ways. Decent folk use other words for them that follow that particular profession." She compressed her lips. "Have you talked to the bear trainers by the Hippodrome? But no, it's a bull you recently visited, not a bear. She claimed to work with them. Bears, I mean."

"And Triton, what profession did he follow?"

"He was like her. Had all sorts of notions, but rarely worked. Fancied himself first an actor, then a bear trainer. The girl knew some of the trainers, as I said, and got him a job with them. It didn't last long and no wonder, if he mistreated the bears as badly as he did her."

She hugged herself suddenly. "If you don't mind, sir, there's bit of a chill in the air. I need to warm up inside and then I'm off to the Great Church. I spend as much time there as I can."

John remarked that one's faith could be a great comfort in such trying times.

Glykeria gave another cackle. "It's the incense that draws me there these days, sir. Yes, the blessed incense. It's the only thing that banishes the stink of death from my nostrils."

Chapter Nine

Anatolius loped through the high-ceilinged halls of the Baths of Zeuxippos, exchanging hurried greetings with one or two of the scanty number of bathers availing themselves of the facilities. It was remarkable, his poetic nature noted, how even as the shadow of Thanatos lay across the city, some residents still clung to their everyday routines.

What was even more remarkable, his practical side immediately asserted, was that there was still enough manpower and fuel to provide enough hot water for the baths to continue to operate.

The corridors were eerily deserted as he made his way toward the private baths. His footsteps, slapping against an uncharacteristically dry marble floor, sounded far too loud.

He remembered a dream he'd had more than once. In the dream he arrived at the baths only to find himself alone. The water was cold, the corridors all empty. As he wandered the lifeless labyrinth panic began to swell in his chest. Suddenly he knew, without question, he was the last person left alive and that when he emerged from the impossibly deserted baths, Constantinople would be just as empty, and all the towns beyond its walls, and all the lands beyond the seas—all would be empty. He could feel the emptiness inside him as well as all around him.

Had that recurring dream been an omen?

He had begun to form the uneasy feeling that perhaps he was dreaming again when he arrived at a semicircular area graced by a platform facing a number of empty benches.

At least this lecture room was occupied, if only by a single person, the glum-faced Crinagoras.

Seeing Anatolius, his expression brightened and he leapt up with an eager grin. "How kind of you to attend my recitation! I feared my genius had frightened off my fellow devotees of Calliope. Until you arrived, as someone once said, my audience was made up of three benches and four walls. Well, if you want to be entirely accurate, not even four walls, just a single curved one."

Not certain whether his friend was jesting or not, Anatolius mumbled apologies for arriving late. "I visited the Lord Chamberlain on the way here, and we talked about Gregory's murder. Remember, I was telling you about that after you mentioned you'd witnessed—"

"Oh, don't worry about that. What matters is that you've managed to finally get here!"

"Yes. That's the important thing, naturally."

Crinagoras ignored the ironic comment and chattered on.

Anatolius occasionally wondered why he tolerated Crinagoras. They'd been tutored together as boys. Their shared horror of the hypotenuse was the foundation of their friendship. The two aspiring poets had always preferred Homer to Pythagoras.

Crinagoras had grown up to be slightly taller than Anatolius, bigger of frame, and with a tendency to plumpness. Although the same age as his fellow, his ruddy face, framed in sandy curls, retained the pudgy, unformed look of a child, a face that might be characterized as a not quite completed marble likeness still awaiting time's final, telling cuts.

"We may as well begin, I suppose." Crinagorus fussed with the voluminous folds of the old-fashioned toga he'd donned for the event. A disappointed scowl displaced his welcoming grin as he ruffled through several parchments. "It's just as well I didn't bring my lyre."

"Perhaps notice of your recitation has not yet reached your patrons?" The prospect of maintaining a semblance of enthusiasm as an audience of one in the face of his friend's lugubrious verses made Anatolius squirm as much as the sight of a equilateral triangle on a wax tablet had upset him in his youth. "Might I therefore suggest you delay it until they have received the news? Doubtless they'd all be sorry to miss such an opportunity! Instead, perhaps we could…." He cast about for inspiration. "…go off into the country for a little fresh air?"

"What? But we'd have to go to the stables. I'd need to change my clothing. What about our midday meal?"

"Oh, you don't need to change," Anatolius replied hastily. "It will be an adventure. John was telling me just now that he hadn't learned anything when he visited Nereus' residence except that the household has moved out to his estate. It's up by the northern end of the Golden Horn. Perhaps we could find out something useful for him."

"I'm not certain if I want to go, Anatolius. Riding always upsets my humors."

"We could stop at the cemetery on the way and inspect your latest inscriptions."

"Well, there's that, certainly! It may be that some of my dear patrons no longer draw the breath that sang my praises. What a cold mistress is the grave, yet none can resist her blandishments. Alas, that men would desert my verses for death."

"Aptly put, my friend. You must write it down for posterity as soon as possible."

"Anyway, it would be best to reveal my newest inspiration to several of my patrons simultaneously, wouldn't you say? Then no charge of favoritism could be leveled at me if one should hear before the rest."

"A circumstance that would certainly create difficulties in the way of obtaining new commissions, if someone thought another had heard your most recent creations first."

"Exactly so. I hope you don't mind, Anatolius, but I shall not let you read my new poems either, even though you are a close friend!"

"Of course." Anatolius attempted to look disappointed. "Even friends cannot always ask for special dispensations."

"I can tell you, however, that one of them is a most personal poem about my beloved Eudoxia and the agonies of longing I have suffered ever since her death. I am quite painfully honest about my anguish. Courageously honest, if you will. It is my duty to keep her dear memory alive."

"You don't have to explain. Your patrons expect nothing less of you. Alas, I know how difficult it can be, pleasing one's patrons."

Crinagoras looked thoughtful. "I said I would not reveal my latest poems to you, but I will tell you I have composed several more of my epigrams on architecture. You see, my thought is they might eventually be chiseled on the architecture in question for a reasonable price. You might describe them as little bricks of poems. Businessmen are not always interested in the finer feelings. Ordinary subjects are what they prefer. For instance—" he glanced through the parchments in his chubby hand— "you've already heard my Ode to a Granary. Another one proclaims the Mese. I call it Forked Like The Serpent's Tongue. There's pathos in stone, you know, if you can just find it."

Anatolius stated he was absolutely certain if pathos could be found, Crinagoras would be the one to find it.

"You're right. It's an amazing talent once you realize you have it. Here's another. It's about the fortifications on the land walls. Ninety-six Towers, I call it."

"Speaking about land walls and towers reminds me we were going on a little journey, so let's be off."

They strolled out, taking a leisurely pace through the rambling edifice. Glancing at the numerous bronze and marble statues of heroes of mythology and prominent Greek and Roman poets and philosophers with which the baths were decorated, Anatolius found his attention straying somewhat from his companion's recital of his latest misfortunes.

"But then we must all be men of philosophy in these sad times," Crinagoras concluded, "especially poets."

Anatolius agreed. "Yet consider," he went on, "sometimes it's less their writings, but rather the lives of philosophers and poets that provide the lessons." He gestured at the statue of Aeschines they were approaching.

Crinagoras laughed. "The orator who was a sausage-maker's son?"

"We should not scoff at sausage-making. It's honest work, after all. However, more importantly, his statue reminds me he failed in the perfume business."

Crinagoras inquired as to the moral of the tale, other than that it proved sausage-makers' offspring should not nurse notions of entering a more fragrant profession.

"The lesson, my friend, is that anyone can aspire to greatness, even if he loses all he has by failing in the attempt. Is it not true that the courage to try, however hopeless the task might be, is the mark of the hero?"

"Now you sound like our old tutor," the other grumbled. "However, you've inspired me with a wonderful idea. I'll write a series of poems relating lessons we can learn from all this wonderful statuary." His face flushed with excitement. "Yes! Just think, I could lead my patrons around the baths, give a short lecture at each statue, and then declaim my verses!"

Anatolius wondered uneasily what he had unwittingly unleashed on Constantinople's literary community as his companion plunged ahead, eagerly laying out plans for his new enterprise.

"Take, for example, Erinna of Rhodes over there. A poetess, and one who died at a tender age. I could make much of those crocuses at her feet. Something along the lines of, oh, it would be sending crocuses to Cilicia looking for poets of my quality in Constantinople, for I never hesitate to give acknowledgement to my fellow writers." His expression clearly conveyed his opinion of his rivals.

"Not to mention that such appearances would naturally lead your audience to recollect your services are available for hire?" Anatolius suggested.

"Indeed!" They turned a corner and entered a corridor lined with bronze statues.

"Writers should always be subtle in offering their compositions," Crinagoras continued. "Look at this representation of Isocrates. Wonderful orator, no doubt about it, and there's his famous tomb with a column supporting the statue of a siren. An absolutely inspired choice for symbolic decoration. Are not sirens the most persuasive of creatures, even to the extent of leading men to their deaths? I've made this very observation more than once. Yet how often when Isocrates' name is bruited about does someone immediately recall that the orator owned slaves who were expert flute-makers? Isocrates' slaves are as famous as he is and none of them ever wrote a line!"

Anatolius observed it was certainly a strange circumstance that servants whose names were not known to history could become as famed as their master.

As they emerged into an atrium graced by a fountain set about with curved benches, Crinagoras' commentary ran on as ceaselessly as the water splashing into the pink marble bowl.

"Sometimes it's as hard laboring to find the right word as it is to dig a ditch. On the other hand, now and then inspiration strikes as suddenly as the tortoise that fell on the head of Aeschylus over there. Though not as fatally, of course."

Anatolius, ruefully remembering a few of his youthful more than impertinent verses about Empress Theodora, thought that in some circumstances poetry might indeed prove fatal.

"Now, take Demosthenes," he replied, unable to resist playing the game Crinagoras had started. The statue to which he called attention depicted a man in his later years, his thin face wrinkled and brow furrowed. "No doubt he would have orated at length about Diogenes there going about with a lantern looking for an honest man in broad daylight! Considering the lurid reputations of some who regularly patronize of this establishment, his would be a lengthy task, I fear."

Crinagoras nodded appreciation. He fluttered a hand toward the marble Alcibiades standing guard at the entrance to the baths.

"Handsome fellow, isn't he, especially for a general? Even if he did wear his hair at such barbaric length," he sniffed. "I suppose when one is successful one can carry it off. Anyway, it isn't going to grow any longer!"

Anatolius scowled. His companion's hair did not look that much shorter than the statue's. Worse, the comment had reminded him of a man named Thomas, whose hair had been overly long, and who was a barbarian to boot. Not to mention he'd paid far too much attention to John's daughter Europa.

Why should he suddenly think of people he had not seen for years?

Crinagoras' prattling about his long lost beloved Eudoxia must have put the thought in his mind, not to mention his own preoccupation with Lucretia, another person from his past. With death everywhere, those who were gone, who were dead, seemed no less substantial than the living. All might soon join together in the legions of memory.

Even as the thought occurred to him he visualized his old mathematics tutor again, as harrowing a presence as if he were actually standing nearby.

Anatolius had truly tried to put Lucretia out of his memory as surely as her marriage to Balbinus had removed her from his life.

She simply refused to leave.

Perhaps Crinagoras, with his endless agonizing over the departed Eudoxia, was not entirely wrong about the way of things.

***

It was late morning by the time they reached the cemetery between the city's inner and outer walls. Crinagoras climbed off his mount with the grace of a one-legged septuagenarian, lamenting about the sad state of his nether regions.

They might have ridden all the way to Rome rather than up the Mese, Anatolius thought in exasperation. "Let's have a look at some of the epitaphs you wrote," he suggested.

They picked their way between innumerable fresh mounds of earth. Surprisingly no burials appeared to be in progress in the necropolis.

The wind had shifted and the smoke that had so often shrouded the city in mourning during the past weeks drifted overhead in ragged clouds. Anatolius could taste it in the air. The sudden thought that the smoke carried specks of the dead chilled his blood.

Crinagoras limped theatrically to a modest tomb, little more than a marble box with a steep roof and pillars at each corner.

"Here is the very first verse Paraskeve commissioned." He read the chiseled inscription. "It says 'Here lies the earthly husk of Didia, beloved wife of the baker Julius.' Husk, you see, because the husband made his living from grain. Much more subtle than the tomb-maker's notion of appropriate decorations."

He pointed at the carved wheat sheaves embellishing the pillars, all that distinguished the tomb from many of its neighbors.

"The architecture may be less than classic," Anatolius ventured, "but marble will preserve your words long after the last piece of parchment touched by your kalamos has crumbled into dust."

Crinagoras sniffed. "This dreadful smoke is burning my eyes. I am not ungrateful for the work, you understand. It's just that I feel I'm neglecting my duties toward my dear Eudoxia. It's been a while since I've composed a poem for her and even longer since I sold one."

They walked through the miniature city of tombs. A bird sang, bees buzzed in the grass.

Crinagoras stared thoughtfully in the direction of the inner wall from which they had just ridden. "If it weren't for the smoke, it'd be hard to imagine what we've just left. All those deserted streets, the endless lamentations reminding us how near we are to death."

"Not to mention it is right underfoot."

Crinagoras looked down hastily. "How could I forget!"

Strolling along, they stopped to admire other examples of the poet's work.

"'Do you caress my cold stone, tickle my mossy epitaph with your warm fingers? Alas, I know not, for I am dead,'" Crinagoras declaimed.

"I like this one," Anatolius said. "'You have journeyed far, now here you are.'"

"It is just as I told you," Crinagoras declared suddenly, seemingly in response to a conversation he'd been carrying on in his head. "You scoffed at the notion, but you are blessed because Lucretia is still alive. With life there is hope and with the odious senator on his deathbed, you may well be reunited with your beloved after all. Fortuna smiles on you."

"Yet why on me and not on Balbinus? Am I more deserving?" Anatolius smiled wanly. "That is a question not worth asking, for it is unanswerable."

"It's the unanswerable questions that are the most interesting. Besides, I can tell you why you deserve Fortuna's favor. You are a man of tender feelings, my friend, just like myself."

Anatolius came to a halt. "I can't help my feelings, Crinagoras. Yet it's wrong to wish for happiness at another's expense."

"The senator stole her from you. Her family arranged the marriage. She didn't want it. Would you wish Lucretia to be deprived of her happiness as well?"

"I admit it," Anatolius confessed shamefaced. "I am hoping her husband will die."

"Believe me, Anatolius, I know how it is. Lucretia is the sun in your sky. When she married, I feared you might throw yourself into the sea."

"I try not to recall that time. Not to mention it's just as likely the fellow who sells me wine threw himself into the sea when I regained my senses and his sales declined so drastically."

They resumed walking, completing a circle around the lonely space. Not far from the narrow road by which they had entered, a particularly unusual tomb caught Anatolius' eye. It resembled the Great Church, but reached only as high as his chest.

"Come along." Crinagoras sounded impatient. "We don't have time to dawdle over every monument in the place. Remember, it's some distance yet to Nereus' estate."

Anatolius' gaze slid across the miniature edifice. "You're in a hurry all of a sudden. I see there's an inscription on this tomb. It's one of yours, isn't it?"

"Well, yes, but do hurry up. At this rate it'll be dark before we even get to the estate."

"What is it? Why don't you want me to read it?" Anatolius bent slightly to make out the epitaph carved into the small church replica. "'I am only a dead dog, but my tomb is more magnificent than the candlemaker's.'"

***

The muscular, bare-chested man unloading amphorae from a wagon parked outside Nereus' villa looked up as Anatolius and Crinagoras approached. His hair was cropped to a black shadow, matching poorly shaven cheeks.

"I am Cador, assistant to the master's house steward. How can I assist?" The man's Greek was hesitant.

"We're here to ask a few questions concerning your master's death," Anatolius began, trying to remember how John conducted similar interviews. "Could we speak to the steward?"

He glanced toward the doorway, flanked by two massive, elaborately carved columns. The house was otherwise unadorned, a low, plaster-faced structure with a colonnade running down one side. It stood in the shade of a variety of short ornamental trees.

"Calligenes is gone. I am in charge until the master's legal affairs have been concluded."

"Your accent tells me you have traveled far, Cador," Crinagoras broke in.

The man nodded. "You are most perceptive, sir. It's been a long time since I last saw Bretania's rocky shore."

Anatolius scowled in annoyance. He'd taken the man's stilted speech and hesitancy as indicating he was slow witted. Now he noticed Cador had the reddened, peeling skin of those used to less sunny climes. "How did you come to work for Nereus?" he asked quickly, before Crinagoras could beat him in extracting more revelations.

"I was a tin streamer, sir. The brooks I panned were cold and seemed to get colder every year. Eventually I crossed the water and before I knew it, I was in Constantinople. Master Nereus was engaged solely in the tin trade at the time and gave me a job because of my experience."

Cador spoke as if he were weighing every word. The hard stare he directed at his visitors made it obvious to Anatolius that the man was highly suspicious. Extracting information would be as difficult as panning tin from a stream.

"Well," Anatolius said, thinking flattery might work and drawing on the few comments John had made about his sojourn in that distant land. "I have never been to Bretania, although a friend of mine was there many years ago. He described it as wild but beautiful."

"He was correct," Cador replied, his gaze never wavering. "Too cold, though. But that is enough reminiscing. There is too much work and too few hands. I have my own tasks and all the tasks my superiors left undone besides." He pulled another amphora off the back of the wagon. The brilliant sun glistened off rivulets of perspiration running down his sides.

"We just want to ask a few questions about your master's final hours," said Crinagoras. He was sweating too, or perhaps, more correctly, stewing. Swathed in his heavy toga, he didn't appear to be enjoying the heat as much as Cador. "What exactly happened?"

Cador set the amphora down. As he looked up at Crinagoras his eyes narrowed. "My apologies, sir. Now I recall, you were at the master's bedside. I did not recognize you in that strange garb."

Crinagoras bit his lip and flapped the folds of his toga sorrowfully.

When Cador didn't deign to actually answer the query, Anatolius took the chance of asking again. For a moment, caught in Cador's insolent glare, he was sorry he had.

Then, however, perhaps remembering his station, Cador nodded and spoke. "I can't tell you much about it, sir. The master was sinking fast, but insisted on seeing all his callers. There was a seller of antiquities and oracles. The master had done business with him before. This time Aristotle arrived with a very large oracular head."

Anatolius expressed surprise.

Cador allowed himself a slight smile and then continued. "The master asked it what course his illness would take. He was told, 'By tomorrow it will be forgotten.'"

"A delightful bit of ambiguity," pointed out Crinagoras. "How did this strange oracle make its predictions?"

"It was a hollow brass head of hideous visage," Cador replied. "The method used was placing a lantern inside the head and then interpreting the shadows it cast on the wall."

"An interesting notion," Anatolius put in. "What happened next?"

"Less than an hour later, the master took a turn for the worse."

"That was when he decided to execute an oral will?"

Cador nodded. "First he asked for Calligenes, the house steward, but he was ill also. We couldn't rouse him, so I served in his stead."

Crinagoras looked puzzled. "Calligenes was the first witness your master specifically requested?"

"Actually, sir, as you know from being present, there were already—"

"He must have trusted this Calligenes fellow then," Crinagoras mused. "Unduly, perhaps. What do you make of that, Anatolius? Something doesn't seem quite right. A fascinating problem, one to consider carefully, over a few cups of wine, in the shade of my garden."

"Excuse me," Cador interrupted, "but Calligenes was a loyal employee who had served Nereus well for many years. There's nothing more to it than that."

Crinagoras glanced at Anatolius and raised his eyebrows meaningfully.

"I know how valuable he was to the master," Cador went on. "I've been trying to complete all the work he left unfinished. The correspondence alone…well, before traveling here I trudged around half the city, delivering missives Calligenes had drawn up. He left a mountain of them on his desk, sirs. Letters, contracts, who knows what, all addressed in the fine hand on which he prided himself so much. In the course of carrying this out, I met bakers and bankers, importers and exporters, shopkeepers of various sorts, a perfumer, a lawyer, a bookseller—"

Anatolius broke in. "A lawyer? Can you tell us who this was?"

"Well…if I can remember…yes, it was one Prudentius to whom I delivered a letter."

Crinagoras clapped his hands. "There! You've discovered what we need to know, Anatolius. The murder has to do with the will. Where there's a will, there's a lawyer. This particular lawyer will settle it. Just in time, too. I'm famished and we still have our homeward odyssey ahead of us."

Anatolius had the impression that Crinagoras might begin to tug at his tunic and whimper if they didn't soon leave. Besides, he was right. Nereus' lawyer would certainly be able to shed light on the shipper's affairs. He thanked Cador for his help. "One last thing. Did you notice anyone following Gregory when he left?"

Cador shook his head. "I don't recall seeing him leave, sir."

As they walked back to their horses, Crinagoras suddenly spoke. "I wish I'd continued to escort Gregory after he left Nereus' house. If I had, he might still be alive."

"Or you might also be dead."

Crinagoras came to an abrupt halt. His eyes widened with alarm. "Why, I hadn't even considered that. You don't think we could have been followed here, do you?"

"What I think is Gregory was killed during a robbery. If not, John will surely find the culprit. Now we've discovered the name of Nereus' lawyer, once John has the information, he'll know best what to do next."

Chapter Ten

The mud-spattered apparition arrived at John's door well after dark. Peter, who had answered its frantic knocking, stepped backwards with a cry of horror.

"Anatolius!" John called from the top of the stairway. "You look as if you've been—"

"Buried and dug up," Anatolius said ruefully. He stepped into the atrium, dripping on the tiles.

Peter returned upstairs, looking reproachfully back over his shoulder.

Anatolius' gaze followed the elderly servant. "I know I'm not exactly a sight for innocent eyes, but surely Peter knows me well enough not to take fright at my appearance?"

"He's not himself right now. Come up to my study."

Anatolius looked down at his waterlogged garments and shook his head. "I think I'd better not. I'm making enough of a mess as it is. Besides, I need to get home and change."

John came down to the atrium. Heavy rain rattled impatiently into the impluvium.

"Crinagoras and I rode out to the countryside today. We were only half way back when the skies opened," Anatolius explained. "Crinagoras had composed ten new epitaphs for himself by the time we'd reached the city."

"I can imagine, but frankly I'd rather not. Be careful, Anatolius, you're dripping water on one of Hypatia's pets."

Anatolius stepped away from the clay scorpion stationed near the door.

"They make Hypatia happy," John said in reply to the unspoken question. "I consider myself fortunate my servants haven't deserted me for the safety of the countryside."

"Speaking of those who flee the city, Crinagoras and I were searching for just such a household. We made a discovery you might find interesting."

"That explains this late-night visit. I was afraid someone had died. Senator Balbinus, perhaps? Usually only bad news comes calling well after dark."

"No, there's no such bad news." Anatolius ran a hand through his sodden curls. "Have you learnt anything further about Gregory?"

"Nothing that would help me find the person I seek." John had not mentioned Peter's misconceptions about his friend to Anatolius. The younger man had a loose tongue and might let the knowledge slip. John was more guarded or possibly less straightforward, a thought that made him uneasy.

"Then I'm having more success than you are! I've found out the name of Nereus' legal advisor."

***

Prudentius' house sat behind the Hippodrome, just beyond the row of dilapidated wooden tenements piled at the base of the arena, like shipwrecks against a line of rocks.

John knocked and waited.

He seemed to be spending an inordinate amount of time standing on doorsteps of late.

The house front presented the anonymous facade common to Constantinople's dwellings. Its door displayed the usual nail studding and metal strapping. Here in the city, even the homes of the well-to-do resembled crates stacked in a ship's hold, all identical from the outside, but each holding…what?

Which door would open to the solution he sought?

This particular door opened on an unexpected cacophony—shouts, the buzz of conversation, a snatch of laughter, the clatter of a pan, the thump of a heavy basket. It was as if Constantinople had been turned inside out. The quiet of home lay in the street, while the bustle of the byways had come into Prudentius' house.

The young servant girl who opened the door carried a squalling infant in her arms. The girl ineffectually tried to shush the child. "I'll tell him you're here," she said in reply to John's inquiry. "Hurry up and come inside. Otherwise the geese'll get out."

John followed her into the atrium. She was short, her brown hair pinned up securely. A loose, undyed tunic revealed a slightly built frame which was nevertheless broad in the hips. Her face was an attractive amalgam. She had the aquiline nose of a Roman, but full lips and dusky skin spoke of the empire's eastern fringes. The exotic effect was somewhat diminished by the number of teeth her smile revealed as missing. John could see no geese, but stepped carefully around the evidence on the atrium tiles that proved their presence in the house.

Inexplicably, the atrium resembled nothing so much as a public square. An assortment of people wandered through it or stood about talking. Others sat leaning against its walls. They could hardly all be servants.

"Your master's given shelter to his family?" John ventured.

"You might say so. Prudentius says everyone is his family." The infant in her arms seemed to find this information highly disturbing to judge by the increased strength of its cries. Answering wails from elsewhere revealed that the girl was not alone in her efforts to increase the population of the house.

John followed her past two men squabbling over a basket filled with vegetables. The house might almost be termed the Forum Prudentius, he thought.

As he went up three wide steps leading into Prudentius' office, John felt a tug at his cloak.

The beggar squatting on the bottom step looked up at him. "Please, excellency, a nummus or two. My family is hungry."

The girl slapped the ragged man's hand down. "You're no hungrier than the rest of us! Does Prudentius have to tell you again? No begging is allowed here at any time and especially not from prospective clients."

The beggar mumbled a number of obscene comments concerning the girl taking advantage of being the master's favorite and her arrogance in assuming this allowed her to order everyone around, especially honest workers and decent folk who had unfortunately fallen on hard times. Such as himself.

John followed her through the lawyer's office and out into the garden. He was not surprised to see several crudely constructed shelters propped against the pillars of its peristyle. Numerous people were lying in the shadows. The garden itself resembled a long-abandoned field, overgrown with straggly bushes and spindly saplings sprouting from beds of weeds. Ashes filled the basin of the dry fountain.

"It seems he must be out somewhere." The girl stroked the scarlet-faced baby, whose keening now turned into huge gulping sobs, soon quieted by the brown breast she popped out from her tunic. "I would be happy to take a message. He's likely looking for more mouths to feed."

The baby's puckered mouth moved contentedly.

"Who are these people?"

"I don't know all their names. Mine is Xanthe, by the way. They're unfortunates such as beggars, out-of-work stone masons, orphans, impoverished widows, even a few whores, if you'll pardon the expression."

There was a rustling and a huge black cat exploded out of a patch of weeds nearby, collided with John's boot, did a somersault, and raced away, pursued in an instant by a much smaller, tortoise-shell kitten.

"As you see," observed Xanthe, "he also takes in stray cats. There's a not a finer Christian in the city. He took me in off the street. I've served in his household for years and he's been like a father to me."

"Giving up so much space in his home must be difficult. Most would choose to donate to a hospice or some similar institution rather than fill their houses with the destitute."

"Not Prudentius! He likes to do heaven's work with his own hands. Needless to say, we have regular visits from a prelate, who reminds all these fortunate souls where their aid really comes from."

John produced a handful of coins. "Give these to your master and this one is for your baby." John had found coins unlocked tongues more quickly than wine. "Do you know when he might return?"

Xanthe gazed down thoughtfully at the nursing infant as if it might have the answer. Then she looked up.

"Ezra!" She accompanied her cry with an energetic wave of her arm, which dislodged the baby's mouth and set it instantly screaming.

John followed her gaze. A thin, half-naked man with a wild beard and straggling hair sat hunched near the peak of the roof.

"Ezra! Did you see Prudentius go out?"

"He visited the sick in the garden just after dawn. Haven't seen him since." The man's croaked reply was scarcely audible.

Xanthe turned back to John. "Sorry. You may have to come back tomorrow. Prudentius doesn't often go out these days. Just as well, really, since every time he does, there's yet another mouth to feed."

"The man on your roof…."

"Ezra's been here for months. He used to be a stylite. Prudentius found him lying at the base of his column. Fortunately for him it was not very tall. The master hired a cart to bring him back here. The poor fellow's legs are like sticks. You could use them for skewers. It's a sorry state of affairs, when stylites are falling off their columns like so many poisoned crows."

"I gather he stays on the roof because that's the only place he feels comfortable?"

"That's exactly right! How did you know?"

John smiled enigmatically.

***

"Tell your master he can preserve his bacon in a dark place. I've got no dill left. None." The vegetable-seller leaned over a display of limp greens of other descriptions to deliver her emphatic message.

"I can pay—"

"You can see what I have to offer, you old fool. Can you see any dill? No! So no matter how much you say you can pay, I still can't sell you something I haven't got."

Peter turned away, his face flushed with anger and frustration. A fine thing for a Lord Chamberlain to eat boiled bacon prepared with insufficient dill. What did that silly girl Hypatia know about cooking? Running out of dill, indeed! It was intolerable.

He'd been to the stall of every vegetable seller between the Great Church and the Golden Horn, or so it seemed. None offered so much as a stalk of dill. Other households had probably stocked up on herbs as a precaution against hunger while he'd been brooding over his poor friend.

He had failed his master.

It was true the Lord Chamberlain had ordered him to take time off from his duties, but now see how it had turned out? Why should he make matters worse by heeding his master's order not to venture into the streets? Especially when there was no dill in the house.

"Old man! Are you all right?" The seller called after him as he walked away.

He ignored her. His heart thumped in his chest. If only it weren't so hot. The sun seemed to beat all strength out of him. The colonnade he was walking toward kept moving sideways.

He stared out at the harbor. Across the Golden Horn, pillars of coiling black smoke rose into the bright air, reminding him of pillars holding up the ceilings over the flaming pits of Hell.

He knew of one last market he could try. He forced his heavy feet to keep moving, just as he had when he had been marching though the rocky passes in Isauria. When he had thought he could not lift his boots again, even though the sun had not even begun to slide down the slope of the blazing afternoon sky. Somehow he had taken another step, then another, until he lost count of the number of impossible steps he had taken. He and Gregory, he thought, reminding himself he was blessed he could still march through the city, however reluctant his aging legs might be.

Gregory could not.

He became aware the sun had stopped torturing him and looked up, expecting to see gathering clouds. Instead, he saw tenements leaning drunkenly over a street as narrow and winding as a dry stream bed.

An unfamiliar street.

He did not remember taking a wrong turn, but now he might as well have been in Antioch. Was it because the street was so silent? When had it become deserted? There had been people in the market he had just left, although not the usual jostling crowds. He had passed others going about on the first street he had turned down. Where had they all gone? To what sort of place had he found his way?

Peter forced himself onward. He felt dizzy. A low humming filled his head. He began to sing a favorite hymn, "Though Thou Didst Descend into the Tomb." It failed to lift his spirits. The buzzing in his head increased. Then he turned a corner and found his way blocked by a pile of dead, overhung by a thick, swirling cloud of flies.

He hastily retraced his steps.

The dim way was no longer deserted.

A lone figure approached.

Peter could not make out its face.

Suddenly the figure broke into a loping run toward him.

Peter fled as best he could.

He veered into an alley, staggered briefly against a wall, stumbled onward.

It was not so much an alley as a narrow space between two buildings whose walls almost touched overhead, blotting out light. In near darkness he trod on as best he could. His chest felt on fire. He prayed for strength, but slowed and stopped.

He bent, gasping for breath.

There was no sound of pursuit.

Had he managed to elude the strange man?

Unfortunately, he had not.

A black figure floated silently toward him, seeming to draw nearer without actually traversing the filthy ground. Rather than growing more distinct as it approached, the figure grew blacker and more impenetrable, a vortex of darkness in which Peter perceived only shifting shapes he could not name.

It stopped in front of him.

With relief, Peter saw that it was just a man in a black cloak.

But where was his face?

Peter trembled. He felt a terrible cold emanating from the approaching figure. The cloak flapped like a raven's wing and a tremendous blow to the side of his head sent Peter sprawling in the slops and debris littering the narrow space.

In an instant Peter knew, it was death come for him, as it had for Gregory.

He lay almost insensible as the dark shape leaned over him.

Another shadow appeared.

Demons, Peter thought in terror. Had he not been a good enough Christian? He waited for the claws, the razor-sharp teeth.

He awoke, propped up against a wall.

Someone crouched beside him.

He tried to turn his head to take a closer look. The pain in his neck brought tears to his eyes.

"You were attacked by a thief." The voice was sibilant. "It is fortunate I happened to pass by just now. Although I have a way of happening to pass by at the right time. You will not die, Peter. Assure your master of that."

Peter tried to respond, but could not.

His rescuer patted his shoulder. Peter glimpsed the face. A face across which countless years and endless roads had scrawled a palimpsest of wrinkles in which everything was written, but nothing could be read.

Then the strange man was gone.

Chapter Eleven

ohn followed a limping man carrying a sack down a short, narrow alley that opened unexpectedly into a dark courtyard. The place was not far from the Hippodrome, but sunk as it was between looming granite cliffs of surrounding warehouses, its cobbled space resembled a cavern. Several restless bears, growling and snuffling, were suitable inhabitants. John came to a halt, then, as his eyes grew accustomed to the gloom, thanked Mithra the beasts were locked inside iron cages.

Beyond the cages, a few shadowy figures—bear trainers, John supposed—sat hunkered down around a bonfire, roasting chunks of skewered meat. By the evidence of the scattered amphorae and the scurrilous songs they were singing, the men had been drinking steadily for some time.

The fellow whom John had shadowed stopped at the closest cage and emptied the contents of his sack through its bars.

"You haven't finished all the wine, I hope," he shouted to his companions. "It's all right for you lot to sit around and drink and gorge since it's not your turn to scavenge for our friends. Took me longer than I expected. Do you know how many rats it takes to feed even one bear?"

"Rats?" someone observed. "How dainty. You've been gathering little rats when the streets are piled with corpses."

"Have some decency!"

"Besides, you don't want them getting a taste for human flesh," another trainer added.

"Well, the owner of the wine shop didn't like the idea of a bear getting a taste of human flesh either, especially his. Samson hadn't even got to the end of his chain and the owner was halfway down the Mese like a deacon with a demon on his backside, leaving all those amphorae untended."

"You've told us all this before! Wait till the Prefect's men are back on duty and start asking questions. You won't be so clever then. 'And what did you say the thief's weapon was? A bear?' How hard is it going to be for even that stupid bunch to point the finger?"

"Well," grumbled the thief, "I notice you haven't refused to drink the wine Samson got you." He turned to the fellow with the sack of rats, who was now sitting by the bonfire. "Have some meat. It's excellent."

The rat catcher picked up a skewer, sniffed at the slab of meat it held, and spit into the flames. "Not dog again!"

"This isn't your scrawny, stringy street mongrel. It's a well fed watchdog. Quite succulent, it is. It was chained in the courtyard of a deserted mansion. Its master probably died. The poor thing would've starved to death. We did it a good turn, and saved it from a terrible end."

"You ought to be working as a thief," grumbled the new arrival. "Why do you bother to train bears?"

The thief shrugged. "I love bears, my friend! Beautiful animals they are. Bear training isn't all about nomismata, you know."

John strode forward, past the cages.

"Ah," the rat catcher said with a leering grin, catching sight of him. "Looks like a visitor from the palace!" The man was snaggle-toothed, John noted.

"Then you better be polite," the thief hiccoughed, contriving to bow while still remaining seated on the straw-strewn cobbles.

"Have you come to tell us the games are to start again?" the first speaker asked, looking hopeful.

John shook his head.

"See, see, I told you!" shouted a man perched on a stool. "When Sappho left, she not only took my good fortune, she took everyone else's as well!"

Fortuna may have frowned upon the bear trainers, John thought, but perhaps at last her humors had improved so far as his quest went. "It's about Sappho I wish to question you."

"Is she at the palace now?" The man he addressed looked incredulous. "Not but what she was always very lucky, for me at least. Whenever she was with me and I rolled the dice, I won."

"She wasn't lucky, it's those weighted dice you use!" one of his companions remarked.

John quelled the man with a glare. Turning back to the fortunate wagerer, he asked his name.

"Theodora's father," someone muttered loudly.

"Her son!"

"Brutus," said the man to whom John had directed the question.

"No, he isn't," revealed the rat catcher. "Brutus died last week. The man you're talking to is Epiktetos."

"Bastard!" Epiktetos shouted.

"Oh, you mean, he's the one who's Theodora's son?" hiccuped one of the imbibers.

"No matter, I'm interested in Sappho," John said.

"I'll wager you are!" The speaker followed the comment with a snigger.

John turned and stared at the man, who suddenly got up, announced he had to relieve himself, and left the courtyard. The staccato sound of his running steps echoed around the small space as he took his chance to flee.

"About Sappho," John went on. "What do you know of her whereabouts?"

"Nothing, sir," Epiktetos responded. "I haven't seen her since last winter."

"She's probably dead by now, like so many others," the thief put in helpfully.

"Not so!" another voice contradicted. "I saw her only last week!"

"You saw her and didn't tell me?" Epiktetos' voice rose in outrage.

"Well, I'm fairly certain it was her. The woman I saw looked like her, only she wasn't wearing yellow."

"Then it definitely wasn't Sappho, you fool," Epiktetos said, an opinion the other trainers appeared to share.

John turned to go. It was obvious he would learn nothing here.

He glanced at the Hippodrome as he retraced his steps. The great building was silent, waiting for horse-racing to resume, but would its thousands of marble seats ever be as crowded as they had been in the past? So many in the city had died, and among them a number of charioteers.

The horses, however, had long since been removed to one of Justinian's country estates. Although it was not known to the populace at large, as his confidant John knew the order had been less due to the emperor's concern for the teams than to avoid the animals' being stolen and eaten. As the plague maintained its grip, the usual foraging by half wild curs had become easier. Fattened on abundant human flesh, the packs were now beginning to be hunted for food in turn, as attested by his recent interview with the bear trainers.

John recalled the hot, oily taste of grilled fish. Very few fishermen brought their catches to Constantinople now. Neptune's bounty was largely unharvested.

What macabre chance had carried his thoughts from horses to fish, he wondered.

Because Neptune created the horse, his memory told him, and horses race at the Hippodrome.

"But none are so fair as the team pulling Neptune's chariot, his horses tossing manes of gold and skimming over the sea on gleaming bronze hooves," John said out loud.

Chapter Twelve

John emerged from the gloom of a narrow alley into the light of a nondescript square near the docks. If strangers could not assist him in furthering his investigations, it might be time to seek the aid of old acquaintances.

As he had hoped, Pulcheria perched in her usual spot on the steps leading to a warehouse portico. Tripod, her three-legged feline companion, frisked around beside her, worrying at a small rat as Pulcheria braided together several pieces of red cloth. The bright strip of fabric thus created would doubtless soon join other colorful scraps ornamenting her tangled hair, complementing the rainbow of rags in which she was dressed.

It was a homely scene, more so than the bedlam at Prudentius' house despite the fact it was outdoors.

Pulcheria looked up at the sound of John's quick step. She smiled and cocked her head artfully, presenting him the half of her face that was still a pretty woman's rather than the melted wax horror of the other side, the result of burning lamp oil thrown by an angry client.

"Ah, it is my friend from the palace." She climbed to her feet and gave an exaggerated bow. "How may Tripod and I assist you today?" she asked as she took her seat on the worn steps again.

John sat down beside her. "I shall naturally make any time I take worth your while, Pulcheria."

"Oh, I do like dealing with men from the palace. They're always so very generous."

John took the hint and handed her an appropriate amount. She studied it carefully with her one good eye and then, with a satisfied nod, tied the coins into the hem of the tunic she wore beneath her gaudy rags. The action momentarily revealed legs streaked with dirt.

"Ah," she said with a sly laugh, "of late life has been so hectic I have been unable to make my accustomed regular visits to the baths."

"Hectic, you say?"

"Yes, hectic!" Pulcheria flung her thin arms wide, setting their attached rags and ribbons fluttering and startling Tripod. "With the city in the grip of sudden and painful death, it's hardly surprising the churches have never been so full. A friend of mine who ministers to weaknesses of the flesh in the Augustaion complains the constant singing and praying coming night and day from the Great Church is very bad for her trade."

John ventured the suggestion that it might also be likely that such constant reminders of sin would dampen the ardor of prospective clients.

"That's exactly what I said! It's as obvious as fleas on a mangy dog, excellency. In fact, I strongly advised her to move to another square right away. Just so long as it wasn't this one."

"This is a tranquil spot compared to where I've been recently."

"A rare lull. Already this morning I've entertained six clients. However, that's no surprise since so long as heaven has been satisfied with prayers and a coin or two given in charity, once men are well away from all that singing and praying, it's time for them to satisfy their bodies. Yes," she mused, absentmindedly scratching a grubby ankle, "for some of us city dwellers, the plague has been a godsend of a different sort."

John asked what she meant.

"For one thing, with so many lying dead in the streets beggars have been having a much easier time. The departed are less inclined to refuse the outstretched palm, aren't they? Yes, beggars all wear new boots these days."

Glancing at Pulcheria's ragged garments, John observed that evidently she had not taken advantage of the unexpected bounty to be harvested in every square and alley.

"Well, excellency, I must admit I've borrowed a few smaller items no longer needed by their owners. Yesterday, however, I had a very distressing experience. I chanced upon a woman wearing a most beautiful garment, brilliant blue it was. Very striking. But when I turned her over, I saw it was not a wealthy stranger, but a woman with whom I had some slight acquaintance."

Pulcheria's expression was sorrowful as she continued her tale. "She was an elderly widow who had been forced to live on the street late in life. She'd had a very hard time, as you might imagine. Just think, excellency, those blue robes were the finest garments she'd worn in years. I wonder where she got them from. Perhaps a cast-off from some aristocratic lady, such as she'd been once? I just didn't have the heart to take them. It would've been like robbery."

She began threading the braided red strip through her dark hair. "It's as well that the theater is closed just now. A lot of my clients used to go there and then visit me afterwards, so with the sudden rise in other business I'd certainly have my hands full." She gave a lewd laugh.

"Your knowledge of the theater is in fact why I'm here, Pulcheria. Do you happen to know an actress going by the name of Sappho? You may have seen her in the company of the bear trainers quartered near the Hippodrome."

"Sappho, you say? I don't recall her immediately, I admit, but you know how it is, they change their names all the time. What does she look like?"

"I'm afraid I can't tell you. I've only heard about her from a person who wasn't able to give me much of a description, except that this Sappho puts on airs."

Pulcheria laughed. "If you'd told me she didn't put on airs, I'd be able to identify her right away, since she'd be the only actress in the city who didn't. I'll ask around and see if I can find out anything about her for you. Ah, I see a possible client approaching. Notice the furtive look?"

She shook her head. Several of the ribbons and cloth scraps in her hair fell down in a colorful veil that partly obscured the ruined side of her face.

A portly, middle-aged man strolled slowly across the square toward them. His face was as pink as a baby's, as if he'd just come from the baths. The buckle on his belt was silver. He appeared to be studying the empty porticos on the other side of the square with great attention and then transferred his gaze to the sky. He nodded a dignified greeting to another man who hurried past, paying him no heed at all.

Pulcheria giggled. "See? What pains he takes to declare to the world that of course he is not considering hiring a prostitute to satisfy his lust, as if anyone were thinking he was, or would even care."

As predicted, the portly man passed in front of John and Pulcheria and then turned back suddenly and hastily tossed a handful of nummi at John. "I'll borrow the woman. Here's her hire."

***

"And what did you do with Pulcheria's fee?" Isis asked, pouring John wine. They were seated on a soft couch in her private apartment on the upper floor of the establishment.

"I've still got it," John admitted. "I'll give it to her on my way back to the palace."

"Why didn't you wait until she emerged from the alley?" Isis went on with professional interest in carnal transactions. Now that she had become owner rather than employee she had allowed herself to grow plump, but her soft prettiness concealed a business acumen that was one of the sharpest John had encountered.

John considered the question for a short time. "To preserve her dignity," he finally replied. "It's one thing to talk about her life, but quite another to...."

Isis nodded agreement. "That certainly wasn't her usual fee! The ignorant fellow must've taken note of those expensive garments of yours. Apparently it didn't occur to him in the heat of the occasion that you'd never be able to buy clothing like those if you were living off a street whore. For that price he could have had a nice bed at his back rather than a brick wall. Mind you, there are some who'll pay extra for someone like Pulcheria."

John asked what she meant.

"Why, she's exotic, John. A woman with two faces. Some men say women are both angels and demons, and Pulcheria resembles just that strange notion. Then too, some clients might relish a demon lover and would be more than glad to anticipate being punished by a demonic visitation even while they were satiating themselves."

"I had thought Pulcheria was reduced to plying her trade on the street because she was, well, damaged," John replied.

Isis formed her red-painted lips into a rosebud smile. "It's all in the way it's presented, John. I once tried to persuade her to work for me, but she likes her independence too much. Mind you, she's right about one thing. Even with half the population gone, my girls are seeing as many visitors as ever. We must be one of the few businesses still turning a profit."

She paused. "Not the only one, however," she went on with a glimmer of a smile. "One of our regular patrons visited us yesterday and was particularly generous in showing his appreciation. I gather from the girl he favored that he's making a fortune right now. What do you suppose he's selling, John?"

"Wine?"

Isis laughed. "You're not that far wrong, if you consider, as many do, that wine is the way to oblivion. Only in the case of our suddenly wealthy client, he's purveying eternal oblivion, or possibly not depending upon your religious views. No, he is selling hellebore."

"Poison? Yet can we be surprised? He has a popular product to offer, given many prefer to depart in a hasty fashion than suffer for days," John said thoughtfully. "No doubt he can name his own price for what he offers."

Isis nodded. "Indeed. Apparently, being a charitable man, he accepts payment in clothing and jewelry as well as coins, not to mention the occasional, shall we say, personal favor of an intimate nature. And this reminds me. You are an old and very dear friend, John. If it should come to it, I have purchased a good supply of his wares and I can easily spare enough to set your feet on the ladder to heaven within an hour or two."

"Thank you, Isis, but I hope not to have to accept your more than generous offer," John replied with a thin smile. "The more so since, before that time comes for me or for Peter, I hope to find a particular woman who may well be able to give me important information in the matter."

Isis settled back into the embrace of her well-cushioned couch. "You mean this actress called Sappho? The bear trainers were not able to assist, I take it?"

"No. I visited them as soon as I'd left the apartment of the wayward son I was telling you about. The only thing that I learnt was she has not been seen for a few months. As I left they were all telling each other how they knew Theodora when her family was still involved in the profession, not to mention much winking and suggestive gestures and hinting that they knew her better than they are now willing to admit. Even the ones half her age, I may add."

"Theodora was a whore once, as we all know. Most of the men in the city have had their way with her at one time or another, according to them, and now that she's co-ruler of the empire, well, men do boast about the oddest things at times."

John smiled wordlessly.

Isis laughed. "They do! Of course, it's very possible this so-called Sappho could be dead. All the same, I'll ask my girls to keep their ears open in case one of their clients mentions her. Information such as that often comes knocking unasked on our door."

"Perhaps that's why I haven't been able to find anything out, despite all the doors I've knocked at this past day or so. The truth's been away calling on you. But then, as I've said, that is why I came to see you, Isis, to ask about this Sappho."

"Not to reminisce about the old days in Egypt?"

John smiled again. Isis often recalled every smallest detail about their days in Alexandria, except the fact that their paths had never crossed while they lived in that huge city. "That too, certainly."

"I always enjoy your visits." Isis patted his knee with a chubby hand heavy with rings. He shifted his leg away reflexively. "Don't feel obliged to visit just for the sake of chatting with an old friend. Avoid streets and public places as far as possible right now, that's my advice."

"According to Gaius the plague strikes at random."

"Gaius? And what does that physician know? The last batch of contraceptive pessaries he made for my establishment would've been more use to a rabbit breeder. Then when a number failed, he charged me double his usual fee to get my girls fit for work again. I might just as well have instructed them to make their own from linen and vinegar."

She selected a fig from a silver tray of sweetmeats and dried fruit on the small ivory table beside the couch. "Speaking of employees, I need a new doorkeeper," she continued as she munched. "The current one is not very reliable. Arrives late, departs early, and what's worse is getting much too interested in a certain young lady here."

"Always a temptation for a man working in your house."

"Indeed. And speaking of houses, I've been thinking of changing the decor again, provided I can find the necessary craftsmen. What do you think about a religious theme? If the Patriarch anathematizes me, so much the better! My house is already one of the best and most patronized in the city, but given the seal of disapproval from one of the highest church authorities, ah, think of the trade it would bring in from people who would like to see the place for themselves!"

The madam beamed with delight, although whether at the prospect of being anathematized or considering the increase in business, or indeed at both, John was not certain.

"Mind you," she went on in a confidential tone, "I'd rather be visited by ten religious figures seeking to convert me to their ways than have to deal with my girls' latest complaint. It's about one of our regular patrons."

John gave her a look of inquiry. He knew Isis made it a rule never to talk about her clients and insisted on the same discretion from her employees.

"Oh dear," she giggled. "You do loosen my tongue, John. I suppose if I leave out the fellow's name…? He's a regular visitor and not at all bad-looking. He could spend more time at the gymnasium perhaps, but then so could most of my girls' admirers. Even so, whenever he appears at the door, they take flight like a flock of seagulls at the sight of a stray dog."

John, realizing hearing the rest of the story was unavoidable, asked as tactfully as possible if this particular client was more demanding than most.

"That is it, precisely." Isis took another fig and chewed it thoughtfully. "It isn't so much the act itself. It is the indecency to which he expects them to submit afterwards." She puckered her rosy lips. "You should hear the girls, John. 'Oh, Madam, don't make me be the one to go with him. We can't stand it!'"

John raised inquiring eyebrows.

"What happens is, well," Isis continued, lowering her voice and leaning toward him, "afterwards he insists on reciting his dreadful, whining poetry. Can you imagine? Of course, he is charged for the extra time, but if you ask me, having to pay whores to listen to your poems is the gods' way of indicating you should find another profession."

Chapter Thirteen

"You'll never become a physician, Farvus. What do you think you're doing? The poor child will be sorry she was brought here!" Gaius irritably pushed aside the young man laboring over the injured girl.

Hypatia had found Gaius in a room at the back of the hospice, futilely attempting to teach his assistant how to bind up a broken arm. Farvus' face, Hypatia noted, was paler than that of the patient he'd been trying to assist.

"You have to place the first part of the bandage on the fracture itself, to drive the humors into the extremities. As I told you, if you don't do that, the humors end up in the fracture. You do at least have the right amount of cerate on the compresses this time."

Gaius began rewinding the woolen strips around the girl's arm. She winced and bit her lip, but remained silent. "You see? Start wrapping at the fracture and move outwards. The further from the fracture, the less the compression. It's easy to remember if you concentrate. Here, do you want to try again?"

The injured girl's eyes widened with alarm.

"Oh, never mind," snapped Gaius. "I'll finish it myself. Get about your regular business."

His assistant left the room.

"Hypatia, come in." Gaius wound the bandage nimbly around his patient's arm. "Broken bones can be disconcerting for a beginner, even though from a medical viewpoint, they're simple enough to treat. They usually take care of themselves so long as you get the bones aligned properly from the outset."

He finished the task and murmured a few words of encouragement to the girl before motioning Hypatia to follow him out into the hallway.

"The girl was found in the Augustaion, screaming like the Furies. Children will insist on trying to climb statuary. She belongs to one of the shopkeepers around there, but we can't spare anyone to go and find the parents. Eventually someone will turn up looking for her."

He rubbed his eyelids. His eyes were red. He looked exhausted. "So you have taken up my kind invitation? I'm more than happy to see you, even if my expression doesn't show it."

His face, Hypatia noted, was as red as if it had been cooked, his nose as dark as a carbuncle. She would make him a batch of invigorating Pharaoh's Elixir, she decided as she followed the lumbering physician along the corridor, stepping deftly around sad clusters of people squatting or lying outside rooms filled to overflowing with patients who were presumably even sicker.

"We've got very few of our usual sorts of clients," Gaius noted as they turned a corner and threaded their way between several patients fortunate enough to have been allotted cots, if not rooms in which to put them. "Not so many cart accidents, there being fewer carts and people about the streets, for example. I suppose we should be grateful for that."

A hoarse shriek rose wavering into the malodorous air.

Gaius gave Hypatia a wry grin. "Sounds as if a patient is calling. He probably needs more of our pain-killing potion. Could you see to that?"

He nodded toward the room at the end of the corridor. "The colleague overseeing this wing mentioned a young man who emerged alive from one of the towers being used to dispose of the dead, according to the excubitor who brought him here.

Seems the patient had a bucket of lye emptied over his head as he emerged, but was lucky enough to keep his eyesight. Not that he'll consider himself lucky when he sees the face he'll live with from now on. All we can do is keep him as free from pain as possible and hope he eventually heals. Haven't attended on him myself. I've been busy enough looking after those who need some expert care. Now, do you think you can cope with an injury like that?"

"I'm not as squeamish as your assistant," Hypatia responded.

"Good. You'll like it here."

***

The young man lying half-naked on a soiled pallet may well have once been handsome. Now his face, arms and shoulders were a mass of angry red burns and blisters. As Hypatia carefully carried the prescribed painkiller to him, he gripped the sides of his pallet and shrieked again.

"Shut up, you noisy bastard!" the man sitting on the next bed shouted. "Did you expect to be a lady's man all your life? How can we get any rest with all that racket you're making?"

His sentiments brought forth a chorus of agreement from two neighbors. All three were nursing broken limbs.

"Ah, but he's found himself a lady friend already," one of the sufferer's roommates remarked.

"The wheel that protests gets the greasing. I'm in agony over here, girl. Why don't you help me instead?" leered the first speaker.

"Wait until she gets a good look at his face," his friend callously observed. "She'll run for the shelter of your outstretched arms."

"They're both broken, you bastard!"

Hypatia ignored them and knelt down by the suffering man, whose dark eyes stared at her pitifully. Tears rolled down his raw cheeks.

Hypatia offered the cup, wondering if salt from his weeping would worsen the pain from his ravaged face.

"Drink this," she said. "It will help."

He greedily drained its contents, thanked her in a hoarse whisper, and began crying again, much to the obscenely vocal delight of his fellow patients.

Hypatia looked around angrily. "Be quiet!" she ordered. "Or I shall be forced to ask Gaius to immediately send you all home, even if you have no homes to go to."

The trio looked at each other and then resumed awkwardly throwing knucklebones on their pallets, pointedly ignoring Hypatia. The man with two bandaged arms protested bitterly that his friend had not shaken the bones enough to his liking before throwing them for him.

"Thank you," the young man said again. "It's hard to be helpless." He glanced over at the players and clenched his fists. "As soon as I am well, they will pay mightily for their behavior."

***

By the time Hypatia emerged from the hospice, the foul atmosphere in the city streets seemed fresh by comparison.

She stood in the middle of the great expanse of the Augustaion, pulling in big mouthfuls of salt-tinged air. She would have to change her tunic as soon as she got home, for the stench of the hospice had clung to it. She feared it also lingered in her thick hair, but she would have to forgo the baths for now.

She had an urgent errand.

Dill. She must find dill.

Peter had obviously taken the notion to torture himself over its absence. Doubtless his friend's death had made him unlike his usual self. She hated to see his grief exacerbated by the lack of something so minor.

She walked down the Mese. Most of the emporia gracing its colonnades were closed, protective grates pulled down and locked to rings protruding from the concrete walkways. The ripe, overpowering odor of spoilt produce assailed her.

So many hungry in the city and food going to waste.

Gaius had kept her out of the plague wards, away from most of the hospice in fact, even though he claimed no one had fallen ill simply from nursing victims. She had therefore spent her time there treating patients with more usual and tractable conditions, applying poultices and ointments or administering painkilling potions.

Even after all the wounds and infirmities she'd witnessed that day, the face of the pitiful burnt man clung in her memory.

When she arrived in Constantinople from her native Egypt she had entered a new, alien, and harsher environment. She suspected the young man, so changed in appearance by his terrible injuries, would find himself in a far different world than the one to which she supposed he had been accustomed.

She had looked in on him just before she left. He had been mercifully sleeping, his rest brought about by Gaius' potion.

Her thoughts were interrupted by a boy who darted out of an alleyway, calling to an unseen friend. "Quick! I found one! Back here! See, I told you so!"

The friend emerged from another alley further down the street. "Aw, you're always finding them. Why do I never get there first?"

"That's four for me and only one for you."

"You always get the best alleys," his friend grumbled.

"Shut up and come and see this one. It's really horrible! All puffy and smelly, with worms and everything."

The two boys scurried out of sight down the narrow way.

Searching for bodies? To rob them, Hypatia wondered, or simply because they were young and foolish?

She kept walking and arrived at the long hill leading into the Strategion. She started down, allowed her strides to lengthen. On a sudden impulse she decided to run. Her hair lifted back over her shoulders and flapped out behind her. She felt as if she were flying.

Those over a certain age did not usually race through the crowded capital. The streets were not thronged today, however, and in a city where children made a game of searching for corpses, there no longer seemed to be such a thing as a recognized standard of appropriate behavior.

The sound of women wailing, accompanied by the mournful sound of flutes and snatches of song, floated from the side street Hypatia was approaching, and she came to a halt behind a pair of men who stood on its corner.

A funeral procession moved slowly down the hilly byway toward them, led by three musicians ambling in front of a pair of singers whose melody was largely drowned by the lamentations and weeping emanating from further back in the shuffling line.

A dozen men—servants, Hypatia thought, or perhaps slaves newly freed—trod proudly along after the singers, and behind them came the departed, a richly dressed and bejewelled woman lying upon a narrow couch carried on the shoulders of four bearers. A dozen adults dressed in mourning followed the couch of death. The women beat their breasts and ululated their sorrow.

"They're burying their dead in the old Roman style," a florid-complexioned man near Hypatia gasped in horror. "And it's a woman at that! They're obviously pagans! Pagans, I say, and parading their foul practices around the city at a time like this!"

"And where's the Prefect's men when you need them? This should be stopped immediately!" declared his companion, a pale man with scanty hair and even less flesh on his bones.

"Yes, well, when you get down to it, nobody in authority particularly cares how the dead are buried, with rites or without them, Christian or pagan, just as long as they're not in the way when they go about the streets," his friend remarked.

"The household have obviously all lost their senses," returned his friend.

"Nonsense! They're just taking advantage of lack of civic order, that's all! They should be punished!" The man picked up a stone as the musicians drew level with the small knot of onlookers.

Hypatia stepped back a few paces, offering a prayer to the gods of her country for the departed woman.

Just as the outraged pedestrian prepared to hurl his missile, a man in a filthy, hooded cloak erupted from an alley a short way up the street, dashed past the musicians, and grabbed the woman from the couch.

With a discordant clash of music and even louder screams and curses, the procession immediately halted. Several men leapt forward to grab the interloper, but the cloaked figure whirled around out of their grasp with a clumsy, dancing step.

The dead woman's head lolled backwards, her heavy, golden necklaces bouncing on his chest as the man began to sing a mournful hymn and continued to dance, forcing the woman clasped to him to move in a mimicry of life.

The onlookers stood frozen in place, uncomprehending, faces aghast as the blasphemous scene unfolded.

Hypatia stared hard at the dancing man, but the hood drawn over his head allowed only the merest glimpse of a face that was brown and criss-crossed by a myriad of lines that reminded her of cracks on a sun-baked mud flat along the Nile.

"Demon!" one of the women mourners screamed.

"Blasphemer!"

"Kill him!" one of the musicians shrieked.

The few passing pedestrians began to gather on the corner, shouting imprecations at the dancing man and his pitiful partner.

"Desecration!"

"Stop him! Do something!"

"What's the matter with you, you fools? There's only one of him!"

Just as it appeared to Hypatia that the small crowd were preparing to attack the man, he dropped his victim, swayed, and toppled forward. He hit the cobblestones face down with the crack of a shattering amphora and lay there motionless.

A few brave souls sidled over to look at him.

"Take care," someone whimpered. "It's a demon."

"Not so! That was nothing more than his own death fit," remarked a new arrival knowledgeably. "That's all it is. Sometimes people stricken with the plague have hallucinations and become quite crazed. My physician mentioned this very thing to me only yesterday and he has treated the emperor on occasion, so his word is hardly to be doubted."

The pompous speaker nudged the demon with the toe of his boot.

Bringing it immediately back to life.

The cloaked figure leapt to its feet, flourishing the dead woman's gold necklaces.

"You call me a demon?" the creature shouted at the horrified crowd. "Don't you believe the dead will rise on the day of the resurrection? Which of you would refuse to dance with your savior on that glorious day? You can say I'm a fool for reminding you of your sins, but you'd do better to look around the city and tremble at the warning being given. I say, the faster off to bed, the sooner the blessed morning arrives. Today buboes, tomorrow the heavenly banquet!"

***

"Peter. I found some dill!" Hypatia called as she pattered lightly upstairs.

There was no answer. The house was silent.

The fire in the kitchen brazier was almost extinguished. Peter's well-scrubbed pots and cooking utensils lay undisturbed on their shelf. None of the comfortingly familiar smells of a cooking meal hung in the air. A neatly jointed chicken sitting on a platter on the kitchen table was the only sign Peter had been at work.

By now the fowl should have been boiling in a pot for John's simple evening meal. Instead, it provided a feast for a swarm of flies.

"Peter!" she called again.

There was still no reply.

A pause for thought and then the young woman ran along the hallway and upstairs to the third floor to pound on the closed door of Peter's room.

"Peter! Are you all right?"

The answer came in a wavering voice.

"Yes, Hypatia, I am all right, for I am in the Lord's hands now. Tell the master I regret the inconvenience, but I don't expect to emerge alive, and if any attempt is made to break the door down, I intend to jump out of the window."

Chapter Fourteen

John pounded again on the door to Peter's room.

The sound echoed in the hallway, but Peter did not respond.

Even in his own home, the Lord Chamberlain was being thwarted. It was as if he had succumbed to the plague and unknowingly entered a dreary afterlife where the pagan dead knocked forever at doors that refused to open.

"Peter! Answer me! I order it!"

A pause and then a reply. "Master, forgive me. I'm waiting to die. Everyone must stay away. I would not want my last act in this world to be to give you all the plague."

Hypatia, standing behind John, leaned forward to address the door. "Gaius told me it was all a matter of chance! Come out right now, Peter. The Lord Chamberlain's has been tramping about the city all day on your account and it's getting late. Do you want to leave this world disobeying the master's orders?"

"Please, master, don't order me to open the door," Peter replied with a hoarse sob.

Again the sound of knocking echoed in the hallway.

"There's someone at the house door," Hypatia said and ran downstairs.

John remained outside Peter's room. He heard the clatter of Hypatia's footfalls on the steep wooden stairway to the second floor, followed by their more muted sound as she went down the final set of stairs into the atrium.

"Peter, we can't help you if you won't let us in," John said quietly.

There was no answer.

John turned away.

Hypatia met him before he reached the kitchen.

"Master, there's a pair of impertinent vagabonds outside. They claim they know you. One of them's armed. I locked the door."

John's hand went to the blade at his belt. "I will attend to it, Hypatia."

Had he been summoned to the emperor? Or had his frequent comings and goings been observed by someone who hoped to find a poorly guarded house and a naive servant who would allow them to enter?

Hurrying to the atrium, he threw open the house door.

"Lord Chamberlain!" declared his unexpected visitor. "I thought I would call on you since I find myself in the city."

The man's Greek was heavily accented, the booming voice familiar. The speaker was a burly fellow with long red hair and a ginger mustache. His scuffed leather boots and dust-covered clothing attested to a long journey. He was indeed armed, but the broad smile on his face indicated good will rather than evil intent.

Even though his presence was improbable, John recognized him instantly.

"Thomas! I never expected you to set foot in Constantinople again!"

Before John could say more, his second visitor stepped into view.

A slim young woman with dark eyes and an exquisite face.

Europa, the daughter John had not seen for seven years.

John gestured them inside wordlessly.

Europa hugged him awkwardly.

"Thomas," John said over her shoulder, "you know I don't allow anyone to carry weapons in my house. Leave your sword by the door."

"I know we've taken you by surprise, father, but it was rather a good jest, wasn't it?" Europa giggled, stepping back.

John smiled down at her. "So it was, Europa."

When John had last seen his daughter, the only time he had ever met her, Europa was still a girl. Now her figure was the slightest bit fuller, her features thinned and sharpened, her demeanor more adult. She had become a woman. He couldn't help looking back at the door.

"Mother will be here shortly," Europa said, as if reading his thoughts.

John nodded. "I see."

He found himself in the kitchen with his visitors, unable to remember having climbed the stairs.

Hypatia poured wine and set out honey cakes, all the while peering curiously at the strangers until John, tersely, explained who they were. She left, with obvious reluctance, to work in the garden.

For a while the three of them sat and stared at each other, sipping wine.

Suddenly Thomas set down his cup and laughed.

"Well, John, here we are again. Doesn't seem that long ago since we said farewell, does it?"

"Indeed not," John replied. He did not add that their visit was unwelcome in one sense. He did not want his daughter and her mother living in the city. Powerful men made inviting targets. In his deliberately solitary life, John could employ a staff of only two servants, could both keep a house and walk in the streets unguarded. But how could he ask Europa and Cornelia to also live in such a dangerous manner?

"Many things must have changed since then, but I have to say these honey cakes are as good as I remember," Thomas said.

"Either your cantankerous old servant is still with you, or he taught his successor how to make them."

Europa brushed a crumb from Thomas' ginger mustache. "Mother's not far away. A few hours' ride at most. She's still at the inn where we were staying."

"The last time I saw you, you were bound for Crete, Europa. How long have you been living on my doorstep?"

"Not long." Thomas took a swig from his cup and grimaced. "I must have neglected to finish that last cup of ghastly wine when I was here last. My thanks for saving it for me all these years."

"Where have you been all this time?" John looked toward Europa, but again it was Thomas who answered.

"It's more a question of where haven't I been? Egypt, Gaul, Germania, living by sharp wits and a sharper blade."

"And you, Europa?"

"Mother and I remained in Crete for a while and then rejoined the troupe. We were traveling with them until quite recently." She glanced at Thomas, who appeared only too eager to take up her story.

"As I said, John, I found myself in Egypt. It was some months ago, in Pelusium, to be precise. Visiting the baths, I heard much talk about recently arrived entertainers, said to include a pair of bull-leapers in the ancient tradition. Could it possibly be the friends I'd last seen some years ago in Crete, I asked myself. After all, you don't stumble over bull-leapers every day."

Thomas offered Europa a broad smile. "I made some inquiries and finally found the troupe, or what was left of it. The company was in the process of disbanding. The plague had just appeared and had already taken a few of them. It was time to leave."

"And what's more, our bull had been stolen," Europa put in. "I fear he ended up butchered. A beautiful, intelligent beast like that." Her eyes glittered at the memory, although whether with tears of sorrow or anger John couldn't tell.

"I don't think those pagan priests would have allowed that," Thomas observed. "But in any event, the disaster sweeping the city put an end to my business there as well."

He paused and John wondered exactly what business Thomas had been pursuing so far away. "In any event, I suggested to the few remaining performers that we stick together and move along the coast, earning our way by impromptu performances in towns as we went. Alas, I fear I am not cut out to be an entertainer."

The admission caused Thomas to pick up his cup, which turned out to be empty. Before he could say a word, Europa refilled it.

Thomas fortified himself and continued with his story. "Unfortunately, the plague appeared to be pursuing us. No sooner had we arrived in Ephesus, but the plague appeared. We hastened on to Smyrna and Nicaea and the same thing happened. You'd have thought we were carrying the disgusting sickness on our backs. Eventually we parted company with the rest and gradually worked our way up the coast to Nicomedia."

"Naturally at that point it seemed an excellent notion to come into a city where the dead were piling up in the streets," John observed.

Thomas began to mumble a reply.

"Mother asked Thomas to escort me here," Europa interrupted. "She was trying to protect me." Her tone and accompanying frown made it plain that she considered the effort unnecessary. "We knew Constantinople was being ravaged. Is there anywhere that isn't? Yet, she said, to survive in the midst of such a horror, what better chance could one have than to live in the household of the Lord Chamberlain?"

"She's a practical woman, is Cornelia," Thomas put in.

"You say Cornelia is still at the inn where you were staying?"

"A place called the Inn at Stephen's Column, on the road from Nicomedia. It's not far from a stylite's column. Stephen isn't there any more, just the column. I suppose the place was built to accommodate passing pilgrims."

"Why didn't she accompany you?"

"The innkeeper owes us money," explained Europa. "We'd paused there for a few days, performing in the courtyard to entertain guests. He was awaiting payment for something or other himself. I'm not certain of the details, but in any event, mother didn't want to arrive on your doorstep empty-handed. Isn't that what she said, Thomas?"

Thomas' head bobbed in agreement.

"That would be her way," John said. "A very proud woman, Cornelia. As if I don't possess more than enough wealth!"

"I notice you still haven't spent any of it on new furnishings," said Thomas.

Before John could reply, there was a rap at the house door.

John leapt to his feet and went to the top of the stairs.

Hypatia had come in from the garden and already opened the door, but the figure who rushed inside and loped frantically across the atrium towards the stairway was not Cornelia.

"Anatolius! You look as if you've had a terrible shock. Come up into the kitchen."

"Fortuna has smiled on me, John." The young man was out of breath as he reached the top of the stairs. "Balbinus is sinking fast! I called at his house again. The place was in an uproar, but I gathered that when Lucretia looks out of a window tomorrow, the sun will shine in on a widow."

John caught his friend's arm a stride's distance from the kitchen and spun him around.

"Anatolius!"

Anatolius looked at him, amazed at his harsh tone.

John released his grip. "You're wishing for Balbinus' death!"

"I'm thinking of Lucretia—"

"No doubt. But the Lucretia you knew is gone, Anatolius."

"No, John, never."

"Lucretia has shared the senator's bed for some time now. It's true she left him once, but she returned."

"John, I would rather not think—"

"You had better think about it, Anatolius. However much we may desire it, the past can't return."

Even as he uttered the words, John realized he had been giving voice to what he had been trying to tell himself ever since his visitors had arrived, counseling himself not to hope too much, not to build dreams.

As Anatolius turned toward the kitchen doorway, John saw
Europa seated at the table, a living refutation of everything he
had just said about the past.

Chapter Fifteen

John chose to cover the short distance between his house and that of the lawyer Prudentius by taking the back streets behind the Hippodrome rather than walking up the Mese.

It was just as well.

Those streets being less frequented, there were fewer citizens to draw back fearfully from the tall, grim-faced Greek who was obviously, from his demeanor and dress, the bearer of some grievous trouble from the palace. Those passersby who scuttled out of his path were more frightened still by his lack of a bodyguard.

It was obvious to anyone he was as dangerous and reckless as he was powerful.

Despite his grim face, John was not contemplating the infliction of harm on anyone. He was merely thinking, as he liked to do as he walked. The harder he thought, the faster his feet moved.

Despite his rapid pace, he could not find any ready solutions to the myriad of problems posed by the unexpected arrival of his daughter in the company of Thomas. At the realization, his mouth settled into a hard line.

Then too there was Anatolius' dangerous pursuit of Lucretia. Why hadn't that young man grasped his opportunity and taken her to wife before she was married off to Senator Balbinus?

Most importantly, there was the matter of Peter's illness. If his elderly servant were indeed dying then it was even more urgent that John find Gregory's murderer. Or so he'd told himself upon waking that morning after a restless night filled with dreams he could not recall.

The evening before had been trying enough, brief as it had been thanks to the hour at which Thomas and Europa arrived. Hypatia had prepared rooms and they'd been happy enough to retire early, leaving John alone with his thoughts and Zoe.

All in all he felt he could hardly linger at home and chat with the new arrivals this morning. There was work to be done.

As Prudentius' house door opened, a voice in the back of John's mind insolently suggested that duty could also be a convenient refuge.

The exotic servant Xanthe greeted him. This time she did not carry her infant, which was doubtless one of those John could hear crying lustily in the far recesses of the house.

John was indeed fortunate today, Xanthe indicated. Prudentius was at home and receiving visitors in his office.

The lawyer had closed the room's inner screens, barely muting the clamor from the atrium, while leaving the rest open to the garden.

The man John had arrived to interview turned out to be as tall as the Lord Chamberlain and hollow-chested with a long bony face, sporting as much bristling white hair in his eyebrows as on his balding, cropped scalp. He gave the impression of a patrician who had become a desert hermit, particularly in his garments. The gold embroidery around the collar of his well-worn robe had begun to unravel. Stray threads stuck out untidily, mirroring the hairs over his deep-set eyes.

He offered John the chair beside a dainty lacquered table whose legs terminated in carved and gilded swans' heads. The delicate piece of furniture apparently served him for a desk.

"May I offer you wine and perhaps some of this excellent cheese?" Prudentius indicated a silver platter on the table. "It's one of the smoked varieties. It's flavored with thyme and very difficult to obtain of late. An unforgivable luxury under the circumstances, really, yet we all have our weaknesses."

John politely declined. Aside from the incongruous table the room was utilitarian, its walls covered with niches overflowing with codexes and scrolls. More than a few were piled haphazardly on the floor. Several marble busts set on tall pedestals glowered balefully into the distance, like irate judges. The brass water clock sitting prominently in one corner doubtless served to remind Prudentius' clients that his time was their money.

"There's never been a slab of grilled meat of any kind that I find as tasty as this particular delicacy," Prudentius said. "Like our emperor I choose not to sully myself by eating flesh."

John gave the lawyer a thin smile, thinking of grilled fish.

Prudentius smiled in return. "I see you agree. Now, sir, Xanthe is a sweet child, but not much good at announcing visitors, I fear. To whom am I speaking?"

At the words Lord Chamberlain, the lawyer's expression became grave. "How can I assist you, excellency?"

"I would like information concerning a client of yours, a recently deceased shipper by the name of Nereus."

"Nereus? Deceased, you say?"

John stated the cause of death.

A breeze wandering in from the sunny garden gently rustled legal documents in their niches.

Prudentius bowed his head. "Of course. Does anybody die of anything else these days?" He directed a sharp look at John. "How did you know he was my client?"

John mentioned the letter Cador had delivered.

"Of course. You understand, excellency, I must be cautious in matters concerning my clients. Any assistance I can offer therefore depends on what sort of information you seek."

John outlined the little he had learnt about Nereus' final hours. "Had he consulted you about making a new will?"

"Yes, he had, but it was more to confirm what he thought was applicable law. He owned a set of Justinian's Institutes, and when laymen seek to interpret such technical writings, well…but there again it is a point of pride for many aristocrats to write their own wills. Since he apparently made an oral will, I would have to assume he never got around to actually writing a new will."

"Do you know anything about the provisions in the will he intended to change?"

"He never consulted me about it."

"When he asked you for advice, did he indicate what it was he wanted to accomplish?"

Prudentius leaned back slightly in his chair. "You put me in a difficult position, Lord Chamberlain."

"I regret the necessity, but refusal to answer as far as you are able might put you in an even more difficult position," John replied.

The lawyer's shaggy eyebrows went up slightly. "I see. Very well. Nereus asked specifically about an oral will. He said he felt in these troubled times it was a very wise precaution to understand how to do it, just in case he needed the knowledge. Naturally I urged him to allow me to draw up a written will, since it would be much easier to administer. Then too, while he did not say as much, I formed the distinct impression he was considering disinheriting his son. He expressed some anxiety about Triton getting involved with, as he expressed it, a low class of woman who would find a liaison with a rich man's son an attractive notion. And now I have told you everything I know and more than I should have." He began to stand.

John remained seated. "A murder is involved."

Prudentius settled heavily back into his chair. "You said my client died of the plague!"

"That is correct. However, one of the witnesses, a customs official named Gregory, was stabbed to death not long after he left Nereus' bedside."

Prudentius began to pluck absently at a loose thread protruding from his tunic sleeve. "Surely that is nothing but a sad coincidence, Lord Chamberlain? When there's an estate in dispute people generally tend to attack the testator, not the witnesses. And how could anyone outside Nereus' house possibly know what the oral will said? It had only just been made."

"It's possible Triton somehow learned of his father's intent and wanted to prevent himself from being disinherited."

"You mean by removing all the witnesses to his father's final will?" Prudentius shook his head and chuckled. "One can't disinherit a blood relation that easily. There's the Lex Falcidia for one thing, whereby an heir is entitled to a portion of the estate, unless there's ingratitude on his part, or what is legally termed ingratitude. Nereus should have been asking me for advice on that. Then there's the matter of diminishing the estate by the granting of legacies rather than outright disinheritance, both of which may involve different procedures to be valid depending on the circumstances, I might add. And that's just the start of the difficulties. Put the idea out of your mind, Lord Chamberlain. Your theoretical murderer wouldn't know whether he'd gained anything from the crime until after the matter had been litigated for several years."

He paused. "Besides, how could Triton know about his father's will unless he was standing there, listening at the door?"

"True. But consider, he might have bribed a servant to bring him word if Prudentius made a new will. However, you are correct. Murderers don't necessarily consider all the details or think like lawyers."

A clattering from the garden interrupted their conversation. Wheezing shouts followed. "Beware! Beware! The mighty fist of heaven descends on all sinners!"

John glanced out. Ezra was crawling rapidly over the roof tiles like a raggedly dressed crab.

"You are a person of great charity," John observed.

"I hear that compliment often, Lord Chamberlain. People seem puzzled when I explain I try to give back to the poor some of the wealth the rich pay me to assist them with legal matters. I look on myself as a kind of tax collector, levying largely on greed. For example, an importer sells a shipment of sour wine and is promptly sued by the buyer and so finds he needs my assistance. A few waifs here are fed by my fees."

"We were talking about oral wills. What exactly is the law concerning them?"

Prudentius' long face grew longer. "I'm afraid the law is rarely exact. It's complicated. Mens' eyes read free, so if the law was only what is written down, why would anyone wish to employ me? No, what matters is not what is laid down, but what the judge thinks it is, or more precisely whether the litigant and the judge interpret it the same way."

"I can see that might cause difficulties, but what do the laws say?"

"Very little. A testator may make an oral will in the same manner as a written one, that is, by calling seven witnesses, stating his intention to do so, and then declaring his will before them."

John nodded. "The man who delivered the letter to you was one of Nereus' witnesses, as was the murdered man and an acquaintance of a friend of mine. That leaves four whose identities are still unknown to me."

"He couldn't have called on any slaves he owned, I can tell you that." Prudentius gazed out toward the stylite on the roof, as if the holy man was an aid to his memory.

He held up a hand and began to tick off various possibilities on slender fingers. "A woman can't be a witness, nor can anyone who has not reached puberty. Needless to say neither can anyone who is dumb, deaf, or insane, not to mention a person who has been deprived of the control of his property or who has been declared infamous and incapable of testifying. On the other hand, witnesses can be related, but a party under the testator's control, a minor for example, is barred as a witness. So is the heir. Legatees and trust beneficiaries are not disqualified."

Ezra began to sing unintelligibly in a grating voice. Several birds perched unseen in the wilderness of the garden formed the chorus. John was reminded of Peter, who sang hymns just as tunelessly while he worked.

He thanked Prudentius for his assistance and got up to leave.

"If this murder is connected in some way to Nereus' will as I suspect, then any of the witnesses might know something that the murderer would not wish revealed," he told the lawyer. "That being the case, keep in mind that if a witness is in danger because of his connection to the will, the testator's legal advisor might well not be safe either."

Chapter Sixteen

"You say I'm possibly in danger just because I was kind enough to escort an old man around the city? That's not fair! Not fair at all, is it, Anatolius?" Crinagoras' soft mouth settled into a petulant moue as he looked away from John to his friend, seated beside him in the Lord Chamberlain's study.

Anatolius pretended to be looking at the scene outside.

"And so now going in fear of my life is how my kindness is to be repaid!" Crinagoras concluded angrily.

"If any of the witnesses are in danger, I'd suspect it would be because of some connection they had with Nereus or an interest they had in the will, which obviously does not apply in your case," John pointed out wearily. "Nevertheless, exercising caution would be the best policy for now."

Crinagoras shifted uncomfortably on the hard wooden seat set in front of the bucolic mosaic. "Lord Chamberlain, is there no cushion to be found anywhere in your house?"

Thomas, leaning against the door-frame, laughed. "A hard seat's exactly what you need right now, Crinagoras. Less chance of dozing off. Remember, a murderer might be seeking you."

Crinagoras shot an accusatory look at the red-haired Briton. "Why did you have to say that? I'll have difficulty enough sleeping as it is."

Thomas grinned. "What you need is to hire a bodyguard. As it happens, I'm looking for work and I'm also very handy with the blade, as the Lord Chamberlain can confirm from our adventures together during my last visit to your city."

"It's certainly a good offer," Crinagoras mused, "but what kind of remuneration would you require? My poems and epitaphs are not selling very well right now. So many of my patrons are at their country estates."

Thomas tugged thoughtfully at his mustache. "Ah, but there may be someone out there who'd be happy to write your epitaph free of charge."

More than one person, John thought. "I realize you can't afford to spend the entire morning answering questions, Crinagoras, so I will take as little of your time as possible. As I explained, there must be seven witnesses to an oral will. You and Gregory were two and there was also Nereus' servant Cador. Did you recognize anyone else at Nereus' bedside?"

"Half the population of the city was present, Lord Chamberlain. A riot might have broken out at any time, there was such chaos."

"And who might all these people have been?" John asked patiently.

"Servants. Slaves. Common laborers." Crinagoras sniffed at the memory. "I recall a rustic fellow and a very strange person who insisted on dancing with a man in ecclesiastical garments."

Thomas didn't quite stifle a laugh.

John glared at him.

"I'm sorry, John," Thomas grinned, "but I had forgotten how entertaining Constantinople can be."

"You may not find it quite so entertaining after a few days' stepping over the dead," Anatolius remarked. "How entertaining do you suppose Europa finds it?"

"The riotous scene at Nereus' bedside will not be re-enacted in this room." John's tone was sharp. "Now, Crinagoras, you say someone from the church was there?"

"Yes. In fact, I remember that he had something to do with the Church of the Holy Apostles. What a memory, eh, Anatolius? I learned that from the servant who showed Gregory and me out. She mentioned, for some unfathomable reason, that the preserved nose of some saint or other is on display there and said if she had to go through life wearing a nose like that, she'd as soon not be a saint."

He paused thoughtfully. "A comely young lady, and obviously quite taken with me. What do you suppose she meant by telling me she didn't want to be a saint? Perhaps she was hinting...?"

John ignored his ramblings. "And this person you describe as very strange?"

"The fellow wore rags and had skin so leathery he looked as if he'd been left on the brazier too long."

Thomas observed it was a description that fitted many residents of the city.

"But how many of them insist on dancing with a churchman while a man lies dying in the same room?" Crinagoras asked. "Not to mention knocking over the water clock. His rustic companion appeared to find that remarkably comical."

He wrinkled his small nose. "It made an awful mess, of course," he went on. "I couldn't help thinking how appropriate it was, in a terribly poetic way, since poor Nereus' time was about to run out all at once, just like the water in the clock."

"Time was about to run out for Gregory too," John reminded him.

"Yes, unfortunately. We'd talked on the way to Nereus' house," Crinagoras recalled. "As a poet, I make a study of humors, of character, the ways in which men express themselves. Naturally, Gregory was impressed when he learned about my poetic skills, so I asked what he did for a living. Alas, the poor man had passed much of his life as a customs official."

Crinagoras sighed at Gregory's misfortune. "He did however purchase a poem from me, composed on the spot. I borrowed a kalamos from one of Nereus' servants to write it down. One never knows when the Muse will favor one. It was a wonderful piece about the tragic story of Leander and Hero."

That explained the dreadful poem he had found on Gregory's desk at the customs house, John realized. Which in turn meant that the customs official must have returned there before he died. Did that shed new light on anything he had learnt?

"I would still prefer to fight with a sword than a kalamos any day," Thomas was saying.

Anatolius continued to devote most of his attention to what was going on outside, as if he'd never seen passing excubitors or foraging seagulls before.

Crinagoras squirmed on his chair and grimaced. His attention was caught by the mosaic. He reached out suddenly to run an exploratory finger over the image of the girl Zoe.

At John's sharp glance he drew his hand back as if the tesserae were red hot.

"And finally about the oral will itself," John asked. "Think carefully. What did Nereus say?"

Everyone looked expectantly at the young poet.

"I have no idea," he confessed, red-faced. "With all the commotion, I could hardly hear a word."

Mithra! John thought. Was every avenue he found to be barred after he had taken only a few steps down it? "I see. Very well, Crinagoras, I won't detain you any longer."

"Yes, I'm certain you have some verses to write," Thomas put in, "but make sure you bar your doors and windows first."

Crinagoras struggled up from his chair. "How would you like some of my poetry?" he asked Thomas as he drew level with him. "The ladies all love to be wooed with a good romantic poem. I'll trade my verses for your blade's protection, what do you say, Thomas?"

The burly knight exhibited a grasp of Greek vernacular John had not realized he possessed and then shrugged his shoulders.

"For today, it's a bargain," Thomas concluded, following Crinagoras downstairs.

John glanced at Anatolius' doleful face and suggested a stroll around the garden.

Soon they were pacing around the peaceful space. Heavy dew still spangled its bushes, shimmering on spiderwebs and dripping from leaves and branches.

"So many shades of green, all different and yet all known by the same name," Anatolius mused. "Perhaps I should write a verse or two about that…."

John changed the subject. "You've been so quiet today I assume Senator Balbinus awoke with the sun this morning, despite his servants' dire predictions to the contrary?"

"Yes, Fortuna smiled upon him." Anatolius looked glum. "Crinagoras and I visited his house on the way here. It is only a matter of time, however, since Lucretia could not leave his bedside, or so we were told."

He stopped at one of Hypatia's herb beds and drew in a deep breath. "A pleasant fragrance, is it not? Especially after the streets. Father was never one who cared much for flowers and such, so my garden is rather plain. Perhaps I can borrow Hypatia some time to rectify the situation?"

"Can you be trusted with her?" John asked with a smile.

"I admit to the occasional infatuation, but you needn't worry, they are all behind me. There is only Lucretia. There's never been anyone else, not really, and there is always hope….Haven't you always longed to be reunited with Cornelia?"

John plucked a leaf from a bushy herb. It felt slightly furry. He crushed it and brought his fingers to his face. The odor was familiar. Was the herb something Peter used when cooking?

"There are certain subjects it is best not to discuss, even between close friends," he said quietly.

Anatolius was silent for a time. "Thomas and Europa seem very fond of each other," he finally ventured.

"I had noticed."

Anatolius glanced upwards abruptly. John saw what had caught his friend's attention. A tiny, brown bird had dropped out of the sky to perch on a limb of the olive tree beside the fountain. It sat for an instant, then fluttered away and up under the peristyle surrounding the garden.

"There's more than one nest there," John explained. "My house is like an avian inn these days."

"It will be more home-like when Cornelia arrives."

John shot him a warning glance.

"Er...speaking of lovers, try not to mention the subject to Crinagoras."

John observed it was not one of his usual topics of conversation and in any event it would certainly not be something he ever expected to discuss with Crinagoras.

"Just as well. His dear Eudoxia wasn't more than fifteen or sixteen, you know." Anatolius stared toward the pillar behind which the bird had disappeared. A faint chirping could be heard.

"Crinagoras and I grew up together," he went on, "and it gets tiresome to constantly hear about this great love of his. He has himself half-convinced she threw herself into the sea in despair because they were forced to part. Yet as far as I know, all she did was step onto the ship taking her family to Egypt. Her father had been appointed to some high administrative position there. Crinagoras rushed to tell me as soon as he heard she had gone."

Anatolius struck a dramatic pose. "How could Eudoxia leave me? No, no, never could she leave me willingly. She must have thrown herself over the rail and into the winey waves. That was his reasoning." He paused. A cloud passed over his face. "If I really believed she'd killed herself I couldn't tolerate Crinagoras' company for an hour longer. She's probably married with five children by now. I asked him once why he didn't go to Egypt and find out exactly what happened to her. He said even looking at the sea made him nauseous. Do you know, I've never been to Crinagoras' house. We arrange to meet here or there, just like Peter and Gregory did. It's because Crinagoras still lives with his family. There's not much money in poetry and epitaphs. It's just as well Crinagoras' father deals in sewers and such rather than verse."

He paused for an instant. "And what he said when Crinagoras announced his ambition was to become a court poet rather than dabble in drains, well...."

***

When Anatolius departed, John secured the house door and visited Peter's storeroom to replenish the kitchen wine jug, deriving some amusement from the realization he was performing tasks for both his servants. Then he sat in the garden for a while, mulling over his next course of action.

Europa appeared. She perched at the side of the pool, dangling a hand into the water. Her tunic sleeve was pulled up to her elbow, revealing a slim, muscular arm.

"It's cool here, isn't it? I suppose it will be another hot day." She turned her face toward him and smiled.

His breath caught in John's throat. Europa looked like her mother.

"Cool water feels wonderful, especially after all those dusty roads we traveled and the public squares we performed in with the sun blazing down on us all day long."

"How is your mother?"

Europa looked down at the water, rippling with her hand. "As always. In Egypt she still insisted on dancing on the bull from time to time."

"And otherwise?"

"She never married."

Was his interest in that direction so transparent, he wondered. "And you haven't either, it seems."

Europa's hand churned deeper, raising a series of waves. "Not yet, father."

John drew a slow breath. He felt overheated. He would have found it easier to attend a midnight audience with Theodora than to try to talk to his own daughter. "And Thomas?"

"He has been nothing but helpful to mother and me. He's different from when we met him years ago, when we were here the first time."

John uneasily noted the secret smile that passed over her lips. "He may not be a man you want to think about too seriously, Europa."

"Perhaps. But don't be deceived by his barbarous looks. He is not as unsophisticated as he appears."

The waves she was making lapped over the pool's edge. She pulled her hand from the water and wiped it dry on her tunic.

"Please don't worry about me, father. I am not certain what we will do after mother arrives. Considering the life I have led, what can I know about being the daughter of the Lord Chamberlain? Would I have to sit in the garden and sew dainty things all day or compose pretty verses like that fellow you were questioning just now? No, I'm happy as it is. Thomas says he'll find a suitable bull to replace the one the troupe lost and then we can start traveling again."

"If that is what you want, Europa, I can obtain an animal as fine as any in the empire before the sun sets."

"Thank you, but I would rather Thomas and I found one for ourselves."

John went indoors, leaving Europa sitting by the pool. Thomas again! What had Thomas been doing since they had last met? He had not exactly been forthcoming when questioned about it.

If Peter had been dead, John's knock would have roused him.

Though he had nothing to say beyond asking that water be left at his door, Peter's voice sounded weaker.

John debated ordering him to open the door. Then he could consult Gaius on suitable treatment.

But what if Peter died anyway? In that case, he would die without his dignity.

With a sigh John turned away. He couldn't allow that, any more than he could permit him to die without knowing justice had been done for his friend.

Chapter Seventeen

"I'm off to visit Scipio, my bookseller. His shop's just across the Augustaion," Crinagoras told Thomas, as he led his newly hired bodyguard through the huge, bronze gate of the Great Palace and across the square beyond.

"What do you intend to buy?"

"I don't purchase literary works, Thomas, I write them. Scipio handles the occasional copying job for me. He also sells my poems."

"Does he? You mean to say you can make a living in this city by scribbling poems? What a strange place!"

"Yes, well, I have been known to turn my golden verse into silver now and again. Tell me, Thomas, what do you do for a living?"

Thomas slapped the hilt of the sword hanging from his belt. "My blade's my livelihood."

"You've killed many men?"

"Do I look like a butcher?"

Crinagoras scowled at his red-headed companion, uncertain whether he'd been given an answer or not. "So you have spent a lot of time employed as a bodyguard?"

"Not that much."

"Well, where is it you've been when doing this work of yours?"

"Is your bookseller more than a day's march from here? If not, you don't have enough time to hear all the places I've traveled, so ask me instead where I haven't been."

"Anatolius said you were from Bretania. Have you returned to that gray and misty island recently?"

"No. That's one of the few places I haven't been. Another is Armenia."

"You haven't been back to your homeland, despite all these wanderings to and fro you mention? Why not?"

Thomas simply grunted.

They crossed the great square of the Augustaion. The gulls had most of its cobbles to themselves today. Across the way, a donkey cart stood in front of the Great Church. Two men came out, carrying a limp form between them. Another plague victim. The sight was so common, it had become almost homely, as one with grubby street vendors hawking their wares or malformed beggars with outstretched palms.

Crinagoras was disappointed. He had rather hoped he and his impressive bodyguard might run into one of his acquaintances. "It's a fine adventure to sail the seas and travel in distant lands, I suppose." He sighed. "Frankly, I prefer to explore my imagination. Sometimes I think it is vaster than the whole world. I might appear to be sitting in my room, day after day, but in reality, my friend, I am braving the unruly waves, visiting foreign shores, walking with mythological beings."

Thomas observed that he had not met any of the latter, but quite understood the attractions of sea travel carried out under one's own roof.

"You grasp it exactly, except the sea…ah, well…for some it signifies excitement or adventure. For me it held tragedy. I can never look upon its sparkling water without remembering my lost beloved. Poor Eudoxia. In the lonely silence of my room, I shed rivers of tears for her."

"Men do not speak of such private matters," growled Thomas.

"A pity, isn't it? We don't mind at all, nor think it unmanly, to bare our bodies to one another in the baths, but to bare our souls—"

Thomas cleared his throat loudly. "As to what I do for a living. As I mentioned, I live chiefly by my blade. You see, for years now I have sought the Holy Grail."

"The Christian relic? But I don't understand how you can make a living seeking something if you never actually find it."

"You make a living seeking truth and beauty, do you not?"

Crinagoras smiled. This barbaric fellow was apparently not so dull-witted as he appeared. "Now that you mention it...."

"In my case," Thomas continued, "I have not yet found what I seek. However, when an adventurer from Bretania, who's been to the ends of the earth searching for the Holy Grail, arrives in a new town on his quest, word gets around quickly. And there's always someone who has a job just waiting for a bold fellow like that."

"I should think so! Do you know, a few months ago I misplaced my best ink pot. I spent days searching for it. I penned a most amusing poem about the experience. Humorous, yet poignant. Losing that ink pot reminded me of losing—"

"Here's a better idea," Thomas interrupted. "Why not write about my search for the Grail? The stories I could tell you would sound like invented and quite fantastic tales! I won't charge you much for them. Buy me a few cups of wine, and that will suffice."

Crinagoras clucked with disapproval. "No, no. I fear you are not an authority on literature, Thomas. Whoever would want to read about a fellow from barbaric climes running about looking hither and yon for a musty old relic? As if we need any more relics in this city when it's already full of them!"

He gestured at a shop doorway. "This is where today's quest ends. We have reached Scipio's emporium."

Crinagoras and Thomas stepped from the street straight into what might have been the library of a wealthy household, except that few rich men owned the number of codexes and scrolls arrayed on shelves or laid out on tables, some opened as if the master had just been perusing them. Latin and Greek texts occupied opposite sides of the shop, whose painted walls depicted Romans from all walks of life in the common act of reading. Emperor Augustus and an anonymous young pupil of Socrates appeared to be held equally in thrall by the scrolls they perused.

Thomas chuckled and when Crinagoras glanced at him nodded at the wall painting beside the entrance. The scene depicted several octopii hovering over a burst crate of codexes, part of the cargo of a sunken ship.

Scipio's emporium did not smell of ink and parchment, but rather of the huge bunches of freshly cut flowers filling a multitude of glass vases set on every side. Ink was, however, very much in evidence on the tunic of the proprietor, not to mention under his fingernails, and along the side of his nose. There were even traces not quite concealed by the cropped furze covering the short man's scalp.

"Ah, Crinagoras, how nice…um…yes…why, it seems just yesterday you were here." Scipio's smile looked forced. "And who is your friend?"

"Thomas isn't a friend, Scipio. I have hired myself a bodyguard!"

"Why, are you afraid someone's reading your poetry?"

"What do you mean? Have you sold any of my work? Any more since yesterday, I mean?"

Scipio scratched nervously at his head. "Let me see, I don't believe I have. Business isn't what it used to be. Mind you, with the plague, people are buying a fair number of saints' lives, and I'm doing a brisk trade with the Institutes. They always sell. Can't copy them fast enough, and that's the truth. But my customers just don't seem to be in the mood for poetry. I'm having a hard time making ends meet."

"That's a very good reason to put more of my poems on display, don't you think?"

"Of course, of course! Except, as I just explained, business is not going too well right now. Writing materials are expensive, and my copyists won't work for nothing. However, I have had a wonderful idea. I've been keeping track of the doings of the holy fool. That's something people are bound to be interested in reading about. I could tell you what I've learned and you could write it down. We could call it The Chronicle of the Fool, that has a learned air to it."

Crinagoras sighed. "I might as well be young again and working away at my tutor's lessons. Everyone has a copying assignment for me today. I'm sorry, Scipio, but you know I only write from the heart. I do have some very deep and sincere feelings about the plague."

"You could fit those into such a chronicle easily, couldn't you?"

"The fool's an actor, a fraud. I write about real life, my friend. Real people. My subject is always truth, never lies or made-up stories."

Crinagoras strolled around the emporium, his gaze flickering over the shelves. "Now, about those poems of mine. I'll give you a share of my profits, Scipio. I see since yesterday you've sold all my collected epigrams. Why don't you keep the proceeds from those for now and use them to pay your scriveners to produce a few more copies for sale? I always like to assist a friend if I can."

"That's very generous of you, Crinagoras. I'll see what I can do."

Thomas made a circuit of the shop and examined the wall paintings. He paused near the back of the room, plucked a codex out of a crate, and ran a finger over its ivory cover.

Scipio looked alarmed. "Be careful! That's not supposed to be out here…it's a very valuable item." He took a step in Thomas' direction, but Crinagoras was already looking over the burly Briton's shoulder.

"What's the title?" Crinagoras asked.

Thomas held the codex up so the poet could read it.

"'A Bouquet of Crocuses.' By Erinna of Rhodes." How very remarkable. I thought only a few of her verses were known." Crinagoras opened the codex. The ancient, stained parchment pages crinkled noisily as he thumbed through them. He stopped and began to open his mouth, as if to read aloud.

Scipio plucked the codex away. "One of my assistants must have left this here by mistake. It's a special order. Fragments from an old scroll, which I was asked to bind into a codex, as you see."

"I was certain almost all of Erinna's poetry was lost to the ages, Scipio. Who could this gem possibly belong to? The emperor?"

"No. It belongs to a dealer in…such things. He brought it to me. The bits of the old scroll, that is."

"How fascinating." Crinagoras peered at his thumb. "Yet, I seem to have picked up some fresh ink from handling it…."

"Yes, well, being of great age some of the verses were exceedingly faint, you understand, so I was asked if I would highlight the writing a little here and there, to make it more legible. You cannot appreciate beauty if you cannot see it, can you?"

"A very poetic comment, Scipio," Crinagoras observed with approval.

"You never know what's going to happen next in this city," Thomas grinned. "There's no end to wonders here!"

"Quite so." Crinagoras rubbed his smudged fingertips together. "Now what about my offer, Scipio?"

Scipio rubbed his scalp. It seemed less a nervous gesture than a sign of an incipient headache. "Parchment has gone up in price, you know," he replied doubtfully.

"And why would that be, if people aren't reading very much?"

"Perhaps it's due to all those wills being made," remarked Thomas.

"That may well be so," replied Scipio. "How about this, Crinagoras? Jot some of your poetry down. Any old scrap of parchment will do. Then I'll keep them on hand, and if anyone wants to purchase one it can be copied out nicely. I'll be happy to keep a selection of your work on hand for my customers' perusal. I'll only charge you a nomisma."

"What? You want a nomisma, even though you won't have a proper copy on sale?"

"But you see, when anyone does ask for a copy I'll split the profit with you."

"I don't know, Scipio. I'd have to think about it."

Looking unhappy, Crinagoras walked from table to table, eyeing their offerings. He plucked a ragged piece of parchment from an enameled box full of similar sheets and scowled at the sign propped up nearby. "What does this mean, Scipio? Your sign says 'Pre-inspired writing materials.' What's that?" He held the sheet up and squinted at it.

"Oh, it's just something I offer at a reduced price. For poor poets. That's to say poets with more inspiration than means."

"I've heard poor poets tend to be poor poets," put in Thomas.

Crinagoras suddenly reddened. "But…but…this was one of my epigrams! I can still see the words. You've scrubbed the parchment, Scipio! You're selling my work as cheap writing material!"

"Pre-inspired parchment, my friend," Scipio corrected him. "It helps to get the imagination going. The poet doesn't have to supply the whole of the inspiration himself, because the parchment has already been imbued with previous genius. Think of it as a collaboration between you and some lesser writer, if you will."

He snatched the scrap from Crinagoras' trembling hand. "Besides, this particular parchment being in the box was a mistake," he went on. "I shall have to rid myself of that bumbling assistant, I can see. This was never intended to be sold as writing material. It was…that is to say… I merely felt the verse was so strong, its emotions so overpowering, that, well, I thought it best to lighten the writing a little, to protect the reader's sensibilities. Now, about that offer we were discussing…."

Crinagoras sniffed, then sneezed. He wiped his suddenly streaming eyes and sneezed again. "Yes, yes. I'll bring you some poetry to keep on hand for copying, Scipio, but I'm only paying you half a nomisma. How much extra work can it be to keep a sheet or two of parchment sitting about on a shelf? Now I must leave. The scent of these flowers is overpowering. Where did you get the notion to fill the place with such heavily perfumed blooms? I much prefer the smell of ink and dust."

Chapter Eighteen

"Yes, Lord Chamberlain, children can sometimes be trouble-some." Archdeacon Palamos looked sorrowful as, with a wave of a pudgy hand, he directed an urchin approaching with a jug of oil toward a flickering lamp suspended from an ornate silver stand.

"He's one of our young orphans," he went on with a fond smile. "Alas, there are so many in Constantinople these days that I fall into despair thinking of them being left all alone to fend for themselves."

John offered a compliment on the ecclesiastical care given freely to the sick and helpless. "I shall endeavor not to detain you too long from your good works. Speaking of which, I hope this will be of some assistance." He proffered a suitable amount.

"Most kind, Lord Chamberlain." The man's bow was impeded by his ample stomach, noticeable despite his volumi-nous robe.

There was an unnatural pallor to Palamos' face. He looked perfectly at home among the bones and scraps of desiccated cloth and flesh that had at one time or another been mistaken for part of a departed holy man. As he'd approached John, moving through isolated pools of lamplight, he'd resembled a phantom.

"You were inquiring about Nereus' will. It's so sad that such a good friend has departed and died, worse than that, vexed to his soul by that troublesome son of his. Even so, he still remembered the unfortunate with his generous gift to the church."

John had recognized Palamos. He had met him briefly years before, but the recollection was not mutual. Much had changed since then and the lighting in the crypt of the church was extremely poor. "Nereus left a legacy to the church?"

"He did." Palamos peered first into a large box filled with irregular bundles tied with cords and then examined several dusty baskets whose contents John could not make out. Crates lined the walls, vying for space with more baskets and bundles. The air was thick with a sharp incense composed of dust and mold.

"And the son?"

"The legacy to the church reduced the estate to a small plot of poor land to the west of the city, holding the ruins of the house where Nereus was born. He stated he was leaving it to Triton because that was all he himself had inherited, so that his son could have the benefit of making a fortune by his own labors. Just between us, Lord Chamberlain, I believe the young man was fortunate to get even that."

"I understand Triton had been involved with an unsuitable woman?"

"Unsuitable is hardly a strong enough word. An actress, a friend of bear trainers! We all know the way such women earn a few nomismata extra, don't we? Every night I pray my dear parentless boys will escape the fleshly fish hooks dangled by such low women. They drag such innocents down, straight into the clutches of the demons of lust, and then it is eternal agony and for what, I ask you, for what?"

"Could you describe who was there when Nereus made his will?"

"Nereus was frantic, poor man. There was a great deal of confusion and difficulty finding the required number of witnesses." Palamos gazed up at the shadowy ceiling, recalling recent events. "I had gone to offer him spiritual comfort, having heard he had been taken ill. He asked me to assemble witnesses. I discovered his house steward, whom he had specifically requested, was himself too sick to attend. However, his assistant, Cador, a man from Bretania and well trusted by his master, was able to take his place."

Palamos knitted his brows and glanced up again as if invoking heavenly aid for his memory.

"It was dreadful, Lord Chamberlain, seeing my dear friend sinking so fast." A vague smile flickered across his face. "Dear me, that could almost be the sort of jest a callous person would make, given Nereus' shipping interests. To return to your question. Also present were a couple of men I did not know, these being a cart driver and that obscene simpleton who has been running about the city lately holding himself out as being a holy fool. Can you imagine the dreadful anguish of being on your deathbed with a pair like that standing next to it?"

An outraged tone crept into Palamos' voice. "Do you know, this so-called holy fool started telling what he considered humorous anecdotes, despite my pleas to respect the situation. Why, the more I protested, the more lewd they became!"

He paused and looked around the gloomy surroundings. "I should not be saying this within the hearing of young ears. Children will creep down here to play, no matter how often I warn them not to do so. The other day I caught two of them testing the sanctity of Flavian against that of Gorgonius, or so they claimed. To me it looked more like a sword fight. Well, as much as you could recreate one when your weapons are a bit of thigh bone and a mummified forearm."

John remarked that the incident sounded even more blasphemous than joking lewdly beside a deathbed.

"I would certainly agree, except the relics kept down here are those whose authenticity has been doubted even though their donors were perfectly sincere in their belief they were indeed what they purported to be."

John asked him why such dubious items remained in the church.

"An arm or a thigh bone once belonged to some poor soul even if he wasn't a saint or a martyr, Lord Chamberlain, and therefore should rest on sacred ground. Then too, we may at times be mistaken. For example, the Patriarch recently ruled our finger of St. Luke is authentic after all and ordered it put on display because of Luke's connection with the healing arts. Heaven only knows where we stored it, though." He poked forlornly at another bundle.

"About this holy fool…?"

"If you must insist on hearing the sordid details, Lord Chamberlain, after that the disgusting fellow began to sing a filthy song about the empress and a number of ecclesiastical dignitaries! I will say he seemed to have a fair grasp of the church hierarchy. Then, and I shudder to relate this, he actually seized my elbows and pulled me around Nereus' room in a horrible sort of dance until I managed to shake him off. Dreadful, just dreadful. I practically fainted between dizziness and the sheer horror of his blasphemous behavior."

John expressed sympathy.

Palamos shook his head. "And then this unspeakable fool finished his performance by leaping up on Nereus' bed and bouncing up and down! I thought we were in the presence of Satan himself. Yet what can you expect when time is of the essence and you are forced to drag rascals in off the street?"

"Certainly you could anticipate they would not be models of courtiers' behavior," John observed. "Are you certain the man you mention is the one claiming to be a holy fool?"

"Definitely, Lord Chamberlain. He invaded this very church not long ago and tried to make off with our fragment of the Column of Flagellation."

John mentioned he had seen several boys and two men pursuing the would-be thief. "They did not catch him?"

"No. However, I'm glad to say we haven't seen him since."

"What about the cart driver?"

"I regret I cannot tell you who he is. Light!"

John heard running footsteps and another urchin emerged from the shadowy stairway to hand a clay lamp to Palamos.

"Have you seen the finger of St. Luke?" Palamos asked the boy. The boy reddened. "Oh no, sir. I haven't touched it and neither has anyone else." He nervously licked his lips. "What good would an old dried-up finger be in a fight anyway? It would probably break soon as you poked anyone with it. If anyone did, I mean. But nobody broke it because we didn't have it, you see."

"Yes, I think I do see." Palamos shooed the boy away and led John to a table standing in a corner. In the lamplight, beneath thick cobwebs, glinted what might have been the eyes of malignant spiders. Drawing closer John saw several jeweled reliquaries.

"They hold several pieces of the leg bone of John the Baptist," Palamos explained. "From their size and number it would seem he was twice the height of an ordinary person. Very convenient for river baptisms, wouldn't you say? I'm certain he would forgive me for saying that." He gently brushed cobwebs from the reliquaries.

John described the witnesses he had already identified: Crinagoras, Gregory, and Cador. "With yourself and the holy fool and a cart driver that makes six. Do you know who the seventh was?"

"Aristotle of Athens," Palamos replied immediately. "He tried to pawn off some questionable relics on me whenever I happened to meet him at Nereus' house. He presents himself as a dealer in antiquities and oracles."

Palamos coughed. Was he choking on the cobwebs he'd stirred up or the thought of the dealer of antiquities?

"Did Nereus transact very much business with this Aristotle?"

Palamos nodded. "I regret to say it of a good friend who is now gone, but Nereus exhibited a certain gullibility at times."

"Where is Aristotle's establishment?"

"I'm afraid I can't tell you. I never ventured there myself. His regular discovery of ancient oracles struck me as highly suspicious. In fact, on one occasion I questioned him most closely about it. And do you know what he said, Lord Chamberlain?

He claimed he was born on the fifth day of the fifth month and as Virgil observed, when gamblers wager, Fortuna favors uneven numbers! Thus, he said, he trusted to Fortuna that the antiquities and oracles he bought and sold were as represented and since he has not been prosecuted so far, obviously that proved his wares were genuine."

"It's extraordinary how many are placing their trust in Fortuna these days. Her name seems to be on everyone's lips."

"True enough. We should rather be praying to the Lord, but there are those, I am sorry to say, who are reluctant to trust one whom they believe responsible for the pestilence. In fact, many say we have brought the plague on ourselves."

"Do you know the lawyer Prudentius?"

Palamos had picked up a small, exceedingly ugly reliquary which resembled, no doubt quite by accident, a jeweled toad. He looked up from it in surprise. "I do know Prudentius. Very well, in fact. Another pious man full of charity. He was another orphan like the boy you just saw and again like him brought up in the church. Now he not only donates regularly to our charities, he also takes outcasts and dear children into his own home. As you see, Prudentius' kindly nature and actions prove that charity begets charity. If you're thinking about the will, though, Nereus formed his own opinions about that."

John asked what he meant.

"Recently Nereus mentioned to me he'd consulted the law on the matter. I think he meant he had been leafing through that set of the Institutes he obtained a while ago. He consulted them as often as he did those oracles in his garden. Well, as far as the latter goes, superstition isn't a sin, but what sense he could have made of something as confusing as the Institutes, I can't say. One needs suitable training to disentangle the entrails of the law."

He tugged at the tiny door of the reliquary. "You haven't told me why all this interests you, Lord Chamberlain, not that I have any right to ask. It isn't about his generous gift to us, is it?"

John assured him that no one was thinking about confiscating the church's legacy and then briefly explained Gregory's fate.

Palamos looked distressed. "Gregory was another of our benefactors. And he's been murdered, you say? I didn't know him too well, although I've occasionally seen him here. He'd come in now and then and just stand silently for a time, contemplating our relics of John Chrysostom. I did not think it unusual to see him at Nereus' house. People who worship at the same church tend to get to know one another, conduct business together, and so forth. Have you spoken to his widow?"

"There was no one at his house when I called."

"I believe her sister lives nearby. She may be staying with her."

Palamos finally managed to pry open the reliquary and extracted from it a finger with a cracked and blackened nail. As he held it up, it appeared to be pointing at John.

Palamos smiled. "The finger of St. Luke!"

***

Angelina, Gregory's widow, was spinning wool in a sunny room at the back of her sister's house, a short walk from her own home. A small, plump woman perched on a stool, she reminded John of a dove. A dove whose feathers were, however, a blue and dark as the waters of the Sea of Marmara under the glare of the midday sun. In one hand she held a clump of wool. A weighted spindle dangled from the other.

She greeted John with a timid smile, indicated he should take a seat, and continued working. "My sister's husband has been taking care of such matters that need to be taken care of, I am thankful to say. The news was a terrible shock. A man from the palace administrative offices came to tell me. It all seems a terrible dream."

John offered condolences.

"Thank you. As you see, I am keeping myself busy. Not crying in lamentation or any such extravagance. A nasty pagan practice, excellency. They might well tear their hair at the mouth of Hades, but why should we when our loved ones are standing at the gate of heaven?"

The widow's cheeks were rosy without the aid of makeup, her skin unlined, her hair, pulled away from her face, dark brown. It struck John that Gregory must have taken a much younger bride, until he noticed the joints of the hands that tugged at the wool and twirled the spindle were swollen and knobby with age.

"Not that the journey there is easy unless one is a saint," Angelina continued. "My poor husband must be braving the toll-houses at this very instant, arguing over his baggage with demon tariff collectors." A brief smile illuminated her face. "He always said he'd be well prepared to deal with them, having been a customs official himself."

John remarked that such a position would certainly be of great assistance in the circumstances.

"He was a good man, excellency. A good husband. I never wanted for anything. If he is facing some satanic judge right now, he surely has a score of angels defending him."

Not to mention angelic messengers seeking justice on his behalf, John thought. "I would say Gregory is not carrying the sort of baggage that would interest demons."

Did a wistful look cross the round face before him? "None of us are without sin, I fear," Angelina said.

The room had whitewashed walls lined with chests and baskets of wool. A shaft of light from the open window fell across the dark floor tiles, touching the stool where Gregory's widow worked. John told her, without elaboration, he was investigating her husband's death.

She accepted the statement without question. It would not be unusual for the palace or the City Prefect to take an interest in the murder of a high-ranking customs official.

"I understand your husband was once a military man. How did he come to be a customs official?"

"John Chrysostom got him the post," was the surprising answer.

"But he died almost a century and a half ago!"

"My husband had a great and abiding interest in him, excellency. When he served in Isauria he would visit every church he saw to ask if it owned any copies of the man's writings. Whatever he found, he committed to memory as best he could. Thus eventually he carried in his head a library no ordinary soldier could possibly have afforded."

John realized that the young Gregory had probably shared this knowledge with his friend Peter. "How did he become interested in John Chrysostom?"

"It was because John was exiled to that part of the world near the end of his life. He was part of the history of the mountains, if you wish. The beauty and power of his writing impressed Gregory." Although the old hands continued to work the wool and spindle, a quaver crept into her voice. "Gregory chose a phrase from them for his tomb inscription long ago."

"Since he was a Christian as well as formerly a military man, might I venture to guess it questions the supposed victory of the grave?"

The spindle stopped for an instant. Then she plucked hastily at the thread, smoothing out an errant thickening. "Why, yes, excellency. You are also a man of the church?"

"I am often at the Great Church." John did not explain that, as Lord Chamberlain, it was part of his duties to arrange and oversee the emperor's ceremonial entrances into the church, and that further, it was extremely wise for him to attend its services, despite holding other religious convictions.

Angelina forced a smile. "But I was telling you how Gregory obtained his post, wasn't I?"

She lifted the spindle and pushed down the multiplying coils of thread. "It was in Isauria that he took a spear in the arm."

There was the slightest hesitation in her words. The ancient wound she had mentioned might well have reminded her of the more recent and fatal wounding.

"He couldn't remain in the army," she continued. "He always said it was a sign sent by heaven. In any event, he came back and took a clerical job at the customs house. As it happened, one of the higher officials there was also a student of John Chrysostom's writings. He learned that Gregory shared his interest and when they began discussing matters of religion he soon recognized my husband's intelligence and talents."

Her hands continued like separate creatures, going about their own business. "He was blessed to be given a path leading so sure-footedly from a soldier's life in the wilderness to great wealth here in the capital," she went on. "I know Gregory wouldn't like to hear me complain it ended as it did. That would be ungrateful and unreasonable, he would argue."

"Did your husband discuss his work much with you, Angelina?"

John was not surprised when she told him he had not. Was there any connection between Gregory's post and his death? Was his death related to Nereus' oral will? Tariff collectors were so much disliked that it was not surprising that the church, seeking to remind the faithful of future accountability, had populated the soul's road to heaven with demonic customs officials.

John asked whether anyone with whom Gregory had recently transacted business might hold some resentment against him.

"No, excellency. He felt he was simply taking wealth on behalf of our Christian emperor from those who had more than enough. He personally donated a great deal of his own wealth for charitable purposes, particularly to the Church of the Holy Apostles."

"Did he receive any unusual visitors during the past few weeks?"

The spindle was full. Angelina placed it in the basket set beside her stool and brought her gnarled hands together in her lap, folding them together as if in prayer. "As I indicated, I did not know much about my husband's business. Indeed, you exhibit considerable knowledge of him."

"Peter related a few things about your late husband to me," John explained.

"Peter?"

"Gregory's old army friend."

"I've never heard Gregory mention him."

"Peter is the man Gregory met every week or so to talk about theology and—"

John was unable to finish because Angelina sprang off her stool, a dove taking awkward flight.

"Bless you, excellency!" She burst into tears. "You were sent from heaven. Now I see it all! Sent from heaven!"

She looked up at the whitewashed ceiling. "Gregory, forgive me!" she cried, and then addressed John. "All these years when Gregory was going off to his meetings with this Peter you've just mentioned, and never saying why or who he was visiting, oh, Lord forgive me, I supposed he had been seeing another woman."

Chapter Nineteen

Loud voices from the atrium distracted Hypatia. The scorpion's tail snapped off in her hand.

She set the lump of clay she'd been modeling on the kitchen table and quickly wiped her hands on a rag. The door slammed below and someone stamped angrily upstairs.

Europa burst into the kitchen, eyes bright with anger.

"I wish we'd never come here, Hypatia! I'm telling Thomas I want to leave!"

She found a cup, filled it from the wine jug, and drank thirstily.

"You didn't enjoy your visit to the Great Church?"

"I'd hardly reached the Mese when a man accosted me." She took another gulp of wine. "It was my father. I've just been escorted back home as if I were a child. Now he's gone out again. The streets are dangerous, I was told. Ha!"

Europa's tone of voice, her slim physique and deeply tanned skin, the mouth set in a thin line of anger reminded Hypatia of how much his daughter in some ways resembled the Lord Chamberlain. She murmured sympathetically.

Europa continued to fume. "I didn't notice any danger in the streets. The last time I visited this city they were swarming with people. Now it might as well be some old ruin in the middle of the desert. The most threatening thing I saw this morning was some half-naked old man singing lewd songs."

"That sounds like the holy fool everyone's talking about, mistress."

"I've heard better lyrics on the docks."

"I saw him dancing with a dead woman," Hypatia recalled with a shudder.

"Let him try dancing on a live bull! Come to think of it, I wouldn't be surprised if father asked me to give up my profession because it's dangerous. I hope mother arrives soon. She'll set him straight." She glared darkly into her cup and then pulled a stool over to the table. When she sat down her movements were as fluidly graceful as a dancer's. She poured out more wine. "Have a libation, Hypatia. You look overheated."

"That would hardly be proper, mistress," Hypatia faltered.

"This is not what many would call a proper household, is it? So it will be all right. How is Peter?"

Hypatia shook her head. "Fading, judging from his voice. I talk to him through the door when I take him food and water. He doesn't eat much, but the water's always gone next time I look."

"He didn't like Thomas when we were here last, I recall, but it's a shame to see him so ill."

Feeling awkward, Hypatia sampled the wine. "You've been involved with Thomas a long time then?" she ventured.

"No. We'd gone separate ways after he escorted mother and me back to Crete. It's just during these last few months, after he ran into us by accident, that I've got to know him well."

"Thomas is a fine fellow, mistress."

"He is, though some might call him a barbarian because he was born in Bretania, practically on the edge of the world. A country permanently shrouded in fog and mist, he tells me. A most romantic place. He's traveled a lot and seen more of the world than I have, and that's saying something."

"I'll wager he has many stories to tell!"

"Oh, he can be a regular Herodotus, if you can persuade him to talk about his past. He's a very discreet fellow."

"A quality to admire." Hypatia shoved her empty cup aside. It had occurred to her that if the Lord Chamberlain were to return, he would not appreciate finding his servant sharing wine with his daughter. She picked up the half-made scorpion and began nervously forming the clay.

"He's a sweet man, Hypatia. Oh my, yes...." Europa smiled to herself, but did not elaborate.

"I met someone sweet recently," Hypatia heard herself confessing.

Europa leaned forward. "Someone special?"

"Well, he might be." Hypatia's voice caught. Surely she shouldn't be confiding in Europa? Yet somehow she could not help herself.

She worked at the clay furiously. "His name is Pamphilos. He's a patient at the hospice where I've been helping Gaius. He was badly burned with lye. Somehow he'd been thrown into one of the towers being used for disposal of the dead."

"How horrible! Will he live?"

"Yes, but his face...."

"He'll need your comfort then," Europa said kindly.

"Once he was handsome, mistress. Even now you can tell that was the case. He is so kind and charming. He thought I was an aristocrat from a rich Egyptian family. I told him I was merely a servant. 'Surely you jest?' he said. 'You don't have the bearing of a servant.'"

"Evidently he is a golden-tongued young man!"

"I admitted my master was not just anyone, but rather the Lord Chamberlain. Pamphilos insisted it was a scandal that I should be anybody's servant and that half the men at the palace would throw themselves at my feet if given the chance."

Hypatia had formed the clay into a rudimentary face. It reminded her too much of her patient. She squeezed it into a lumpy mass. "He is so romantic, mistress! He even kissed my hand once and said all five fingers should have silver rings on them."

Europa, overlooking the fact that Pamphilos had counted thumbs as fingers, asked why he would pick silver rings and not gold.

"He said gold rings were so commonplace that the true romantic would always choose silver. Especially as silver is sacred to the moon, the friend of lovers," Hypatia explained with a blush.

"Indeed. Well, he sounds quite a fine young man. You should take no notice of looks, Hypatia," Europa said. "In the dark, you won't notice a few scars. Thomas has more than one."

They were giggling together when Thomas appeared in the kitchen doorway. "What's so funny? We could hear you laughing all the way downstairs!"

Hypatia blushed.

"How did a great big man like you creep up here so quietly?" Europa demanded in mock anger.

Thomas looked bemused. "You've been imbibing! Both of you!"

Europa pouted and shook her head. "No, no, dearest. Only me. Hypatia has been a good girl."

Crinagoras peered over Thomas' broad shoulder. "Thomas has been escorting me while I visited my favorite bookseller, and I must say Scipio was very impressed. He'd never seen me accompanied by a bodyguard. It makes one feel a new man, walking the streets with a guard at one's side."

Thomas smiled benignly.

"Would you escort me again now, Thomas? I'm meeting Anatolius."

"I think not," Europa said severely. "Thomas' services are needed here."

Crinagoras stepped into the kitchen. "We haven't agreed on a fee for today's work yet, but now that I see you two lovely ladies, let me offer some thoughts, fresh from the oven of my inspiration. I've been summoned to entertain Theodora at the Blachernae, I may add." Crinagoras set his soft hand on Thomas' shoulder. "How much is that worth, my friend? To be entertained like an empress?"

Thomas had no opportunity to answer since Crinagoras began to declaim, waving his hands around after the fashion of an intoxicated mime.

"For you, dear friends, I wish only happiness and the joy of never knowing the suffering experienced by me, sad Crinagoras, parted forever from the maiden Eudoxia by duplicitous death. May the ship of your happiness rise on the ocean of my tears, may you climb toward endless joy up the tower of earth excavated from the pit of my despair. May—"

"Cease at once!" Thomas commanded.

Crinagoras broke off, his face expressing confusion and incipient hurt.

"You must write it all down, lest it be lost forever," Thomas continued.

Crinagoras beamed. "Of course, Thomas. How stupid of me not to think of it. I shall write it out for you to savor at your leisure as many times as you please. You will have it by sunset tomorrow. And now I must depart."

As he scuttled off downstairs Thomas pulled at his ginger mustache and smiled with satisfaction.

Europa broke into a broad smile as Hypatia gave him a questioning look.

"I never learned to read," he told Hypatia with a grin.

Chapter Twenty

Anatolius waited for Lucretia in the atrium of Senator Balbinus' house. Time seemed to have stopped, as frozen as a water clock left outside on a winter's day.

Perhaps he had arrived at a time of crisis? At this very instant Balbinus might be struggling for another breath, one that would never come.

He listened, but could not hear even a muffled sound of a commotion.

Perhaps Lucretia simply did not want to see him?

He reminded himself of Crinagoras' advice. It couldn't have been given more than an hour ago, yet it felt like days.

"Follow your heart, my friend," the other had said. "Where would we be if Cupid were cowardly? Think, Anatolius. If you don't comfort her now, how will you ever be able to approach her afterwards?"

Crinagoras had reached up and tapped the mosaic on the inn wall. "You must emulate these brave charioteers. The first to the turn wins. In romantic matters, propriety must sometimes be left behind in the dust."

Anatolius' feelings about another visit to Balbinus' house were ambiguous, but the statement had persuaded him. Now, however, he had begun to have second thoughts.

Anatolius' mouth tasted sour. Did he smell of wine? He hadn't drunk much. Why then did he feel dizzy?

"Now, off you go." Crinagoras had practically pushed him out of the tavern door. "Fair Lucretia has not forgotten you. Didn't you tell me not long ago that when Senator Balbinus' party passed by you in the Augustaion after they left the Great Church, Lucretia looked back over her shoulder at you? Didn't your gaze nearly meet hers?"

Anatolius' grip tightened on the small scroll he held. The parchment felt damp.

No, he decided, this visit really was not proper.

He turned to leave.

"Anatolius."

Lucretia stepped into the atrium.

The sight of her stopped his breath.

Glossy ringlets, tamed by a mother of pearl comb, surrounded her pale, patrician face. She wore a simple robe of white linen, decorated around the collar with pale blue gemstones unwittingly echoing the purplish smudges under her tired eyes.

She must be exhausted from attending Balbinus night and day, Anatolius thought.

She invited him into a reception room he had never glimpsed. Dazzling bright, with walls of snowy marble, and white alabaster urns in its corners. A couch and two pine wood chairs were inlaid with cream-colored ivory. As he sat down opposite Lucretia he thought she might have been one of Peter's angels, and this the antechamber to the old servant's heaven.

"Why are you here again, Anatolius?" Her voice was low and breathy, as always.

"I wanted to offer any assistance I could render. Because... because...well, you remember...."

"My husband is dying. How exactly do you propose to assist me in the matter?"

Anatolius began to feel ill. "I'm sorry, Lucretia, I realize this visit may seem presumptuous."

"It most certainly is presumptuous."

"I will leave." He stood.

"Wait, Anatolius. I know you have a kind heart and came to see me with the best of intentions. I appreciate your sympathy."

"Everyone at the palace is saddened by his illness, Lucretia. I…I am saddened."

A faint, ironic smile flickered on her lips. "If you have come to commiserate with me on my husband's death, I fear you are somewhat premature."

Anatolius reddened. "He'll be well soon, Lucretia. It's just, I mean, if the worst happens…if there should be any legal difficulties…the Lord Chamberlain has the emperor's ear and as you know he is a good friend of mine. So I thought if I reassured you…well, you would have assistance if it was needed in that, um, remote possibility it would help ease the burden…." He floundered to a halt, having forgotten the carefully constructed speech he had rehearsed.

What a sorry excuse it sounded when spoken aloud.

How could he have taken that fool Crinagoras' advice?

"I see you've thought very hard about how you might help me, Anatolius. Thank you."

He glanced down at the sodden little scroll in his hand. How near she was. He could not recall when last she had been so close. How could he remind her of waking together in moonlight, of worshiping Venus in warm summer-leafed groves, of intimate hours lit by a flickering oil lamp?

He tried to recollect all he had intended to say. The words had fled in abject shame. He felt as if he was a soldier who had girded for battle, only to be struck down in the enemy's first wave of arrows.

"I've been a fool, Lucretia." He felt even more foolish for having said it.

"Who isn't at some time or other?"

"Do you ever think of me?"

"Of course. However, I am Senator Balbinus' wife and have been for some time."

Anatolius set the scroll on the couch beside her. "Something I wrote for you, Lucretia, as I used to do in the old days."

Lucretia looked down at the gift, her face inscrutable. She did not pick it up.

Neither did she push it away.

Anatolius found courage to speak. "Let me believe there is hope, Lucretia."

She did not raise her head. "Believe it if it pleases you, Anatolius."

"Lucretia, if you had not married Balbinus, you would have married me. We both know it."

Lucretia finally looked up at him. "No, Anatolius. I would not have married you."

Chapter Twenty-One

The bellow of a bull greeted John as he turned down a familiar street leading off the Strategion. It was almost as if Nereus' oracular bovine were foretelling his visit. Was it a good omen from Mithra?

Sylvanus stood outside his late master's house securing a basket full of frantically clucking chickens to a donkey cart.

"You've arrived just in time, Lord Chamberlain. I'm about to embark on a new adventure, since I'm off to the master's country estate with my charges. I was lucky enough to be able to purchase this cart this morning. Its owner demanded an exorbitant price, but I won't stay here another night!"

A cloud of feathers wafted out of the basket as Sylvanus struggled to tie it to the side of the cart.

Recalling their previous conversation, John asked what would drive a confirmed city dweller into the countryside sooner than would be necessary.

A puzzled look crossed the rustic servant's face. "You haven't come to investigate the incident last night when someone broke into the house?"

The bull bellowed again. Sylvanus swiveled his head toward the open house door. "Apis!" he shouted. "Don't worry, I haven't forgotten you!" Turning back to John, he invited him inside.

Nereus' house was a shambles. Fragments of terracotta and marble, the remains of lamps and statuary, littered the atrium. John stepped over a pale arm. The marble lump in one shadowy corner might have been a head.

"It's an outrage, sir!" Sylvanus fumed. "As if we hadn't enough to weep over! Yet heaven heaps even more misery upon us."

John glanced into Nereus' office. Whoever had broken into the house had taken the trouble to damage its wall mosaic. Glass tesserae sparkled here and there among the ripped codexes and scrolls carpeting the tiled floor.

"Theft and breaking into houses are becoming the city's main occupations," lamented Sylvanus, "and fine pickings for the dishonest too, what with so many homes unoccupied. I can almost sympathize with those who break into a house they think empty, looking for something to steal and sell so they can feed their families, but wanton destruction...."

"What was taken, Sylvanus?"

"I can't be sure, sir. You'd have to ask the house servants."

The garden had also been vandalized and shrubs uprooted and tossed into the fish pool.

"They left the oracular chickens and fish," Sylvanus pointed out. "I would have thought to a hungry thief both would have prophesied a very hearty dinner."

"You were absent when these intruders broke in?"

"In a manner of speaking. I regret to say I over-imbibed last night and did not realize that strangers were in the house until I saw the destruction this morning."

Bacchus, John thought, had become almost as popular these days as Fortuna.

"You heard nothing at all?"

Sylvanus, looking ashamed, shook his head and then, unexpectedly, beamed as he picked up a metal plate which had been half hidden under a low bush. "Here's another of the master's Dodona oracles. Bent, as you see, but I'm sure it can be put right. That makes three I've managed to find. I wonder where the other one is?" He looked around vaguely.

"You're fortunate you weren't murdered," John observed.

"I keep my door locked at night. It's always a wise precaution." Sylvanus strode over to Apis and grabbed the pitchfork lying by the pen. "If I'd heard the villains at work you can be certain I wouldn't have cowered in my room."

He sank the pitchfork vehemently into the sparse pile of hay and tossed some to the bull. "It might have been demons who did this all by magick, sir. The streets are full of demons these days, looking for victims. Let them strike you once and before you know it the plague is carrying you off."

It occurred to John demons would have found Nereus' garden of pagan oracles a very pleasant place, rather than one to destroy.

Apis chewed contentedly. Sylvanus rubbed the sleeve of his rough woolen tunic over the plate he had just recovered.

John thought it more than likely the stealthy night visitors had been seeking something specific. Could it have been Nereus' last written will?

But the oral will had immediately superseded it, he reminded himself.

"I returned to question you about the man called Aristotle of Athens. I understand your master conducted business with him and thought you might know where I could find him."

"Yes, sir, I do," the other replied. "In fact, I visited him only a few days ago regarding a statue of the oracle of Hermes the master had purchased. But then, I've told you about that already, haven't I? There was some difficulty in making delivery arrangements. Now he will never see that amazing statue and neither, sir, will I."

Taking a key from the pouch at his belt, Sylvanus opened the gate of Apis' enclosure. "I noticed you admiring the beast. You can come into his pen. He sounds very fierce, but really he's quite tame."

Accepting the invitation, John patted the bull's flank as Sylvanus knelt to unlock the creature's shackle.

The click of the lock snapping open drew John's gaze down and then he knelt to examine the bull's restraining chain. "Do you see that, Sylvanus?"

"See what, sir?"

John pointed out a bright, shallow notch in one of the chain's tarnished links. "Someone made a valiant effort to cut this."

"The bastards!" Sylvanus sprang to his feet and stroked the placidly chewing bull's muzzle. "Don't worry, Apis. No one's going to steal you, and soon you'll be frisking about in country fields."

Sylvanus inclined his head toward John and added in a whisper, "He'd feed a whole family for who knows how long."

John remarked it was possible. "Before you leave, I wish to look at Nereus' room."

The room, overlooking the street, showed the same vandalism as the rest of the house. The water clock had been overturned again, and the sheets of papyrus scattered on the floor were sodden, already starting to smell of mold. There had been a cross on the wall. Now it lay on the floor. The bed had been turned over. So too had a heavy writing desk, a few bulky chairs, and a pair of oversized tables.

One wall was covered with a bright fresco depicting a frozen sea populated by numerous vessels swarming with fantastical baboon sailors setting course to far-off lands where buildings sporting spires, domes, and towers could be seen set amid woods and rolling meadows. Closer to home strings of camels brought boxes and bales from the docks toward a house depicted in the lower right-hand corner. It was obviously Nereus' house, and three well-dressed figures, presumably those of Nereus, his late wife, and Triton, stood beside it.

John wondered, if Nereus were still alive, whether he would have ordered his servants to move one of the larger pieces of furniture in front of that portion of the fresco now that Triton had fallen from paternal favor.

It was not a large room. John had a difficult time imagining seven witnesses crammed into it, standing alongside the dying man's bedside as servants rushed in and out. Where had the holy fool found space to dance with the archdeacon?

A number of codexes in a wall niche sat undisturbed. John pulled one out. It was part of Nereus' set of Justinian's Institutes.

His legal oracle. He checked the niche quickly. Nereus had not concealed his last written will there.

John wasn't certain why he had wanted to visit the room. Did Nereus' shade linger? While the departed shipper made his way past heavenly tollhouses or up the heavenly ladder, or by whatever route one imagined led to the afterlife, did he still remain connected tenuously to a world he had not quite left, like a newborn clinging to its mother? Perhaps Nereus was even now discussing shipping affairs with Gregory, both detained by the same recalcitrant demon.

The break-in was as mysterious as the other circumstances surrounding Gregory's murder. Had it merely been vandals? Or thieves? Someone seeking Nereus' will or something else? As he went back downstairs a thought occurred to John.

"Sylvanus, a word of warning."

The oracle keeper was leading Apis across the atrium. He paused and the bull stopped immediately, perfectly obedient. "An oracle keeper never ignores words of warning or he'd soon be out of a job, sir. What is it?"

"It's possible that whoever broke in last night intended to harm you, or possibly somebody else they expected to find here."

"All the more reason to be off for the country as fast as I can, then."

***

John accepted Sylvanus' offer of a ride.

He sat uncomfortably beside the oracle keeper as they lurched away from Nereus' now barred and shuttered house, shifting his lean flanks continually in a fruitless effort to be marginally comfortable.

The chickens in the basket squawked indignantly and water sloshed out of the amphorae holding the oracular fish as the donkey struggled up a steep incline to the Mese and then dawdled along the thoroughfare to the Capitolium, where one branch pointed north, the direction the cart would have to journey in order to get to Nereus' estate, and the other south.

Thanking Mithra and Fortuna both that Aristotle's establishment lay to the south, John climbed down from the cart in front of a looming marble structure that might have been a temple to Zeus, except for the huge crosses adorning the facade. The overladen cart crawled away, the tethered Apis ambling placidly along behind.

John set off at a brisk pace.

Soon he had passed down the Mese and through the Forum Bovis with its huge bull's head. Aristotle had set up business on the seaward side of the Mese, not far from Constantine's wall, in an area of small workshops and private warehouses.

John soon spotted a building that displayed a sign bearing the inscription *Oracles, Antiquities, Bricks*.

The edifice in which Aristotle conducted his trade sat at the end of a narrow road next to a patch of scrubby land. Whatever use it might once have had, the open area was now dotted with heaped mounds bearing silent witness to the continued decimation of the city's population.

However, even proximity to the sad place could not account for the overwhelming, acrid odor that permeated the air.

The pungent smell was immediately identifiable, although a quick glance around did not reveal its source.

John knocked at Aristotle's door.

Another door, he thought wearily. Perhaps he should petition Janus, god of thresholds and of beginnings and endings, for aid in his search.

The door swung open to reveal a man hefting a wooden cudgel. He was short and broad shouldered and wore a soiled leather apron over a grubby work tunic. He warily eyed his unexpected visitor.

With the door open, the source of the overpowering smell of urine was apparent.

It emanated from inside the building.

Doing his best to ignore the odor, John stated his interest in talking to the seller of antiquities.

"Aristotle's not here. Haven't seen him since this morning."

"Did he say where he was going?"

"No."

John curbed his irritation. "You are a member of his household and know when he is expected to return?"

"No, I'm not." The short man spoke in an aggrieved tone. "I'm Anthemius. I'm a brickmaker by profession. Aristotle and I merely share these premises. Rentals in the city are outrageous, not to mention since this cursed plague arrived there hasn't much call for bricks. Yet there seems to be plenty of money for antiquities and oracles. Aristotle brings back huge sums every day. I don't know how he does it."

Evidently Anthemius had been waiting for an opportunity to air his grievances. He scarcely paused for breath as he rattled them off.

"All day long I'm attending the door and it's always Aristotle whose services are being sought. Nobody seems to have any use for a brickmaker any more. However, as I told you, Aristotle's not here right now. Would you care to step in to take some refreshment and wait a while? I could show you some of my handiwork. You might well find it of interest. I do excellent work, sir, if I say it myself."

Declining wine, John followed the man inside. The atrium had been turned into a storage space and held piles of stacked bricks. In the inner garden patches of weeds alternated with areas of hard-packed earth.

John noted the source of the smell. A concrete-lined pit almost filled with urine. A tethered donkey grazed contentedly nearby. Several long mounds of earth, some of them overgrown, testified this house too had seen losses.

Anthemius intercepted his glance. "You get used to the smell, sir. Aristotle keeps talking about going into the leather business, but so far he hasn't done much about it except collect one of what you might call the necessaries."

John commented on the pitiful mounds.

Anthemius scratched his head. "Sad, isn't it? Most of them were there when I arrived a few months back. Don't know who they are, since Aristotle never spoke of his family. They're all gone now. The last one was buried right after I arrived. It was a bit of a surprise to me since there was nobody in the house but us, or so I thought. Then, in the early hours one morning, something woke me up and I looked out of my window and what do you think I saw?"

John indicated he could not guess.

"Aristotle was burying the last member of his family. Well, I couldn't see too well because it was so dark, but the departed was either wrapped in white or stark naked, but either way, it was tragic, sir, tragic. I didn't like to observe such a private matter, so I closed the shutters as soon as I realized it wasn't one of those stealthy nocturnal visitors who come to steal whatever they can run off with."

"Doubtless if it was your cudgel would soon have persuaded them otherwise."

Anthemius lifted the cudgel and tapped it lightly in the palm of his free hand. "Indeed it would and in fact it has done so on occasion."

"You've had to fight off intruders recently?"

"Just a few rambunctious children, actually," Anthemius admitted.

"No one has attempted to break into this house?"

"No. I'd know if anyone had tried to get in. I'm here most of the time right now, with so little call for my bricks. And that reminds me, sir, I was going to show you samples of my work."

He led his visitor across the malodorous garden and through a passage that emerged at the back of the house. A rambling, ramshackle shed occupied one corner of a patch of land surrounded by high stone walls.

"That shed's my workshop," Anthemius explained. "My kiln's been cold for some time, since as I said business is extremely scanty. I do have some very nice samples to show and I can easily produce more if needed. I'm very proud to put my mark on my work, I am, and that's the truth, sir."

Anthemius pointed out sights of interest. Bricks were stacked neatly in straw-separated rows. Their sizes ranged from those that could be held in the hand to others that looked as if they would take a couple of strong men to lift. Some were triangular, while others were decorated or molded specimens.

"I tell my patrons if they need only the common sort of inexpensive bricks to hide behind a marble facade, they can go elsewhere. My work is of the highest quality. In fact, I would venture to say that if the pharaohs had been able to use my bricks for their pyramids, those odd constructions would be in perfect condition today."

Anthemius tapped his cudgel gently on a pair of bricks sitting atop the nearest pile. Larger than average, they displayed a bas relief showing a woman between two beings which were obviously goddesses.

"None of my patrons has ever guessed what these are, sir," the brickmaker continued with a sly grin. "They're Egyptian birth bricks. In the old days the ladies squatted on them to give birth. Sounds most uncomfortable, doesn't it? These of course are replicas and I always make that plain when I show them. There's not much call for them these days, of course, except perhaps as conversational pieces. I enjoy making them. They are much more creative than your typical brick, don't you think?"

John agreed. The brick's bas relief was certainly well executed.

"I give the ones damaged in the firing to Aristotle. He likes to give them as gifts to prospective patrons. They always catch their interest, he says."

John wondered whether the seller of antiquities might be less punctilious than the brickmaker in declaring the recent origin of the birth bricks, especially since damaged bricks would look a lot older than they actually were.

"I see we have a visitor, Anthemius! I trust you've been keeping him entertained." A big man with a mournful face and the bearing of an aristocrat strode into the brickyard. His dark robe was decorated with elaborate, multi-colored embroidery. A mantle studded with glass beads completed the guise of a courtier.

"Aristotle, this gentleman wishes to see you."

The seller of antiquities made a low bow. "Welcome, excellency. How may I assist? I can see you are a man of the world and therefore not too likely to be interested in oracles, but I can also offer a very fine collection of ancient statues and artifacts, including a few that would cause a lady to blush!"

John introduced himself, wondering why Aristotle had formed the impression he was a man who would be interested in artifacts that would make ladies blush. "I regret that I cannot take advantage of your generous offer, Aristotle. In fact, I am here to ask you a few questions."

Aristotle colored angrily. "Has somebody been complaining to the authorities again about my donkey keeping them awake? Or the smell? Why shouldn't I keep a donkey, excellency? They have worse in the palace menagerie! It's a fine thing when an honest man cannot even try to make a living without some dainty-nosed insomniac causing trouble!"

"Is it about the donkey, sir?" Anthemius looked chagrined. "You didn't say it was about the donkey."

Before John could reply, Aristotle spoke again. "I intend to eventually go into selling fine leather goods. It will be a much steadier trade, at least when times are better. Meantime, my donkey will soon earn its living by hauling my larger antique pieces to clients. That's a problem that's caused some difficulties lately. I'm waiting to purchase a cart at a reasonable cost, so the beast is currently enjoying a holiday."

John assured Aristotle he had no questions concerning the donkey.

"I'm pleased to hear it, excellency. Do you know, this lack of suitable transport is costing me money right now? You'd think carters would be glad to have something that never breathed to haul about, rather than someone that once lived. Less offensive to the nostrils, for a start. However, with all the work they have right now, they charge such outrageous prices when heavy lifting is involved that it's impossible to afford very much help. Some of my larger statues, now, I'll gladly part with them for half of what they're worth, if you'd provide your own transport." He paused hopefully, then sighed at John's obvious disinterest. "If it's not about the donkey, what did you wish to question me about?"

"It concerns a will you recently witnessed."

"Nereus' will, you mean? He was one of my best patrons. A man of remarkable perspicacity. It was all most upsetting. It would have made an angel weep to see his departing, for little dignity and a lot of chaos saw him out of this world."

Aristotle frowned at the brickmaker, who was shamelessly eavesdropping. "His was only a small bedroom and for some reason he was fond of large pieces of furniture, so there wasn't much space to begin with, even before we were assembled. Servants were coming in and out constantly for one reason or another and his oracular bull was bellowing as if it knew the master of the establishment was about to start climbing the ladder to heaven."

John observed he could understand how distressing the situation must have been.

"Thank you, excellency. It was a terrible shock to find Nereus in such a dreadful state when I arrived that afternoon. Although, strange to say, the oracular head I had been asked to bring for his perusal seemed to grow exceedingly warm the nearer I got to his house."

John questioned Aristotle further.

"No, I never met the wayward son," he replied. "Even if I had, I doubt he would've been interested in my oracles. He was a man who never looked to the future, going by what I've heard about his behavior."

"Of the other witnesses, I understand Archdeacon Palamos is an acquaintance of yours?"

Aristotle looked outraged. "I hope you pay no heed to anything he says about me, excellency. There are some, and I include certain churchmen among their number, who pretend to doubt the authenticity of my wares. However, that is because they're merely trying to strike a better bargain."

A stray breeze carried the scent of donkey urine more strongly into the brickyard.

Mithra! John thought. It was obvious that he was no further forward in unraveling the puzzle. He wondered if Cornelia had arrived, or if Peter was any worse. For all John knew, Peter might have died while John futilely tramped the streets. He realized his hand had strayed underneath the line of his jaw, where the swellings started.

Nothing.

An hour or two from now, he might not be so lucky.

"Even so, I will admit," Aristotle was saying, "I'd agree Palamos had reason to complain about the holy fool dancing with him while Nereus lay dying."

John forced his thoughts back to the matter at hand. "I understand this holy fool was there only because he happened to pass by when time was of the essence, and also that the driver of the cart he was riding in was another witness. Do you—"

"Byzos," Aristotle answered immediately. "He agreed to carry out some work for me at a reasonable rate. He's not one of your city dwellers, always willing to take more money the less work they do. He's from somewhere out in the country where they deal with you in a fair fashion, or so he keeps telling me. I paid him for a ride back here after leaving Nereus' house. I didn't want to have to drag that oracular head the length of the Mese again."

John nodded tiredly. At least he had discovered the identity of another witness. "Can you tell me where I might find this Byzos?"

"Indeed I can. He's lodging with Scipio the bookseller. His emporium is not far from the—"

John stopped Aristotle in mid-sentence. "I know the place."

Chapter Twenty-Two

As much as John wished to question the cart driver who had witnessed Nereus' oral will, he needed to speak to Prudentius more urgently.

The recent incident at Nereus' house was worrisome. If someone had been looking for the last written will, then Nereus' lawyer would be the obvious next victim, and he was a man who had not struck John as particularly Argus-eyed.

Prudentius immediately dismissed John's fears as he settled into a chair behind the lacquered table in his office. "Strangely enough, though, there was a curious commotion early this morning." He gestured to the waiting servant girl. "Xanthe, my dear, wine for our visitor, if you'd be so kind, and bring along a small snack as well."

A breeze from the garden blew several sheets of parchment off the table. Prudentius shifted the ivory box at the table's side to the top of the pile, weighing it down. The freed sheets drifted around the room.

"The wind has shifted, I see. Perhaps we will have rain." Prudentius glanced outside. "That might serve to temper the terrible smell somewhat. I find it troublesome."

"This commotion you mentioned. What was it about?"

"The commotion? Oh yes. It awakened the entire household. You've probably noticed my guests are quieter than usual? Most of them are still asleep. The sun wasn't even up when Ezra began running around the roof exhorting all and sundry to repent. One thing I'll say about our current affliction is it's certainly turned men's attention toward heaven."

Looking across the garden to the roof that sloped down opposite, John could make out what appeared to be a bag of rags near its ridge. Evidently Ezra the stylite was also resting.

Xanthe reappeared with the wine and a platter bearing a tiny chunk of cheese.

Prudentius frowned and ran a hand over his severely cropped hair. "Is that all there is?"

"I warned you it was almost gone," Xanthe said.

"You're right, my dear. You said so, just last night." Prudentius shook his head as the servant departed to wait just outside the room, in case, as Prudentius put it, the household's esteemed guest needed anything.

The lawyer eyed the platter disconsolately and his long face grew melancholy. "My apologies, Lord Chamberlain. Since I am unable to reenact the miracle of the loaves and fishes, I fear that this is all I can offer you."

John declined and the lawyer popped the scrap into his mouth and then continued. "When shall I taste the like again? I went around to the merchant who sells it just the other day. His shop was closed and none of the neighbors appeared to know where its owner had gone. I wonder if it will ever reopen?"

John took a hearty gulp of wine, temporarily cleansing his throat of the acrid taste of the smoke of funeral pyres. "Does Ezra often have these shouting fits?"

"Yes, but not usually at such an hour."

"Perhaps something disturbed him? Did you notice anything amiss? Anything that might indicate someone had tried to get into the house?"

"No, I haven't. Why do you suppose anyone would want to do that?"

John explained that it appeared an unknown person might want Nereus' last written will.

"What good would it do them, Lord Chamberlain?"

"I thought you might provide the answer."

Prudentius nodded thoughtfully. "People often steal wills in order to destroy them. However, Nereus' oral will immediately destroyed his written one. Anyone who stole his last written will would possess nothing more than a piece of useless parchment."

"On the other hand, whoever intended to forge a will would need a sample of Nereus' signature."

"Forgery? Well, that has certainly been attempted on more than one occasion."

"Then again, supposing the intent was not to make an entirely new will but rather to alter the existing one?"

Prudentius pondered the matter briefly. "Alteration of such a document would be difficult, although not impossible. However, I should point out that this hypothetical person is obviously not well versed in the law, because if they were they'd realize neither plan would serve their purpose. They can produce any will they like, but it would still be a fruitless endeavor because, as I just said, Nereus' oral will supercedes everything. Which is not to say I wouldn't put that sort of knavery past Triton, except that he is dead."

The lawyer offered John a frosty smile. "You really should have told me about that, Lord Chamberlain. After all, a lawyer is not instantly privy to everything that happens in the family of someone who consults him."

"Have you met the son?"

"Xanthe! Another jug of wine, please! The better sort, if there's any left." Prudentius turned his attention back to John. "Although I've heard much about Triton, I met him only once. He came here not long ago and demanded I immediately return something of his I had allegedly stolen. He went so far as to make threats against my life, I may add. I instructed the house steward to remove him from the premises and, further, that he was never to be admitted again."

"Something he owned? What was that?"

"Perhaps he thought I might have his father's will in my custody? He was intoxicated, a regular occurrence with him, I've been told. A violent man too, by all accounts."

Xanthe returned with more wine. Prudentius reached toward the jug, then seemed to think better of it, and set his cup beside the mountain of documents on his table.

"I'm afraid I can't tell you anything more about the man, Lord Chamberlain. He wasn't my client and I wouldn't have worked for him even if he had asked me to."

John gazed outside. The ragged stylite lying on the roof remained motionless. "I believe you were brought up by the church, Prudentius?"

"Indeed I was. My parents died when I was only a few months old. I don't even know what caused their deaths. I am told I was found lying in the Augustaion. In any event, the church has been my mother and father. I do my best to pass along the charity I received, for kindness can only be repaid that way."

"Let me add a kindness or two of my own in return for the time I have taken from your work." John stood and placed several coins on the table. "I will arrange for regular deliveries of food from the palace until the city has returned to normal. We must all do what we can. Meanwhile, however, if my theory is correct, I would strongly advise you to post guards here. Your charitably open door makes it very easy for someone to gain access to your office."

"Thank you for your generosity, Lord Chamberlain. I shall certainly consider your advice carefully. In the end, however, our lives are in heaven's hands."

Chapter Twenty-Three

"Father's out, I'm afraid."

Anatolius peered through the narrow gap between the barely opened door and its frame. A brown, well-muscled arm led back to a slim figure clad in a plain white tunic. The silver chain holding Europa's hair back glinted in the dim atrium.

"How is Peter?"

"Hypatia says he's fading fast. She spends half her time lecturing him through his locked door and the other half at the hospice fussing over her poor young man. She's upstairs trying to persuade Peter to come out of his room right now."

"I'll wager Peter pulls through. He's tough as an old boot."

Europa stepped outside. "It feels strange to be in this city again." She glanced around the deserted square. "I remember last time you bought a lot of birds from an old woman and set them all free. I admired you for that."

Anatolius smiled at the compliment.

Europa closed the door firmly behind her. "I need a breath of air. Want to go for a stroll?"

She didn't look any different than she had seven years before, Anatolius thought. It was almost enough to put Lucretia out of his mind for a brief time. He needed to put her out of his mind.

"As it happens I have to collect a few documents from my office, but if you don't object to a detour I'd be happy to show you some of the palace grounds afterward."

They crossed the square and traversed a colonnaded walkway, passing by several excubitors who greeted Anatolius by name. The administrative building where Anatolius worked was half-deserted, a maze of featureless corridors which might have led to the Minotaur rather than a cramped office, filled with incongruously ornate furniture.

"I've been doing some copying at home." Anatolius rummaged through documents on a writing desk which might have been a reliquary, inlaid with ivory and trimmed with gems and gold. He noticed Europa's stare. "Elaborate, isn't it? Justinian decided his personal secretary should labor at a desk that honored the transcribing of imperial edicts."

"I find it hard to believe you're just a scribbler, Anatolius."

"Actually, Justinian tells me more or less what he wants to say and then I put his thoughts into the form he would have chosen, if he had time for such trivial chores. Mind you, he wouldn't appreciate your telling him I said that."

"I'm not likely to meet him, am I?"

Anatolius pulled a few sheets of parchment from the pile. "You might be interested in this proclamation. There's shortly to be another statue of Emperor Justin erected. It's almost completed and eventually will stand near the booksellers' quarter. No one knows of the decision yet, except Justinian and his personal secretary, one Anatolius—" he bowed— "and now yourself."

"The sculptor must know."

"Well...."

"And someone in the imperial treasury, or whichever office paid the sculptor. And what about the sculptor's wife? Not to mention whoever sold the sculptor the marble, and—"

"You have the same manner of thinking as your father, Europa, and I mean that as a compliment! Ah, here are those documents I wanted."

He led her out of the rambling office complex, through more colonnades, some so overhung with vines they might have been tunnels of vegetation, and down a steep stone staircase that ended at one of the lower terraces.

From a miniature flower-filled meadow at the base of the staircase, the palace was invisible, hidden behind a line of pines rooted in the next higher terrace and seeming to float in midair. The Marmara sparkled before them.

"I'd almost expect to hear Pan's pipes in such a pastoral setting," Anatolius observed. "But it will change soon enough. Justinian has ordered this particular garden replanted with purple-blossomed trees and flowers. Imperial purple." He paused and then added with a scowl, "Personally, I'd have said that plantings of aconite and hemlock and such would be far more appropriate in a garden designed especially for Theodora."

"Poisonous plants?"

"Exactly. Not to mention the added attraction of the shining waters of a nice, deep pool. More than one person has been drowned in the imperial baths, and not by accident either."

Europa looked shocked. "You said that the empress knows just about everything going on in the palace. Do you think she knows Thomas and I are at my father's house?"

"I would be astonished if she didn't."

They gazed silently out over the water for a while and then Anatolius showed Europa a cleverly hidden, twisting path through a thick wall of shrubbery. It led to a clearing holding several rustic benches and a circular, shallow pond graced by a statue standing on a pedestal rising from its center.

"This would be an excellent place to contemplate the inevitable passage of time," Europa guessed.

"Exactly! The edge of the pool is marked with the hours and the shadow of the reed the marble nymph in the middle is holding serves as a pointer. An interesting conceit, isn't it?"

"What a strange place this city is!"

"Strange? To a woman who makes a living leaping from the backs of bulls?"

"We no longer own a bull, alas," Europa replied. "Even if we did, I doubt we'd find much of an audience right now."

"The situation will be back to normal eventually."

Anatolius walked over to the pool and hunkered down. He traced a finger over a name scratched into the low stone wall containing the water.

"'Tarquin,'" he read. "I see Severus, Hektor, and Alexis have also recorded their visits. It seems to have become customary for court pages to scratch their names here."

"Those boys serve as ornaments to the court, don't they? What happens to them when they grow up? Do they then perform administrative duties?"

Anatolius thoughtfully ran his fingertips over the faint scratches. "No, they don't. Their role is being pretty young boys. Occasionally one finds a patron who'll take him into his home, but most of the others, well, they take what remains of their talents out to the streets, I suppose. Like spring flowers, one day they're here, the next they're gone."

He stood. "Which reminds me. Isn't it time your mother arrived?"

"She'll be here by the end of the week at the latest," Europa replied confidently as they began to thread their way back along the path through the shrubbery.

Chapter Twenty-Four

The deserted street drowsing under a light breeze only added to John's sense of unease. It had the aspect of a brightly lit stage, awaiting the arrival of a company of actors to begin playing out dramas of life and death to an unseen audience. Perhaps a Greek tragedy, or a Roman comedy purchased from Scipio's stock.

The door and windows of the bookseller's emporium stood wide open, as if to entice passersby to enter by foot or for that matter by wing. Here, the blank eyes of the windows seemed to announce, is a place where you can journey far away without leaving your own home, go to lands beyond the seas, hear again the great philosophers and poets declaiming honeyed words and calls to war, learn from mistakes of the past.

Mistakes of the past, John thought. Yes, we could all cite our own examples, and as for lands beyond the seas…but no, he must keep his attention focused on his investigation.

He stepped briskly into Scipio's shop and was surprised to find it filled not only with books but also with flowers. The floral perfume was overpowering.

The short, shaven-headed proprietor bustled forward. A welcoming smile crinkled his face. His quick glance at John's garments was followed by a self-congratulatory greeting introducing himself as Scipio, proprietor of this excellent and well patronized establishment.

"Would you care to peruse some of my latest imported works, excellency? Or perhaps you had something specific in mind? Or could it be…" the man lowered his voice, sounding almost furtive, "…you are interested in, er, lodgings?"

It was the same question Triton's blind landlady had asked him a short while ago. John wondered when he had begun to look like a man in need of a roof over his head. Unless Scipio was hinting that his rooms contained what might be called lodgers in the same sense as those ladies housed at Isis' establishment, and for the same purpose?

"Thank you, no," John replied. "Although in fact I am here about a man I've been told is lodging with you. His name is Byzos."

Scipio looked surprised. "You have heard about Byzos already?" He hurried to a table and picked up a thin codex. "I have only this single copy of his work thus far and, under the circumstances, it is sure to become a collector's item. However, I can give you a good price."

"I believe you're speaking about a different Byzos. The man I'm seeking is a cart driver."

"That's right. First a farmer, then a cart driver, then a writer."

"Indeed?"

"It was as I said," Scipio confirmed. "When we talked it struck me he seemed to have a very poetic nature for a farmer, so I wrote down whatever he said. Literature is mostly aristocrats writing for other aristocrats, when you come down to it, but this is something different. *The Rustic Versifier* is my title."

He opened the codex and scanned its contents. "How about this small sample, excellency? 'Country dirt, city dirt. Heaven and hell.' Profound in its rural way, isn't it? But perhaps that was too glib. Here is another, only too appropriate to the current situation. 'The carter calls. Ravens fly up, living ashes from a burning pyre.'"

"Byzos made these observations in conversation with you?"

"More or less. Definitely a born poet." Scipio riffled through the codex. "Here's another. 'Poor fair one. Died with the honeysuckle and only sixteen.' Be a good epitaph, wouldn't it, if epitaphs can be said to be good, that is."

"I'm certain the collection will be of great literary interest at court, Scipio, but my business with Byzos is much more mundane. Could you take me to his room?"

"Very well. This way, if you please."

Scipio tucked the codex under his arm and led John up a flight of stairs, along a corridor, and then up another stairway to the top story. The higher they climbed, the more nervous the man appeared to become. As so often happened in John's experience, this led to a torrent of commentary, much of it apparently intended to distance the speaker from any wrongdoing his guest might have committed.

"Byzos hasn't been staying with me for long, excellency. Ordinarily he could not have afforded my rental, but he came to the city to make his fortune by transporting the dead, and of course in that line of work there is much to be done and a great deal of money to be made...."

They paused on a draughty landing. Scipio looked at John, as if to gauge his reaction to the insights he was providing. "He was a farmer with a large family and too many mouths to feed, trying to grow enough to eat on land blessed with an abundance of rocks and poor soil. There's more silver to be found in a cartload of corpses than a cartload of cucumbers, he told me more than once." He tapped the codex. "That's in here too."

"Indeed," John observed, glancing along the hallway and wondering which of the open doors—Mithra, more doors!—led to the absent cart driver's room.

Scipio did not seem in any hurry to unburden himself of that particular piece of information. "Now you'd think he'd have been afraid to ply such a trade, excellency, would you not? Certainly I would have been, but no, not he. There was a very good reason, for he confided to me when he first took a room that he considered himself protected by a holy relic. Many are buying them, I hear, and in fact I have been considering adding them to my stock to generate a little more income."

John observed that the plague had ruined many businesses, except perhaps for those who sold wine.

Scipio added emphatically, "Oh yes. excellency. However, I've contrived to weather the storm by a most clever notion! It was inspired by a chat I had with Byzos one evening. His room is just down here, by the way."

He led John toward the far end of the hallway. "You see," he continued, "he realized that serving the dead and the bereaved are the most lucrative businesses in the city these days. Then it struck me like a bolt from heaven! Nobody wants to see their dear ones hauled away to leaking ships and sent with hundreds of others out into the harbor to be burnt, or thrown into the sea, or some awful pit. I realized I could offer a service that was sorely needed. In short, the departed stay here as guests until arrangements for proper rites can be made."

Scipio halted and gestured toward an open doorway.

The floor of the room was covered with small stacks of books interspersed with neat rows of the dead.

It was now obvious why Scipio had filled his emporium with flowers and left all the windows open.

"I've always had the occasional lodger to help make ends meet. All these rooms I have, I didn't need them all for storage. Books don't take up that much space, do they? Mind you, I would not have the gossips say I don't practice charity," Scipio prattled on. "I charge vastly reduced prices for the use of my facilities, particularly shared accommodations such as you see here. Still, I do not lose by it since I am able to house many of the departed in each room. Each has his own floor space. I do not stack my guests, excellency. I am very severe about that. After all, even if you were dead, you wouldn't want a stranger lying on you, would you?"

Glancing over the recumbent figures, John wondered that Scipio could be so matter of fact about his latest venture, since no matter how many silent guests he accepted, it could scarcely be possible to become inured to the tragedies they represented. Something deep in one's being wanted to turn away in sorrow.

"I should mention that I only accept the departed of refinement," Scipio was saying. "This guarantees their families don't have to worry about them lodging in the same room as a common beggar. Oh no, instead they sleep with Homer and Plato. Why, even as their earthly remains linger here among the words of those wonderful writers, they are probably conversing with those very men in…well…in whatever after-life they share. It would make for a good way to introduce oneself, wouldn't it? 'Aren't you the renowned orator Demosthenes? My name's Byzos. You don't know me, but right now my lifeless head is pillowed upon a collection of your speeches….'"

"Are you telling me Byzos is dead?"

Scipio scowled. "Certainly. Why do you think this work of his is a collector's item? He's the one in the far corner. He died last night."

Chapter Twenty-Five

"The plague shall not have me! Let it but place its black talons upon my shoulder and I shall cast myself into the waves to join my beloved!"

Anatolius glared at the expostulating Crinagoras, uncertain whether his companion was making an observation or rehearsing his performance for Theodora's banquet. From the fact he spoke in Latin rather than Greek, he guessed it was a rehearsal, not that Crinagoras did not have a tendency to lapse into Latin at the drop of a poetic impulse.

"If you don't let me enjoy the country air in peace, I'll give you cause to cast yourself into the waves!"

The country air smelled of manure from the stables where they'd just left their horses, but it was still a relief compared to the stench of death and burning in the city.

"Now you've fallen silent for a space, isn't that a blackbird? You don't usually hear them in the middle of the city."

"The blackbird sings also for the dead." Crinagoras released a sigh like a dying breath. "Try to remember that, will you? I've left my tablet at home."

Crinagoras' tireless tongue had made the relatively short ride out to Blachernae feel very long indeed. Though it lay on the outskirts of Constantinople, the place gave the impression of being deep in the countryside.

Anatolius remarked that since imperial banquets were normally held in perfumed and gilded surroundings, the location was a novel one.

"I would far rather attend such an event in comfort at the palace," Crinagoras replied, "but we must endure whatever the empress orders. No doubt my recitation will serve to distract her guests from their vexatious surroundings. It's a pity you were not asked to recite, Anatolius."

The other shrugged.

Crinagoras turned the conversation to other matters. "We can certainly expect superb fare. I predict at the very least pigeons' wings fricasseed in wine, honey-sauced lamb, several rich sauces, and exquisite sweetmeats. I do hope there will be poppy seed pastries, they're one of my favorites. And the wines, Anatolius, the wines! Why, by all I hear we'll soon think Bacchus himself is in charge of the imperial cellars!"

Crinagoras talked on about the expected gustatory delights as they followed a pebbled path through a wood composed largely of oaks. Scraps of purple silk fluttered from branches, marking the route to the repast.

While Anatolius was familiar with imperial whims, which could hand an orator gold coins or his own head with equal impartiality, he still considered the idea of an outdoor banquet unusual. There had, of course, been the unforgettable occasion when Justinian held a reception on several ships tied together on the largest lake in the palace grounds. A grin flickered across his face as he recalled how the glittering event had been cut short by a strong wind which had suddenly sprung up and precipitated Theodora's indisposition. It was just as well, he thought, that on that occasion John had not been present. Given the latter's loathing of deep water, he might have found himself more ailing than the empress.

Reminded of his friend, he wondered if John had made any progress in his search. His speculations were interrupted by Crinagoras.

"Bear!" the poet cried.

"For a main course? At a court banquet? Surely not. Then again, with an appropriate sauce--"

"No. No! There's a bear!" Crinagoras staggered backward, practically into Anatolius' arms.

Anatolius heard the rustle of undergrowth and the crack of breaking branches. A dark shape loped through the cedars. An enormous black bear. It came to a halt, blocking their path.

Crinagoras spun around, prepared to run. Anatolius grabbed his shoulder. "Be still."

The beast unleashed a rumbling growl.

Crinagoras made a tiny, keening noise, like a dying rabbit.

There were shouts from the surrounding woods. Crashing, the clash of metal on metal. The bear's head swung toward the racket, its flanks heaved, and it lumbered off with deceptive speed, vanishing into the trees on the other side of the path.

Almost immediately an excubitor appeared from the direction in which the bear had come. He was banging two metal pots together. Other guards appeared, all similarly armed with cooking utensils. They plunged after the bear, yelling and clanking.

Trailing the pack came Felix. The bearded captain's booming obscenities could not conceal the truth that his weapons were a copper night soil pot and a soup ladle.

"I suppose bears flee bad language," observed Anatolius.

Felix launched into an even viler oath, then stopped. "Mithra! My quiver seems to be empty! Not to mention I'm getting hoarse. But you seem to have grasped the situation, Anatolius. We have been ordered to chase Theodora's pet away, without ruffling its fur. It doesn't like loud noises. I hope."

"Is this the bear from the menagerie? I thought you were supposed to let it loose in the countryside?"

"According to Theodora this Imperial estate is the countryside."

"Well," muttered Crinagoras, "there are plenty of trees for the bear to lurk behind if it wants to ambush anyone."

"Bears don't usually bother with people, not even plump poets," Felix informed him. "It's the smell of food for the banquet that's attracted it."

"But having a bear roaming the grounds. Isn't that dangerous?" Anatolius wondered.

"The emperor and empress never go out for a stroll without an armed guard," Felix reminded him.

"But what about guests, or anyone who might wander in by mistake?"

Felix glared into the trees. The sound of the chase had nearly faded away. "Yes, as for such folks, that's Theodora's idea of humor. 'How was your walk? Oh? I thought I'd mentioned my bear!'" The excubitor gave his night soil pot a couple of half-hearted bangs with the ladle and trudged away after his men.

"Oh my," groaned Crinagoras. "All that glorious food awaiting us and now I have the most dreadful stomachache."

They continued more slowly, finally emerging from the wood into a meadow that sloped down from the back of the imperial residence. An enormous purple canopy had been erected in the center of the open space. Diners were already seated at a long table under its shade.

Anatolius could tell that this was what passed, at court, for an intimate gathering. There was a subtle difference in the indecipherable buzz of conversation. The guests were all members of Justinian and Theodora's inner circle, Latin speakers, like the emperor and empress, and unlike most of the population. The emperor, he understood, would not be in attendance, which made the gathering one of Theodora's affairs.

An attendant met the newcomers and showed them to their seats.

"What is this?" Crinagoras stared down at his three-legged stool. "Are we expected to milk goats? Where are the couches? I'm not so certain I care much for the country, Anatolius." He lowered himself gingerly.

"On the other hand, you should be extremely honored to be sitting so near the head of the table." Anatolius pointed out a gilded and plushly cushioned chair set a few arm-lengths away.

As he did, an imperial carriage rattled around the side of the residence and pulled up next to the canopy. As everyone stood, Theodora emerged from her conveyance.

In keeping with the bucolic surroundings, she wore a short brown tunic, one that might well have belonged to a farmer's wife provided the farmer had happened to plow up the chest full of jewels that adorned the rough cloth, and bartered his crops for the golden bees ornamenting her hair.

The obligatory announcements and encomia accompanied her ascent to the makeshift throne. Anatolius paid little attention, having written them.

Servants bearing silver salvers appeared and began a circuit of the table.

Horrified gasps erupted among the guests.

At first Anatolius did not understand, then, as one of the servants drew nearer, he realized with a trickle of shock that those now serving the first course had almost reached their last.

The servants were covered in black boils and their tight-fitting tunics did little to disguise the huge swellings in their armpits.

Theodora emitted a caw of laughter. "My friends, fear not! Is not your righteousness an armor? Eat and be thankful! The entertainments will begin shortly!"

Shrinking away from the slaves circling them, her high-born guests, as frightened by the empress as by the plague, tried to subdue their cries of dismay.

Anatolius looked at the chunk of bread that had been set before him on an earthenware plate and then at the small jug of water beside it. Crinagoras, as pale as a lily, poured water into his cup with a shaking hand.

Theodora, with a scimitar of a smile, nodded to an attendant, who strode swiftly away.

A few heartbeats later, a cart rolled into view and even the presence of the empress could not mute the chorus of full-throated cries that rose into the azure sky.

The cart was piled with half-naked dead and driven by a wizened, sinewy man dressed only in a dusty loincloth.

"It's that holy fool I saw at Nereus' house!" Crinagoras looked prepared to run away as the macabre conveyance rumbled to a halt at the head of the table. "He looks ready to join his passengers at any instant!"

As if to prove Crinagoras wrong, the driver gave a terrible grimace, leapt from his perch, and scrambled onto the table. He danced along it wildly, kicking off plates and overturning cups with filthy, bare feet.

"Eat the bread of affliction and drink the tears of sorrow," he shouted, making an obscene gesture at Crinagoras as he went by. "They're more than you deserve! Eat well and hearty, my friends, for tonight you may be traveling in a cart like mine! For all your finery and fancy airs now, your only attendants then will be the flies, and who will sacrifice on your behalf to Zeus Apomyios?"

Theodora laughed loudly. One or two of her guests tried valiantly to follow suit, but their forced merriment was put to rest when one of the dead suddenly sprang from the cart.

Anatolius nudged Crinagoras in the ribs. "See, they're all alive. It's just one of Theodora's nasty ideas of entertainment."

"Alive?" Crinagoras appeared about to swoon with relief.

It was true. The dead had already risen and were now reenacting the arrival of the plague in the city and its deadly progress through the streets. The plague itself, Anatolius noted, was played by the driver, who, with coarse comments and foul language, strutted about slapping his fellow performers' faces and exhorting his listeners, including the empress, to repent their sins while they still had time. Those struck by the fool staggered, wailed, and fell down in convulsions.

"My friends, eat, drink, as the holy fool bids you," Theodora urged, sinking her teeth daintily into a miniature loaf which, Anatolius noticed, was gilded.

Crinagoras choked down a crumb or two and then asked Anatolius in an undertone if he thought any of the servants really were suffering from the plague.

"Of course not. I told you, it's just something she considers amusing."

The performers, having mimed agonizing deaths, were loaded on the cart by a pair of guards. The holy fool climbed back on the table, waved skeletal arms, and urged the assembled company to sing a blasphemous ditty with him.

"Interesting that Theodora knows all the words, isn't it?" Anatolius noted. "The fool reminds me of someone, but I just can't call him to mind."

Trailing curses, the holy fool finally remounted his cart and drove off as a few of his passengers waved feeble farewells.

Theodora smiled benignly at her guests. "I trust you have taken his exhortations to heart. Now, I have invited a few luminaries to inspire us further during this dark time. Lucilius…." She nodded toward a stout, red-faced fellow seated directly across the table from Anatolius.

The man rose to his feet, revealing that he wore a ludicrously oversized toga. He bowed. "Lucilius is most humbled to be permitted to enter into the presence of our most glorious empress. Were the emperor here I would implore him to commission your fair likeness in gold and silver, marble and mosaic, ivory and paint, for every corner of our city so each of us could always bask in your light. However, I most certainly would not engage the portrait painter Dordanus, who has never yet produced a good likeness, and that includes his own children."

Several of the guests tittered. Crinagoras pursed his lips with displeasure.

"Let us hope that none here need resort to the ministrations of physicians," Lucilius continued. "Why, just last week a physician killed his patient while operating. It was a mercy, he told the widow, because otherwise your husband would have been lamed for life."

Theodora guffawed.

"Did you hear," Lucilius went on, "that the very same physician called on a statue of Jupiter yesterday? And even though it was marble and Jupiter, its funeral's tomorrow."

"I've heard that jest before," muttered Crinagoras, his voice barely audible for the laughter all around.

Lucilius waved his wide sleeves, giving the impression of a fat seagull unable to get off the ground. "Which is it better to trust, a physician or a soothsayer? A traveler went to a soothsayer to ask whether it was safe to sail to Bretania. The soothsayer consulted his oracle and said, 'If you have a new ship, and an expert captain, and set sail in the summer rather than the winter, and the winds are favorable, you will have a safe voyage, unless of course you're captured by pirates.'"

"Nicarchus," Crinagoras said in outraged tones. "Those are all epigrams written by Nicarchus. The villain's stolen them and is passing them off as his own!"

"I shall give you some advice myself, my friends," Lucilius was saying. "Steer clear of toads, vipers, and Isaurians. Also at all costs avoid those afflicted with the pestilence, mad dogs, and Isaurians. Keep far from scorpions and burning tenements, and did I mention Isaurians?"

Crinagoras fretted as the literary thief rambled on. "Why did the empress invite me here, if this sort of nonsense is what her guests are likely to enjoy?"

"They enjoy whatever Theodora says they will enjoy, Crinagoras. No doubt your poems will serve as a welcome contrast."

"Yes, there's that."

Lucilius sat as a last gust of hilarity swept the table. Theodora turned her gaze toward Crinagoras.

He climbed shakily to his feet and muttered the brief words of praise for the empress with which Anatolius had coached him on the ride there.

The empress offered only a glimmer of a smile. "Proceed, dear Crinagoras."

He looked around the table, licked his lips nervously, and began his recitation. "Alas, woe, poor, bereft Crinagoras."

Before he had reached the end of his fourth verse a few guests shielded their mouths to muffle snickers.

Crinagoras stopped.

The purple canopy made snapping sounds in a freshening breeze. A bird called from the underbrush fringing the open space.

Crinagoras cleared his throat and began again, his voice shaking. "Alas, woe, poor, bereft Crinagoras, he who lingers behind fair Eudoxia, she of the—"

More stifled laughter distracted him.

He glanced down at Anatolius, his expression that of a rabbit in a snare, and then soldiered valiantly on.

"—fair Eudoxia, she of the moon-white bosom—"

A strident laugh drowned out the poet's faltering voice.

It was Theodora. Having thus been granted permission, the guests joined in.

Crinagoras sat down.

"No, no. You must continue, Crinagoras," Theodora ordered. "Your poetry is well known at court and we wish to savor it from the lips of its creator."

Crinagoras swayed to his feet.

Fortuna proved more merciful than Theodora. Before he could continue, two guards appeared, dragging the holy fool between them.

Theodora turned to face the arrivals, demanding to know what had happened.

The guards were husky young men, with broad shoulders and wide, bland faces. The fool hung between them, limp as an empty old wine skin, his long hair flopping down and obscuring his features.

One of the guards displayed something that flashed in the sunlight.

"A knife? He intended to assassinate someone?"

"He was trying to steal it from the kitchen, highness," the guard replied. "We caught him with a sack full of imperial silver."

Theodora addressed their captive. "You truly are a fool. I favor you with an invitation to inspire my guests and you attempt to steal imperial silver. Do you realize the punishment you face?"

The fool twisted convulsively, slithering from his startled guard's grasp. Quick as a striking snake, he snatched a gold bee from Theodora's hair.

The two guards stood dumbfounded.

Theodora rose slowly from her chair. Though shorter than the guards, she seemed to tower over them. "What if this man had been an assassin?"

Her tone was low, but many of those present blanched at the venom it carried.

At her gesture, other armed men who had been stationed around the perimeter of the dining area rushed to take charge of the errant guards.

"Pray that you contract the plague immediately," Theodora told the two unfortunates. "Your demise then would be considerably more pleasant than what I am contemplating as a reward for your failure to carry out your duties."

"Please return the knife to the empress," put in the fool. "With this fine ornament, and the other items I've chosen, I would otherwise be over-compensated for the entertainment I provided."

Theodora smiled. "You have a mime's wit, fool. Are your wits nimble enough to explain why you should not join these two in the dungeons? You have, after all, admitted to stealing imperial property."

"Could there be a more heinous crime than stealing from the emperor and empress, our most generous benefactors? Yet how many present would learn that lesson if no one dared to show them by example?"

Anatolius realized from Theodora's laughter that the fool's body would remain intact for another day.

Then again it might all have been planned. "Let's hope this is part of the entertainment too, for the sake of those guards," Anatolius whispered. "What do you think, Crinagoras?"

There was no reply.

Glancing sideways, Anatolius was horrified to see his friend had vanished.

If he had chosen to flee the banquet without Theodora's permission, it would be the worse for him.

Then he noticed the pale hand by the stool next to him and the remainder of the poet sprawled in the grass under the table.

Crinagoras had managed to make his escape by losing consciousness.

***

Gaius straightened up and turned away from the motionless body sprawled on the hospice cot. He shook his head at Anatolius, waiting nearby. "Nothing more than a bad bump on the back of his skull. Nothing to worry about."

The supine figure stirred and whimpered. "Is it safe to move now?"

"You'll feel some swelling there, Crinagoras," Gaius told him. "That's to be expected. However, if the swelling happens to spread to your armpits or groin, do let me know."

Crinagoras sat up, prodded the back of his head, and let out a yelp of pain. His face darkened. "It was awful, Gaius. Everyone was laughing at me."

Anatolius could sense anguish in his friend's tone. "It was Theodora's idea of a jest," he said kindly. "Whenever the empress laughs, her guests have to pretend to laugh as well."

"They sounded very convincing to me."

"You must have noticed that the empress certainly appeared to be enjoying your recitation," Anatolius said. "I'm sorry I had to rush you away from the banquet, but you seemed exceedingly groggy and she kindly allowed us to leave before the entertainments concluded."

"I don't get very many patients arriving in imperial carriages," Gaius observed with a grin.

"You see? The empress lent you her own carriage. Few at court can say that!"

"No doubt Theodora wanted to ensure you'd remain with us and so would be available to entertain her further in the future," Gaius observed.

Crinagoras struggled to his feet. "Perhaps," he grudgingly conceded. He looked down and scuffed his boot on the floor. "I do wish she'd had the bear dung cleaned out first."

"Was anyone else reciting?" Gaius asked.

"Lucilius," Anatolius said. "One of the court poets."

"Not to mention a literary thief," Crinagoras put in hotly. "Although I will admit jests about physicians have always been favorites of mine."

"Do you know why a poet is deadlier than a viper?" Gaius replied.

"Oh, I haven't heard that one! Why is that so?"

"In order to kill, a viper needs to open its mouth and sink its fangs into the victim, whereas a poet needs only to open his mouth."

Anatolius laughed and took Crinagoras by the elbow.

"Nothing like a bit of humor to ease the pain of your patients, is there, Gaius? We'd better be on our way." He stopped in the doorway. "Since we're here, however, I understand Hypatia has been helping you?"

"She just went to the other wing to look in on her favorite patient. If you wanted to stop by and give her some encouragement, Anatolius, it would be a kind gesture. She is a good worker, even if she does need to be reminded now and then that there are sufferers other than the one she's devoted to." He raised a warning hand. "Oh, one thing more, Crinagoras. You must not do anything strenuous for a few days. That means no exertion or heavy work and whatever you do, no writing for the time being either. There's no telling what damage fanning those blazing fires of divine inspiration might cause you right now."

Suppressing a smile, Anatolius thanked Gaius for his advice and hurried Crinagoras through the crowded hospice to the wing where Hypatia was working.

Directed further by a passing assistant, they soon found the hallway indicated and walked down it, glancing into each room.

"That's Hypatia's voice!" Anatolius suddenly declared. "I wonder if this is the room where this favorite patient of hers is—"

He stepped quickly back from the doorway.

"Mithra!" he cursed and hastily ushered Crinagoras outside.

***

"I'm not surprised John isn't here, but the news I have is important. I'll wait." Anatolius was crossing the atrium on his way to the garden before Thomas could reply.

"There's no one here but Peter and myself," Thomas informed him as he followed.

Dusk had settled over the city. Light from torches set in the garden's peristyle glinted on foliage, leaving the deepening shadows beneath trees and bushes untouched.

Anatolius dropped on to the bench beside the pool, "I saw Hypatia at the hospice a little while ago. I would have thought she'd be back home by now."

"She will be here soon. Gaius lends her an escort home, if I can't meet her myself," Thomas replied. "However, just to change the subject, what do you make of that strange object?"

He pointed to the olive tree. A brass plate to which three or four short leather strips were attached hung from a branch. Taking the odd contraption down, he handed it to Anatolius. "I bought it from one of those vendors of trifles you see here and there."

Anatolius glanced at the object and handed it back. "Not many sell portable oracles, I would think."

Thomas looked disappointed as he hung the plate back on the branch. "You know it's a reproduction of the oracle at Dodona?"

"I'd read its description, yes, but this is the first example I've actually handled. Why did you buy it?"

Thomas grinned in an embarrassed fashion. "It's a lot of nonsense, of course, but I thought it would amuse Europa."

"It's often difficult to purchase suitable gifts for ladies." Anatolius sounded wistful. "Mind you, most of the ones to whom

I've presented tokens of my affection would scorn such a simple and useful item. They'd be much more interested in perfume and jewelry or fine clothing, things like that."

"Then apparently being a barbarian has its advantages." Thomas tapped the plate, listening to the leather strips slapping against it.

"It will only work correctly when the wind blows," Anatolius remarked. "Why do you suppose it will amuse Europa? Is there some uncertainty in her future? A decision yet to made?"

"She will make the right decision," Thomas confidently predicted and turned to look at John, who was approaching quietly from the house. "Lord Chamberlain, you have a visitor. I must depart to consult someone about a certain matter, so I'll leave you to talk."

John glanced at the brass plate, then looked after the retreating Briton. He asked Anatolius if he knew where the oracle had been found.

"Thomas mentioned he purchased it from a street vendor. Why do you ask?"

"Nereus' house was broken into and one of his Dodona oracles is missing."

"And you think that someone desperate to purchase food stole it and sold it to Thomas?"

"It seems a reasonable explanation, doesn't it? A plate is easily carried."

"From your gloomy demeanor I don't need an oracle to predict your investigation isn't going well."

John sat down beside Anatolius and briefly recounted his day's efforts, including his visit to the bookseller turned innkeeper for the dead.

"I'm not surprised to hear about Scipio's newest commercial venture," Anatolius observed. "He's always struck me as more interested in coins than words. Oh, he fancies himself a shrewd businessman, but a really shrewd businessman would be selling wine or bread or shoes—anything but literary works. Do you believe this cart driver you sought really died of the plague? It seems very convenient to me. There were no visible wounds, I take it?"

"No. Still, next time you see Crinagoras, you should strongly advise him to stay on guard. He might want to retain Thomas in his employ for a while as well."

"Yes, I'll tell him. But are you really surprised one of the remaining witnesses would be carried off by the plague? I'd have wagered more than one of them would meet the same end. It's almost a race between you and death, John. Are there any of the five witnesses still left alive you haven't interviewed?"

Five for silver, John suddenly thought uneasily, remembering the strange fortune-telling rhyme he had heard so long ago in Bretania. Five witnesses left alive and silver in plenty to be had, given Nereus' wealth. "Only this holy fool who seems to be everywhere and nowhere."

"Perhaps you should try following Crinagoras. The fool seems to be following him around. First he's at Nereus' house, then Theodora's banquet. Crinagoras tells me that Scipio tried to convince him he should write a chronicle of the fool's antics. The bookseller's taken an interest in the rascal, calculating people will want to read about him and his outrageous goings-on. He has a point, I will say, but Crinagoras refused to entertain the notion. He's become quite distressed of late. He keeps telling me the holy man won't let him alone."

"You say the fool was at the empress' banquet at Justinian's Blachernae estate?"

"That's right. I was going to tell you about it." He recounted the fool's performance. "If Theodora had thrown the fool into the imperial dungeons, you'd know exactly where to find him. As it is, he could be anywhere in the city or half way to Egypt by now. However, there is one mystery I have solved for you, even if it has nothing at all to do with Gregory's murder."

"And what might that be?" John leaned forward, picked up a pebble, tossed it into the pool, and watched rings spreading out toward the edge of the basin.

"When I was at the hospice this evening I saw the young man to whom Hypatia has become quite attached, and I'm sorry to say it's that disgusting young court page Hektor."

Chapter Twenty-Six

"If you're looking for Hypatia, I sent her home with a guard less than an hour ago." Gaius looked up from the tray on which he was arranging what appeared to John to be undersized butcher's tools.

"It's just as well she isn't here."

Gaius wiped a fine-toothed saw on a none too clean cloth. "You're as enigmatic as ever, John. I don't suppose you've visited at this time of night to chat. What is it?"

The physician looked as if he hadn't slept for days. The circles under his eyes might have been deep purplish bruises.

"Do you know anything about this favorite patient of Hypatia's? Have you treated him yourself?"

"I've been concentrating on those suffering from the plague. My colleagues are very capable and really, with burns like that, all you can do is bathe them well in water and vinegar and keep the victims supplied with pain-killing potions."

The physician rubbed his face wearily. "Then too we've had a sudden influx of patients who are half dead, but won't die," he went on. "At least not until they really get the plague. All of them are convinced they already have it, and from talking to them I gather they took massive amounts of what was purportedly hellebore, hoping for a quick end. Whatever it was, it wasn't poisonous enough to do the job. I imagine the purveyor of poison will be in some danger once his disgruntled customers get well enough to seek him out again."

"Doubtless a refund of whatever they paid will be the least of their demands," John observed, making a mental note to convey this startling development to Isis as soon as possible.

At John's request Gaius escorted him to the patient's room.

Inside the hospice it might have been midday since the halls were just as crowded, the cries of anguish were ceaseless as ever, the bustling attendants as numerous. Death and illness paid no heed to the hour.

"That's the one." Gaius indicated the room from the end of the hallway. The loud shouts emanating from within made it clear the patients were engaged in a game of knucklebones.

"Gambling seems to be inordinately popular here," the physician went on, "considering we're all rolling the bones with death every day. If you don't mind, I'm hoping to get a little sleep, so I'll leave you."

John watched Gaius trudge off and then strode into the room he had pointed out.

The young man looked up. When he saw John, the suppurating red ruin of his features instantly twisted into a familiar sneer. "The Lord Chamberlain blesses us with his presence."

The other wagerers in the room expressed vigorous doubts, well laced with obscenities, as to the validity of the claim.

John ordered them to leave, his tone and demeanor demanding obedience.

He looked more closely at Hektor. The court page had been a pretty boy who had grown into a handsome young man. Now all that was gone. "I regret your—"

"I doubt it," Hektor interrupted. "At least the injury I suffered has not diminished me as a man. No, rather I consider my misfortune a sign from heaven."

John ignored the insult.

"While the delightful Hypatia cared for me," Hektor continued, "I had plenty of time to ponder my situation. Consider. I have been shown the eternal burning pit of Hell."

John wondered if the young man's experience had upset his humors. It was understandable if it had.

Hektor flung his arms wide. "Yes, Lord Chamberlain, the Lord cast a sinful court page into the pit and a Christian emerged. I intend to enter the church, for am I not a living example of how even the most miserable sinner among us can be saved?"

Justinian's court was Christian and men could advance as far on piety as by their looks. Hektor's intelligence was certainly still intact, John thought. "The truth is you were found intoxicated and unconscious in some gutter or other and mistaken for dead," he said, recalling what Felix had told him about Hektor's recent behavior. "Do you really believe anyone at court will believe you've become a fervent Christian?"

"It has always amazed me what people will believe, Lord Chamberlain. Besides, as you see, I wear the marks of my sincerity." He ran a slender finger across his blistered face. The fingernail still bore a trace of colored polish, the last vestige of the pretty court page he had been.

Hektor's character, however, had not been affected by his terrible experience.

"We shall see. Now, concerning Hypatia—"

Hektor grinned. "She told you I proposed marriage? I am flattered you would personally visit to give me your congratulations. Of course, I'm a few years younger than she, but vastly older in experience. In fact, I believe your friend Anatolius was already composing letters for the Master of the Offices at my age."

"I will strongly advise Hypatia against any such union, Hektor."

"And destroy her happiness? I am surprised at your jealousy! Why, I even gave her my ring as a token of my intentions."

"Hypatia is free to choose her own husband, but don't think you can use her as a means to gain access to my household. I'm well aware of your enmity toward me."

"And if Hypatia marries me?" the young man replied insolently.

"Then she will leave my employ immediately."

***

Outside the hospice, the Augustaion was sunk in an orange twilight. Night never descended entirely anywhere ncar the Great Church, with its hundreds of lamps shining through scores of windows.

John walked away from the direction of the Great Palace. He did not care to return home yet. He stuck to the center of the Mese, avoiding its shadowed colonnades. No stars were visible in the sky. Here and there smoke ascended in columns, glowing in the city lights.

He arrived at the semi-circular courtyard housing Isis' establishment, the gilded Eros outside announcing the business conducted therein.

Zeus opened the door and gestured John inside with a grandiose wave of a gold-painted, wooden thunderbolt.

John, a swift glance encompassing the spectacle before him, from the crown of a well-curled gray wig to the gilt-encrusted sandals adorning large, pale feet, handed his blade to the father of the gods.

The doorkeeper looked highly embarrassed as he placed it with other weapons ranged neatly beside the door.

"Well, Thomas, you certainly appear to have risen in the world since I last saw you. As far as Olympus, in fact."

"You followed me, didn't you?"

"As a matter of fact, I merely decided to call on Isis. What are you doing here? Presumably you have a good reason for impersonating Zeus?"

Thomas flushed, heightened color clashing with his gray wig and red mustache. "I've been contemplating my future, John, and I thought it was time I followed a more regular calling. I'd never contemplated working in a place like this, but when I visited Isis yesterday to…er…renew our acquaintanceship, she offered me the post. I thought well, why not?" He frowned. "I never anticipated it would involve having to dress up in this ridiculous costume."

He paused as light footsteps announced the arrival of the madam. "John! I thought I recognized your voice. What do you think about our new doorkeeper? With Zeus guarding us, how can we fail to prosper?"

Thomas, scowling fiercely, contemplated his flimsy sandals.

"Do I take it that you've decided to change your decor to emulate Olympus?" John asked as he and Isis retreated to her private apartment.

"Not yet." She seated herself on the well-stuffed couch and gestured to him to help himself to wine and sweetmeats. "I've dressed my girls as assorted goddesses to see if there's enough interest to justify all the expense of redecoration. It's going to be costly, what with a certain amount of gilding and a few appropriate busts and statues and perhaps even a mosaic or two."

"When you told me you were contemplating a religious theme I thought you had in mind something Christian."

"I did. Almost everyone in Constantinople's thinking about heaven right now. So it occurred to me it might be a popular theme. Then I thought, no, Zeus is a much more interesting deity from my point of view. Very lusty, for a start. Fortuna must have sent you, because I was going to ask Thomas to convey a message when he returned home."

Home. The word leapt out at John. It had not occurred to him that his house was serving as a temporary home to Thomas and Europa. The notion seemed vaguely unsettling, akin to the queasiness he always felt when crossing deep water. "Has one of your girls heard something useful to my investigation?"

"Not yet, I fear. Rather I have a question for you, concerning a man called Aristotle of Athens."

John arched his eyebrows. "Fortuna has indeed smiled on you, Isis. I spoke to him not long ago."

"Excellent! As I mentioned, if I redecorate I'll be in the market for appropriate statuary and busts. Well, it so happened that during a recent visit one of my girls' regular clients mentioned he'd just purchased an antique marble of Aphrodite in the embrace of Adonis from this Aristotle at a very reasonable price, given its apparent age and the quality of the workmanship."

"Apparent age?"

Isis laughed. "Yes, it seems Aristotle has a fine trade in forged antiquities. The client, who seemed very knowledgeable, indicated the process involves burial of the statues for some time in pits well supplied with donkey urine and cow manure."

John nodded. "He's right. Aristotle's garden is graced, if that's the right description, with just such a pit. He claims he's been collecting it because he's planning to venture into tanning leather in due course. Manure would be easy enough to obtain. I'd heard tales about him burying a body in the middle of the night. Now I see there is a much less sinister explanation than this might suggest. However, why would your patron mention this strange information?"

"You may well ask, John. I certainly did, and in questioning my girl discovered it was not so much the fellow boasting about his knowledge or using it as an indication he could afford artifacts of that sort, but rather the fact that this statue he purchased had inspired him. He wished for its pose to be recreated in the flesh for his enjoyment."

"Surely not an uncommon request in a house dedicated to Aphrodite?"

"True enough. However, it transpired that the immortals were performing an act you won't see on public display among the sculptures decorating city squares or the baths or gymnasium. That being the case, Aristotle sounds like a man who deals in exactly the kind of works I may need, forged or not. So what I want to know, John, is where can I find him?"

Chapter Twenty-Seven

The sound of John's footsteps followed him as he departed homeward from Isis' establishment. Away from its warm lamplight and quiet voices, it was difficult to believe there was anyone left alive in the city.

John reflected that the only apparent result of his investigations so far had been to assist Isis in obtaining erotic statues from a forger of antiquities. If, indeed, she decided to do business with Aristotle. He had counseled against it.

Isis had chuckled and patted his arm. "You declare he's not to be trusted? He's in a suspect business? What would I know of such things, is that what troubles you? I am not the innocent child you remember from Egypt, John."

That was true enough.

Isis' revelation about Aristotle had placed the man's nocturnal activities in a different light. He had been burying a statue rather than a body. On the other hand, the discovery also lent credence to John's theory concerning the possibility of forged wills.

His thoughts invariably returned to the will. Oral wills were not common. That Gregory had been murdered within hours of witnessing such a will strongly indicated a connection. John had hoped that the remaining witnesses would provide information that could indicate what it might be.

He continued along the Mese, past shuttered emporiums. Only a few of the torches shopkeepers were required to maintain at night still burned. Now and again, John traversed pools of almost total darkness.

Could Byzos the cart driver have been the one person who could have illuminated the mystery?

There was also the incident at Nereus' house to consider. Was it possible that the night visitor had expected another witness, the steward's assistant Cador, to be there?

Even if that were the case, why had no one attempted to murder any of the other witnesses?

Did the solution lie with the wayward son who had been disinherited, yet another who had been removed by the plague before John could speak to him? Had that been John's mistake, to overlook Triton's obvious interest in the will? Then there was the woman Triton and his father had quarreled about. Should John again attempt to seek her out?

Of the witnesses, there remained only one for John to interview, the so-called holy fool. The others had revealed nothing useful.

What were the chances that the final roll of the bones would be the lucky one?

Having spent as much time gambling as any military man during his days as a mercenary, John knew the answer.

It didn't happen often, but often enough.

As he rounded the corner of the barracks across from his house John considered whether he should attempt to get a few hours' sleep, or spend the time contemplating his problem in the company of Zoe and resume his efforts with dawn.

Lamplight spilling from the second-floor windows startled him. At this time of night the house should be dark.

He sprinted across the square.

His first thought was for Peter. Had all John's efforts suddenly been rendered pointless?

His next was of Cornelia.

Perhaps the lamps were lit because of her arrival, rather than Peter's departure.

Both surmises were wrong.

John found Hypatia sitting on the edge of Peter's pallet, feeding him gruel with encouraging words and clucking noises, as if persuading a sickly child to take sustenance.

John drew a stool to the bedside as Hypatia apologized for not extinguishing the house lamps. He waved her back to her task, sat down, and scrutinized his elderly servant.

Peter was a wraith. His skin appeared colorless, all but transparent. The notion struck John that if the window were opened, the old servant might float up and rise heavenwards unless someone grabbed an ankle to detain him.

That he had allowed Hypatia into his bedroom and then accepted being fed indicated how feeble was the old soldier's grip on the world.

Peter made a slight motion with his head and Hypatia drew bowl and spoon away. The coverlet tucked up under Peter's chin hid any marks of disease.

"Master." Peter spoke in less than whisper. John was not certain his servant had actually said anything, or if his lips had merely formed the word without releasing a sound. John leaned closer to listen, until he could feel the old man's shallow breathing against his cheek.

"I regret my disobedient foolishness," Peter went on. "I should not have disrupted the household by refusing to open my door, no matter what good reason I thought I had to defy your orders. Please, master, it's best not to come so close."

John waved the apology away. "I see Hypatia's persuaded you to eat at last. It's always a good sign when the appetite returns. It seems then, despite your doubts, you will remain with us a little longer."

Peter released a long, rattling breath. Again his head moved slightly. "No, master. I have a feeling in my bones it will not be so. However, Hypatia can be very persuasive when she wants and, well…as I said…but I also wanted to know if you'd been able to find anything out about Gregory." A smile briefly illuminated his pallid face. "Shouting at each other through the door is not the proper way to conduct a conversation with an employer."

He slumped lower, exhausted by even that brief response.

John exchanged a glance with Hypatia. "I haven't yet been able to find the person responsible. I'm sorry, Peter. I can only hope Fortuna will smile on my labors tomorrow."

"I know you have been doing all you can, master, and that if the Lord wills it you'll find whoever took my friend's life. I only pray I'll live long enough to see justice done." Peter squeezed his eyes shut. When he opened them again they glistened. Hypatia brushed away the incipient tears before Peter could manage to lift his own hand.

Peter offered John a weak smile. "There is one last thing. I wish to leave a gift to whatever family Gregory left behind. He never spoke of that part of his life, although I believe it was because he was too proud to admit his poverty. All he ever said was that he worked near the docks. I am certain you will be able to find his family."

He fixed his gaze on John and went on in a stronger voice. "I've saved a little during my service with you, and while there is not a great deal, I wish it to be divided into three. One portion is to go to Gregory's family, leaving one each for Hypatia—"

The young woman protested, but Peter took no notice.

"No, Hypatia, you and I have been friends since the days we served Lady Anna and you are as close to a family as I have. The third portion I leave to you, master."

"Thank you, Peter. It will be done as you wish if the need arises," John replied. "I give my oath on that."

"Hypatia has promised to attend to the kollyba," Peter went on, his voice fading to a painful whisper. "Some might say that with Hypatia not being of the faith…but it is the intent and not the belief that is important, or so I have concluded after much thought on these matters over these last few days." A look of terror transformed his weary face. As if gaining strength from it, he struggled to sit up.

He no longer seemed to be seeing his familiar room. "Don't let them throw me into the pit, master!" he cried and then fell back.

***

John sensed Zoe glaring at him. He set his cracked cup down and met the mosaic girl's accusatory gaze.

"You didn't tell Peter the truth about Gregory," Zoe told him. Although her lips remained frozen, John could hear her words in his mind, as clearly as Peter claimed to have heard those spoken by the angel.

"Peter should know his friend wasn't a failed ex-soldier," Zoe continued. "Gregory was a successful man, happily married. It would please Peter to know that."

"Wouldn't it distress him more to realize his old friend had concealed so much from him?"

The mosaic girl made no reply. Tonight the slightly curved line of tesserae forming her mouth looked less like a wistful smile than a frown of disapproval.

John glanced toward the door. He half expected to hear Peter's footsteps approach, slow, and halt as he lingered fretfully in the hallway, reluctant to intrude on another of his master's strange soliloquies. John's conversations with Zoe always distressed the elderly servant. If he chanced to overhear this particular exchange he would be even more upset, John thought.

He got up and opened the door.

Only shadows populated the hallway. Peter was unable to leave his bed and perhaps might not rise from it. It occurred to John it was more than likely he would never again glimpse Peter shuffling away down the hall, pretending to have overheard nothing, and muttering a prayer for his master's soul.

"Gregory chose not to reveal the truth to Peter, Zoe. He had his reasons. Should I overrule Gregory's decision?"

Zoe's eyes gleamed in the flickering lamplight.

John looked down into his cup. "I spoke to Gregory's wife for some time. I wanted to know the man better. He was a simple man, a soldier, not the sort one would expect to find working in a customs house's administrative offices. He'd come by his high post almost by accident. It wasn't a position he'd striven to achieve. I believe it never even occurred to him that Angelina might misinterpret his unexplained absences when he met with Peter. Perhaps he felt uneasy about misleading Peter about his station in life, not correcting his misapprehensions, and didn't want to involve Angelina in the deception. After all, Peter is a servant, and Gregory employed servants…if it could in any way be characterized as a lie, it was one born of a kind heart."

But does kindness justify a lie, Zoe wanted to know.

John had no answer. He realized also that Gregory's motivation might well have gone beyond sparing his old friend's feelings. He may have feared Peter would feel compelled to end their friendship if he became aware of the disparity in their social positions. At the very least, their relationship would have changed.

"The whole puzzle has become a labyrinth akin to the Minotaur's maze," he observed to Zoe, "and one that's just as murderous, because you never know who might be lurking around the corner or in some dark alley."

The mosaic girl expressed surprise at his choice of metaphor.

"It's because I'm having a difficult time keeping my thoughts from galloping all over the place," John confessed. "They insist on constantly returning to Crete. Cornelia and Europa returned there when they left Constantinople some years back."

He sighed, took another sip of wine, and continued. "In private I sometimes called Cornelia Britomartis, after the Cretan Lady of the Nets. And why was that, you ask? Because the first time I saw the troupe perform, the sight of her snared me as securely as fishermen catch Neptune's creatures in their meshes. Even so, when I approached her she sent me away after exercising that sharp temper and wicked wit of hers on me for some time. It took me two or three further visits to persuade her to my way of thinking, but then I had to join the troupe since she would not leave it. We traveled with them for a time, and many's the night we spent under the stars away from the others, just us and the kindly darkness...." A smile briefly illuminated his face. "But perhaps I should not speak of such things to a young girl like you."

"Perhaps not," Zoe replied tartly, "particularly since you must keep your attention focused upon resolving the murder of Peter's friend. Yet it seems to me that Gregory also wanted to preserve the past and managed to do so," she went on, "because every time he met Peter he immediately stepped out of his life as an aging customs official and back into his vigorous, military youth."

"As you say."

"For all your wealth, you envy Gregory because he could do that and you cannot," Zoe observed.

John silently raised the cracked cup to his lips.

Chapter Twenty-Eight

John entered Scipio's emporium just as a man dressed in rags and a few stray flower petals was leaving.

The bookseller, fussing over the enormous mound of flowers the ragged fellow had left on a table near the door, looked up at the sound of John's footstep.

"Welcome, excellency! Let me guess the reason for honoring me with another visit. You have been thinking about *The Rustic Versifier* and decided you must have it after all!"

"I fear I must disappoint you, Scipio." John brushed a few stray petals off his cloak. "Aren't all these flowers expensive?"

"My ragged friend offers them for a very reasonable price. Of course, there are many abandoned gardens in the city these days, but if it helps him buy a crust of bread…well…. Are you certain you are not interested in the work of your friend Byzos?"

"No, I'm here to ask about something you said to Crinagoras."

Scipio raised his eyebrows. "You're a friend of Crinagoras? A man blessed by the Muses! But then you will already know that." He tossed down the flowers he had been holding, rummaged in a crate under the table, and pulled out a piece of parchment. "I have a superb selection of his work, ready to be beautifully copied out by one of my excellent scribes."

John found himself asking why Scipio had nothing already copied on hand.

"Why? Well…you know Crinagoras' poetry, excellency. Whenever my scriveners copy it out…uh…they're so moved…well…it's all so tragic…they're no good for anything until the next day, so I try not to overtax their sensibilities."

"There is that, not to mention some might not find his work to their taste."

"Yes. That's exactly what I was getting at," Scipio nodded. "Very upsetting for them, it is, having to copy such, well….Nevertheless, even the poorest words copied out in a fine hand on good quality vellum, perhaps, and enclosed in an expensive leather cover would please a lady. And isn't it true that the most pleasing ladies are not necessarily the most literate?"

"I'm not here to buy Crinagoras' poetry, Scipio. I'm seeking information about the fellow who calls himself a holy fool. I've been told you've been taking an interest in him."

Scipio dropped the parchment back into the crate. "I hope to eventually be able to offer an account detailing his visit to the city and his antics while he was here, but I have yet to find an author. It's a pity, because I'm certain it would sell very well."

"That being the case, have you any notion where I can find the fool?"

Scipio brightened. "We can do business after all, excellency. The fool has been keeping me abreast of his exploits."

John expressed surprise.

"The strange fellow got a ride with Byzos one day," Scipio explained. "By what I hear, the fool has an unhealthy affinity for the dead. After Byzos had disposed of his cartloads of the departed that particular day, he brought the fool around here, to share a meal with him. I suppose Byzos thought he looked as if he needed some nourishment, but that's the nature of these holy men. Always as thin as shadows. However, it gave me an opportunity to strike a deal with the fool. He drops in every morning for a loaf of bread and tells me where he's going to be that day in exchange. I can always find a street urchin to follow

him around and report back on the latest hijinks. I note them
down for the chronicle I am collating. When this plague has
passed, people will want to read all about the fool's exploits. You
can depend upon that, excellency."

"No doubt. Meantime, where will he be today?"

*****

From where John stood at the sea wall none of the burial pits
Peter so feared were visible. A heavy pall of smoke half-obscuring
masts and sullen water alike was the only evidence of municipal
efforts to cope with the grim situation.

The raucous sound of squabbling gulls rose up on cool air
redolent of the sea, overlaid with the sound of voices. Not the
shouts of individual dockworkers, but rather the murmur of a
group of people speaking all at once.

John trod to the bottom of a slippery flight of steps leading
to a rocky strip of shoreline littered with rotting seaweed and
other debris. There he halted to observe the situation.

A short distance away several people talked and gestured
excitedly. A sudden shout directed John's attention toward the
water. Scipio's information had been correct. He could see a
spindly figure some way out.

It appeared as if it were dancing on the surface of the sea.

"Came out of nowhere, so it did," someone loudly remarked.

"It's magick, I tell you!"

"Smoke and sea spray. That's all."

"No, it's him! That holy bastard!" The speaker was a long-
armed, lanky fellow, with shoulders as wide as a spar and an
untidy bowl of blond hair.

"Performing miracles now, is he?" The blond man had a
companion of comparable size, but darker and bearded.

"I'll give him miracles," cried the blond. "He's the bastard
who insulted my wife when the cart came for her!"

The figure identified as the holy fool spread his thin arms
as if they were wings and swayed perilously from side to side,
his feet moving in place as if to keep a precarious balance on
the water.

The fool began to laugh wildly.

His merriment enraged the two men even further. They ran to the shoreline, shouting virulent abuse, which was amply returned in kind.

More epithets followed. Then the pair splashed into the water. It had risen up to their waists before they reached the fool, who was still lurching from side to side.

"Have you been baptized, my sinful friends?" he cried, kicking spray into their faces.

The lanky blond grabbed the fool's arms.

"Now let's see you do another miracle, you old goat!"

He shoved the fool's head under the water.

Eerily lit by strengthening sunlight, the two big men forcing the slight figure beneath the frothing surface might have been chiseled in marble. For an instant John remained frozen in place by the prospect of entering the dark depths in which a murder was taking place.

He ordered himself to move.

He did not have time to obey the order, or to disobey it.

A stiff arm emerged from the roiling water and slapped the blond assailant's leg.

The man let out a yelp of disgust and then he and his companion were retreating to the shore, dragging the fool in their wake.

John glimpsed a bloated face leering from just below the surface and a swollen torso, rotating slowly as it drifted away.

The disturbance created by the fool and his assailants had set in motion the floating corpses upon which the fool had been balancing.

Back on land, the enraged pair began to beat the fool. Between coughs and sputters he taunted them, spitting blood in the bearded man's face.

The onlookers drew back, apparently disinclined to come to his aid.

The blond man pulled out a long blade.

Now John did move, and quickly. "In the name of Justinian, I order this ended!"

Three startled faces turned his way.

"And who might you be?" sneered the man with the blade.

"I know who it is!" came the helpful reply from the fool. "It's the Lord Chamberlain!"

"He's no more Lord Chamberlain than you are holy, you stupid, blaspheming bastard!"

The fool rolled on to his side and propped his chin in his dirty palm. "A fool I am, but not stupid. Look at his clothing."

"It's worth more than I make in a month," growled the bearded man.

"No one'll notice another naked corpse," his companion suggested, lifting his blade.

John turned his head toward the stairs. "Guards!"

The blond grabbed his friend's wrist. "Bodyguards! Now who's the fool? You think he'd be out walking about alone?"

The murderous pair took flight up the shore, not pausing to look back in their panic. The rest of the crowd followed.

John turned his attention to the man he had rescued.

The fool's face was sunburnt and creased with deep, innumerable furrows. His eyes were black and glittering, deep wells sunk in a parched desert.

With a shock, John realized he knew the man he had just saved.

Years before the fool had claimed to be a soothsayer.

***

"Ahaseurus?"

Thomas downed a gulp of wine and wiped his mouth on the back of his hand. "Ahaseurus is the holy fool? I can't say I'm surprised though, since going by what I've heard about his antics, he isn't much of a holy fool. There was one in Antioch you could track through the streets by his spoor. That would have been very useful in your quest to find him, wouldn't it?" He gave a hearty laugh. "But leaving that aside, the question is what's Ahaseurus doing in Constantinople?"

"That's what I hoped you'd be able to tell me," John replied, pouring more wine into his cracked cup.

He had returned to a house occupied only by Peter. After a word or two with the elderly servant, John allowed himself to lie down and awoke late in the day to the fragrant smell of boiling chicken.

Evidently Hypatia had found a suitable fowl in the market-place.

After the evening meal, when dusk cast a kindly veil over the city, Hypatia lit the lamps. As she and Europa chattered in the kitchen, John had invited Thomas into his study.

Thomas regarded the wall mosaic and pondered John's question. "I have no notion why Ahaseurus would be in Constantinople posing as a holy fool. Why do you think I would?"

"Am I wrong to suspect you were associated with the rogue in some manner the last time he was here?"

Thomas ignored the question. "If he really was a soothsayer as he claimed, you'd think he'd have avoided Constantinople, because he'd know if he came here he'd be riding around in a cart hauling the dead or getting himself assaulted by murderous ne'er-do-wells."

"He was fortunate today. Tomorrow he may not be so lucky."

Thomas shook his head in admiration. "Dancing on the sea! What a sight it must have been and yet so simple to accomplish when you know how it's done. Provided one had the agility. I'm sure Europa could have done it. Not that I would allow her to try. Still, why wasn't the trick of it apparent at once?"

"During our conversation he claimed he is able to make people see only what he wants them to see, not to mention that he can also stop them seeing things he does not wish them to see."

"An excellent skill to have, I'd say. Apart from gallivanting about the city getting up to no good and being rescued by Lord Chamberlains, what else is he doing? Is he still working as a soothsayer?"

"He mentioned he continues to practice the art, except instead of reading a chicken's entrails, the chicken itself does the fortune telling. He claims he was recently consulted by the empress at the palace baths, no less."

"He showed a chicken to Theodora in the baths and lived to tell the tale?" Thomas guffawed. "Mithra, but you have to admire the old rogue's tale spinning! Did he happen to mention what the chicken supposedly revealed?"

"Apparently the empress asked it if she would die of the plague and the answer given was that she would not. However, Ahaseurus added that as an oracle the bird was not too reliable because people often don't ask it the right question and it can only answer yes or no."

"I suppose time will tell if Theodora outlives the plague."

"Indeed. On the other hand, according to Ahaseurus, while Theodora definitely will not die of the plague, she also has no notion of just how close she is to the end of her life."

"I wouldn't like to be the chicken that told her that little tidbit, would you?" Thomas grunted. He stared at the mosaic figures animated by the flickering lamplight.

"Speaking of seeing things or not, John," he went on, "that god up in the clouds and the woman with him….It must be the result of working at Isis' establishment. It stirs up one's, um, imagination."

"You mean the flute-player? In daylight she's properly clothed. However, the tesserae are set an angle, so they present a different picture by lamplight."

"Very different! The little girl with the big eyes looks the same, which is to say just as disturbing." Thomas took another gulp of wine. "Did you learn anything useful from Ahaseurus?"

John shook his head. "All he would say about Gregory's death was that it was due to the hand of heaven."

"It would be exceedingly difficult to bring heaven to justice, I fear. Did he happen to say where he'd been all these years?"

"To the ends of the earth. Much like you, Thomas."

The two men sat in silence for a while, passing the wine jug back and forth. Darkness pressed conspiratorially against the room's diamond-shaped windowpanes.

Laughter drifted along the hallway.

His daughter's laughter.

John ran his finger along the crack in his wine cup. He thought of the woman with whom he had shared the original.

"I've noticed you haven't been spending much time here, Thomas. I could almost suspect you were avoiding me."

Thomas denied the suggestion.

"No matter. I wanted to question you concerning Cornelia, but not in front of Europa."

"She'll be here as soon as she—" Thomas stopped abruptly and uttered a ripe curse under his breath.

John kept his gaze level on Thomas' broad, flushed face. Inside he began to tremble.

"I should have told you right away, John, but, well, Europa, I mean, her mother....You've guessed, haven't you?" Thomas fell silent, tugging unhappily at his mustache.

A chill settled over John. "Something has happened to Cornelia? Something Europa knows nothing about?"

Thomas nodded. "Forgive me, my friend. Cornelia charged me with bringing Europa safely to you, and she would never have left her mother's side if she'd known."

"Known what?"

"Just before we left, Cornelia promised Europa she'd send word if she were going to be delayed more than—"

John leapt to his feet.

Dark foreboding encased him in a clammy shroud. "The truth, Thomas! Has Cornelia gone to someone else? Or...Mithra! No! Not my Cornelia!"

Thomas bowed his head sorrowfully. "She didn't want Europa to see. While Europa went to get her cloak so we could leave right away, she told me she had certain symptoms, but insisted I was not to reveal this to Europa or you on any account. Difficult though it was, I have done that. But by now Cornelia...."

He looked up, wiping streaming eyes, as a sudden draft made the lamp flicker.

The study door stood ajar.

John had gone.

Chapter Twenty-Nine

In a cellar hidden at the end of a labyrinth of underground storerooms situated in a remote part of the palace grounds, flickering torchlight gave intermittent life to the sacred scene gracing the wall behind the altar of a mithraeum.

John looked up at it. The familiar depiction of Mithra, Lord of Light, slaying the sacred bull had always been a comfort in times of darkness, but now it merely served to remind him that death was everywhere and none were safe.

He bowed his head, wordlessly pleading again with his god for some revelation, some explanation, of why Cornelia had been taken while he was left behind. He felt numb, as if he had imbibed a poppy potion. Cornelia's loss was a deep pain felt to the bone and yet seemed far away, shrouded in mist, and hidden from view.

Tears welled as he offered a despairing prayer to Mithra.

"Lord of Light, I have always served you faithfully. I ask no intervention for my sake, but for Cornelia's, grant I will find her so I can perform the proper rites…." His petition trailed off incoherently.

Staring up at the bas relief he sought a sign, any sign, that his plea would be granted.

The carved figures remained obdurate, unchanged, and silent.

***

"I'm certain they were the travelers you seek. How could anyone forget a trio like that?"

The innkeeper, who introduced himself as Stephanos, stood a pace or two from the doorway of his hostelry, which is to say in the road itself. Very short and very broad of build, his hair, face, and clothing were the same gray as the dust-coated facade of his dilapidated building.

"They put on several performances in the courtyard. Quite comical, they were too, although I will say the red-haired fellow didn't look very comfortable playing the part of the bull."

"You have paid their fee?"

"Of course!"

"And the older woman who stayed behind?"

"She's not here, excellency. Where she went, I cannot tell you."

An ox-cart piled with household goods rumbled along the road. The hunched driver stared straight ahead over the fly-speckled back of his ox, not acknowledging the two men in front of the inn. As the cart passed John could see blackened swellings on the driver's arms.

A fog of dust billowed from beneath the cart wheels. John tasted grit.

"I have a small bath-house," Stephanos offered. "I'll have my servant stable your horse, if you wish to stop to rest or refresh yourself."

John shook his head. If he rested, he would never rise. Thanking Stephanos, he remounted and continued.

There wasn't a muscle in his body that didn't ache from the long ride. He could feel every rut in the road as clearly as if he had been trudging barefoot along it.

The realization came to him that he had not dared to rest in all the years since he had arrived in Constantinople. Part of him longed for death. Another part, the part who was a follower of Mithra, knew that every day he awoke he had dealt another defeat to the Persians who had captured and mutilated him, destroying the future he might have had.

By the time he had made his way from the mithraeum to the city docks his dark despair had turned to blinding rage. He had hardly noticed the deep waters beneath the prow of the boat he engaged to take him to the Asian shore.

Once on the road he stopped at every inn along the way, in case Cornelia had tried to complete her journey to Constantinople, but found herself unable to proceed.

Proprietors cowered under interrogation from the fiery-eyed palace official.

None had seen her.

Now his anger had drained away. He was no longer certain why he had undertaken the journey.

Had he expected a miracle?

How could he have hoped to find her? Cornelia knew John, knew he would come after her if he discovered the true situation. Of course she wouldn't have stayed at the inn where Thomas and Europa had left her. If she had wanted John to see her die she would have come to Constantinople with them.

Days had passed. By now Cornelia would be dead.

Perhaps John should not be questioning innkeepers, but rather whoever buried those victims who had no families to do so.

He came to a roadside column, most likely the one once occupied by the stylite after whom Stephanos had named his inn. The perch was not very impressive. Made of eroded granite, it was twice John's height. Only a few rusted stubs around the edge of its platform remained of what had once been an iron railing.

There was no reason to go on, he realized. What chance did he have of finding Cornelia?

He was needed at his house.

He had better return as soon as he could.

As he coaxed his horse around, a flash of red caught his eye.

A short, bushy pomegranate, lancet leaves interspersed with scarlet blooms, was growing just behind the deserted column.

John's chest tightened.

He did not know plants. Not even the ones in his own garden. He only recognized it as a pomegranate because he and Cornelia had spent an afternoon in the shade of one such, lying in the grass sampling its fruit, talking about a life that would never be.

John climbed down from his mount.

In the shadow of the column where a Christian holy man had once stood, John opened his wineskin and poured an offering around the tree sacred to the goddess Cornelia had worshipped. He offered a prayer for Cornelia, thanked Mithra for the opportunity to do so, and rode back toward Constantinople.

***

With his gaze turned homeward, John's thoughts again centered on Peter and his murdered friend. Considering the puzzle helped push aside the dark cloud of John's bereavement for a little while.

What had Peter's angel said? "Gregory. Murder. Justice."

He would never find Cornelia now, but perhaps he could still find the justice Peter desired.

Reviewing the events of the past few days and his attempts to form a coherent pattern from disparate scraps of information, John recalled his brief conversation with the bear trainers near the Hippodrome, and his subsequent musings about mythological beings.

Neptune's horses.

The thought persisted and grew stronger.

There was something important, a pointer to the solution, involving Neptune's horses.

Very well then, examine the conundrum logically, he thought.

Neptune was the god of the sea.

Nereus was named after a sea god.

Triton the same.

The sea.

A connection with the sea.

A link with horses.

Neptune's horses, beautiful animals with flowing, golden manes and gleaming bronze hooves, pulling the god's chariot over the surface of the sea.

Yet the thoughts passing rapidly through his mind made no sense, didn't immediately suggest anything that would lead to a leap of deduction, launch him into the darkness with the certainty that his boots would find a firm surface on which to land.

If he could but apply the whip to his flagging imagination, he would have the solution in his grasp. He knew that to be the case as certainly as he knew his own name.

But the only thing that he could think of right now was that there was, in fact, one witness to Nereus' will with whom John had not spoken.

The servant Cador.

It was true that Anatolius had conducted an interview with Cador, and in doing so had discovered that Prudentius was Nereus' lawyer.

Was it possible Cador had other useful information?

John decided he would add a few more hours to his journey and visit Nereus' country estate on his way back to the city.

***

By the time John arrived at the departed shipper's estate, the lowering sun cast a pale yellow light across the landscape, lending it the appearance of an ancient mosaic sorely in need of cleaning.

From Anatolius' description John recognized the muscular man shifting crates in front of the villa.

"Cador?" John proceeded to introduce himself and explain the purpose of his visit. He had to speak loudly to make himself heard over the noise of hammering coming from inside the building. "If we could perhaps talk in private, somewhere quieter?"

"We can step into the kitchen garden if you wish, sir," Cador replied with a keen look at his visitor.

He led John around behind the house. "We're crating up the master's belongings. The estate and its contents are to be sold and the money donated to the church."

The kitchen garden was yellowed from lack of watering. Cador strode to its far end, where a bull grazed in a pen.

As they approached, the animal greeted them with a loud bellow.

Cador looked admiringly at the animal. "He is a handsome specimen, isn't he?"

"He certainly is, Cador."

During his ride to Nereus' estate, John had gone over the questions he intended to ask Cador, attempting without success to identify some stone he'd not already turned over during his interrogations of the other witnesses. No new line of inquiry had occurred to him.

He therefore concluded he would have to ask his usual questions about the will and its witnesses and hope Fortuna might finally favor him. He sighed and gazed at Apis. "Have any arrangements been made for the bull?"

Cador did not reply, continuing to stare at Apis with a smile on his lips.

John repeated his question.

Still the man did not respond.

John took a step backward and spoke the other's name authoritatively, demanding an immediate answer.

There was no response.

John placed his hand on Cador's shoulder. The man turned and looked expectantly into John's face.

"You are cannot hear, can you?" John said.

***

Darkness fell as John questioned Cador further.

No new revelations were forthcoming. Sylvanus brought wine out to them and departed after greeting John and directing a few fond words at his bovine charge.

"I'm sorry I have nothing useful to tell you, sir. Most people don't realize I cannot hear because I can follow their words by their lip movements. If they happen to notice me apparently rudely staring at them, a few get aggravated until they grasp why I must do it. On the other hand, some people will get angry no matter what you do."

"Anatolius mentioned you were from Bretania. I imagine you had difficulty learning to interpret Greek since it is not your native tongue?"

"It took more than a little time. The master was never impatient. There were those who laughed at him because of his great interest in oracles, and though he will never admit it, Sylvanus more than once got into fisticuffs with the other servants, although he never told the master why he had been fighting. Some would have dismissed him immediately, but not Nereus. He treated us all very well. He had a kind heart, sir, and did not deserve to have such an ungrateful son."

"Indeed. You mentioned all of Nereus' possessions are to be sold. Is Prudentius handling that?"

Cador looked puzzled. John wondered if he were having trouble reading his lips in the dim torchlight flickering into the garden from the kitchen windows.

"Is Prudentius, his lawyer, handling the sale of your master's possessions?" John tried to form the words clearly.

"Oh, no, sir. Prudentius is not the master's lawyer. He employed a young fellow with offices not far from the Great Palace."

"I understood that you had delivered a missive to Prudentius."

"That's true, sir. I don't know what it was about. After Nereus and his steward died, it was my duty to do what I could to put the master's affairs in order, so I did what I'd seen Calligenes doing, sorted through the papers on his desk, put aside bills waiting to be paid, that type of thing. There was a letter addressed to Prudentius, so I delivered it when I took a number of other missives here and there."

John stared into Apis' pen.

The bull lay in the shadows, a darker shape identifiable by the odor of dung and hay.

John wasn't looking at Apis.

It was Prudentius he saw, sitting at his ornate office table, explaining to John the law of wills.

A person who could not hear was among those legally barred from serving as a witness to a will.

Nereus' oral will was therefore invalid.

Chapter Thirty

John let himself into his house in the middle of the night.

He had instructed Hypatia not to attend to the door. She would be asleep, exhausted after another day helping at the hospice. Peter and Europa must be sleeping also, while Thomas was no doubt performing guard duty for Isis.

Perhaps Anatolius was correct and John should engage a few more servants. It was unseemly for a Lord Chamberlain to carry a key, not to mention dangerous to maintain a residence so unguarded.

He trod lightly up to Peter's room.

From behind its closed door came the ragged sound of labored breathing.

John turned away and visited the kitchen.

Having filled a plate with bread and olives, he went to his study, lit the lamp, filled his cracked cup with wine, and sat down to his frugal repast.

No one in the house had stirred. If he'd been a thief he would have come and gone unchallenged.

He stared at his mosaic confidante, Zoe.

Tonight her normally expressive eyes appeared nothing more than polished glass.

If he'd been able to seek out Cornelia at once, perhaps Gaius could have saved her.

The thought he had failed his lover was unbearably painful.

On the other hand, his practical side argued, had he not been heavily distracted by the upheaval all around?

Still, the thought of Cornelia dying alone beat at the edge of his thoughts, a black-winged demon tearing at his vitals.

Wiping away tears, he forced himself to focus his thoughts on the puzzle confronting him.

Why had he so readily accepted Anatolius' account of his interview with Cador? How could Anatolius have failed to realize the man could not hear?

More importantly, if the oral will was invalid, then Nereus' estate had passed to his wayward son, Triton, since he was no longer disinherited.

Very well. Then how did this relate to the labyrinth he was attempting to navigate?

Well, since Triton was dead, the estate would have devolved to his heir or heirs.

That was John's understanding of the position.

But did Triton have any heirs?

It was a question John had not hitherto pondered at length since he had believed from the beginning that Triton had been disinherited by Nereus' oral will.

"No wonder you appear so uncommunicative tonight, Zoe," John muttered into his cup. "These endlessly complicated legalities...."

Was there any reason to pursue Triton's connection to the will further, now that that young man was beyond questioning and further had died with no apparent family?

Yes, John concluded, it seemed he had taken the correct course in concentrating on those connected to the will who were still alive and able to divulge information about its provisions and each other.

Although, he ruefully admitted, they'd failed to do much of either.

Then too, John had been ever mindful of Peter's request and the limited time that appeared available to honor it.

Perhaps it was that realization that had caused John to make the wrong deductions.

Cador had mentioned delivering a letter from Nereus to Prudentius, leading Anatolius to leap to the conclusion that Prudentius was Nereus' lawyer.

On the other hand, Prudentius had not disabused John of the misconception. Had Prudentius realized that John was under the impression he was Nereus' lawyer, or had he decided to be circumspect when confronted by a high-ranking official from the palace?

Or had Prudentius lied?

If Prudentius did not serve Nereus in a legal capacity, what exactly was the connection between the two?

Anatolius had been guilty of making an unwarranted assumption, but as John thought back over his interviews he wondered whether he had not unknowingly committed the same mistake.

There was someone he should speak to again as soon as possible.

He slumped back wearily in his chair.

His gaze went to Zoe again, but all the life seemed to have gone from her.

His thoughts returned to Cornelia. Why did the world seem so empty now that he knew she was no longer part of it?

He drained his cup and his fingertip found the familiar crack in its rim.

Drawing back his arm, he threw the cup against the wall.

***

Glykeria's wizened visage peeked around her half-opened door.

She peered at John with sightless eyes. "Ah, the man from the palace who favors vulgar wines has honored me with another visit. Out and about early, aren't you, excellency? Still looking for new accommodations?" She let out a thin cackle, akin to the squawk of a sick crow.

"I wish to question you further about your tenant Triton," John replied.

"Come inside, then. There seems to be a bit of a chill in the air today."

To John, the weather felt oppressively humid, but he was happy to escape the ripe stench emanating from the rotting heap of pelts still lying across the street.

Inside, the kitchen sweltered. The only light came from a dusty slit of a window and a glowing brazier on which a pot bubbled and steamed.

Glykeria made her way without hesitation to a bench beside the brazier. John sat down next to her, wiping away the sweat already beading on his forehead.

"In case you're wondering, I've heard nothing further about the so-called actress friend of his either," Glykeria informed him.

Whatever was boiling in the pot carried a strong odor of herbs, bundles of which hung haphazardly from nails in the walls. Herbs were a perfect decoration for someone who lived largely by her sense of smell, John thought.

"I've been trying to recall the details of what you told me about Triton's death," John began, "and there are one or two points I would like you to clarify."

"If it's the exact day you want, I can't remember. As I said, so many of my tenants have died...."

"You mentioned you thought Triton's death was the most terrible of them all," John prompted.

Glykeria nodded. "It was heaven's justice, excellency."

"You also mentioned he suffered a great deal of pain, in fact, more than most plague victims."

"A lot more, yes. However, that's not surprising since he didn't die of the plague."

John patiently asked her what had caused Triton's death.

"That I can't say. I'm not a physician."

"Then how do you know it wasn't the plague?"

Glykeria tapped her nose. "Didn't I explain? I can smell the pestilence on them. Be happy you've not been blessed with such a talent. No, Triton most certainly did not die of the plague."

She leaned forward and reached unerringly for the handle of a ladle propped up in the bubbling pot and stirred the mixture briskly, sending a fragrant cloud into the dim air.

"You mentioned Triton had a number of visitors?"

Glykeria emitted another grating chuckle. "A steady stream of bill collectors. He was never lonely."

"Could you identify any of them? I'm particularly interested in those who visited him during his final few days."

"Now there I can be of assistance, excellency, strange though that may seem. The very last visitor he entertained was a cheese-maker. I remember the fellow very well, because the smell wasn't just faintly clinging on his clothing. He must have had a whole basket of his wares. I only hope he obtained payment before handing it over."

"Do you know who it was?"

Glykeria shook her head. "No, excellency, but if I passed by his shop I could identify it right away. The cheese was most unusual. Smoky with a more than a hint of herbs."

Chapter Thirty-One

Smoke lay along the Mese, emulating early morning fog on a river. John strode through the swirling gloom, deep in thought. He had not gone directly to his next interview. Instead he had walked in the opposite direction.

He needed time to gather his thoughts. More importantly, he urgently needed to return to his house.

Someone had died.

As he left Glykeria, that conviction had formed in his mind. Where it had come from, he could not say.

Sobs greeted him as he entered his atrium.

John's footsteps slowed as he ascended the stairway. In the kitchen Europa sat beside Hypatia, a hand resting lightly on the young woman's shaking shoulders. Tears shone on Hypatia's cheeks.

Europa murmured to her as John entered. The words did nothing to abate Hypatia's tears. She let her head fall forward to rest against her hands, folded together on the table.

Not folded in prayer, John realized, for the fists clenched spasmodically, as if trying to stave off unbearable pain.

Europa looked up at her father. "It's that bastard Pamphilos."

"Pamphilos?"

"Her special patient. He's discarded her. That's exactly what he said when she went to see him at the hospice this morning, that he was discarding her. He said he was to leave and he couldn't very well be dragging back out all his dirty blankets and soiled clothing and sluts like her with him. How could anyone be so cruel to someone who cared about them?"

John's mouth tightened. Evidently Hektor had taken his warning to heart. "It may not seem so at present, but ultimately the break will be for the best."

Hypatia sniffed and wiped her eyes on the back of her hand.

"Do you know," Europa informed John, "that young villain told her to keep the ring he'd given her. Called it payment for her services. Needless to say, it's worth hardly anything. Pamphilos would probably have thrown it away eventually. A ring off a dead man's finger. What sort of token of affection is that?"

Hypatia opened her fist to reveal the silver band she had been holding. "I shall get rid of it right now!"

Before she could throw the ring into the brazier, Europa grabbed her wrist and managed to extract the unwanted gift from her hand. "You shouldn't...."

Glancing in the direction of Europa's reproachful look, John observed a bowl containing several pieces of a clay cup sitting by the brazier.

"That ring was lucky, master. I believe it saved his life. He brought it out of the tower of the dead with him," Hypatia said mournfully.

"He brought it out of the tower?" John took the ring from Europa and turned it around between his fingers.

Hypatia looked stricken. "Please don't think Pamphilos is a thief, master. He was carried into the hospice clutching that ring. He said he'd grabbed it as he fought his way upwards, that it had came off some poor soul's hand...."

"Don't defend him, Hypatia," snapped Europa. "Whether or not he's a thief, he's still a villain."

John examined the ring closely. It was a strange piece of jewelry. A bent silver coin, to which a band had been attached.

Yet it was not surprising Hypatia had considered it a good luck charm since it bore a likeness of Fortuna.

"Hypatia, does this remind you of anything?" he asked.

The young woman shook her head.

The image was worn, but John had recognized it. If he were not mistaken, he had recently seen an identical portrait of Fortuna. "Is Peter…?"

As if conjured forth by the words, the elderly servant hobbled through the kitchen doorway. "Master! I thought I heard your voice. As you see, the Lord has decided to send me back to work."

Hardly realizing he did so, John murmured thanks to Mithra.

"Well, master, if you choose to use that name, I am sure the Lord will not mind," Peter observed mildly.

Europa stepped quickly to the servant's side. "You're too weak to be up and about. Didn't I tell you to rest?"

Peter reddened. "Master, I did not mean to disobey your daughter, but you see…."

"Never mind, Peter. The household has become rather complicated of late."

In John's imagination Cornelia was looking on with satisfaction. "You see," he could almost hear her say, "Europa is perfectly capable of taking charge. You could join me this very day with no fear for her well-being."

He had had too little sleep, John told himself. The room felt very hot. A droplet of perspiration ran down his neck.

"Peter, the coin in your bedroom. The one from Derbe." John held the ring out. "This was made from a very similar one."

"Of course it is, master. Gregory had his made into a ring. Was it found on him?"

"Gregory wasn't wearing the ring," John replied. "It came off someone else's hand. I have no doubt it was the hand of the thief who murdered your friend. I regret I cannot bring the man to justice, Peter. He was dead of the plague before I even began my search."

"Peter, I'd like you to have it as a reminder of your friendship with Gregory," Hypatia put in.

Peter accepted the ring gratefully. His weathered features tightened with perplexity. "Master, can you ever forgive me?" he finally said, his voice cracking. "I see now my error…the angel who visited me…its message…." He fell silent.

"What is it? You have nothing to apologize for as far as I'm concerned."

"But I do, master. I misinterpreted the angel's message. Now I see the truth of it. The heavenly messenger wasn't instructing me to seek justice for Gregory. It was telling me that justice had already been done."

***

Justice had not quite been done regarding another matter, John told himself as he left his house and set off. Undertaking the task the angel's message had appeared to place before him had not been futile.

Not that John believed in such heavenly messengers any more than he believed in the pronouncements of oracles.

Yet what of the conviction that had sent him home, expecting the worst, only to find Peter recovered and an unexpected solution to Gregory's murder?

Although, he thought, not so much the solution as confirmation of the conclusion he had already reached, that Gregory's death had been nothing more than a random street crime.

Nevertheless, like Peter, John still had work to do.

Rounding the corner of the excubitor barracks across the square from his house, he met a figure shuffling slowly along, head down.

"Anatolius!"

His friend's face was ashen and when he looked up his eyes were as lifeless as those of the statues adorning the baths.

"Anatolius, what is it? You've not been taken ill?"

The younger man said nothing. He gave no indication he'd even heard the question.

John had the impression that had he not been in his path, Anatolius would have continued past without even acknowledging him.

He laid his hand on Anatolius' arm. "Senator Balbinus has died, is that it?"

"No, John," Anatolius choked out. "Not Balbinus. Lucretia. Lucretia has died."

Chapter Thirty-Two

Xanthe opened Nereus' door, her sleeping baby draped like a sack over one shoulder. "Prudentius can't see anyone."

John stepped past the girl. "You are Sappho," he told her.

The girl stared in amazement, lips slightly parted.

"Those teeth you're missing. That's Triton's work, isn't it? A violent man. What is his son's name?"

The girl shut the door quietly.

John looked around the semi-deserted atrium. The few residents in evidence sat or lay quietly. It was as if a great storm had swept through the building, blowing most of the household away, leaving the rest stunned and silent.

"I called myself Sappho once," the girl admitted. "Xanthe is my real name." She gently stroked her baby's back. "He doesn't have a name yet. Or, rather, he did, but Prudentius said he wouldn't allow him to bear the one Triton wanted. But how could you guess I was Sappho?"

"You completed the pattern, Xanthe. I realized there was some connection between Prudentius and Nereus. I originally thought he was the man's lawyer, but it transpired he wasn't. You're the link. You mentioned you'd worked for Prudentius for some time. That was before you moved in with Triton, wasn't it?"

She nodded wordlessly

John explained the solution had became evident by a slow accumulation of small pieces of information, none very striking by themselves, but together forming a clear picture.

"The woman who rented lodgings to Triton described his living with a young woman practicing a questionable profession," John began. "Your master said that Nereus had confided his fear that just such a woman would become involved with his son."

Xanthe was silent.

"Then I discovered someone with a similar past living in the household of a lawyer with whom Nereus had had correspondence, even though he was not his customary legal advisor. And this moreover was a lawyer whom the son had threatened over his supposed theft of something belonging to him. That was extremely suggestive."

He paused. "Then too I couldn't find any trace of the actress with whom Triton had been living, one who apparently hadn't returned to her former profession after leaving him. A bear trainer told me he thought he had seen her, but where had she gone?"

Xanthe knuckled a tear away from the corner of her eye.

"Recently, for no apparent reason, I suddenly became convinced there was some link between the missing Sappho and Neptune. But what could it be, apart from the names of two of the parties involved and the fact that Nereus made his fortune from the sea? Then, as I reconsidered my conversation with Triton's landlady, I suddenly grasped the importance of something she had mentioned in passing,"

He went on. "It was connected with Neptune's horses. They have golden manes. Your name means golden or yellow. If you had not had the pretty conceit of always wearing saffron-colored garments during the time you went by the name of Sappho, it's possible I would never have made the final leap, connecting the sordid life of a brutal man to a young servant with an infant."

Xanthe looked at her sleeping son. "Triton thought I should support him. It was the final straw. But Nereus did not tell

Prudentius the entire story, Lord Chamberlain. What he feared would happen had already taken place. He somehow found out about me. He hated me. After all, I wasn't a suitable companion for his useless drunkard of a son, was I?" She smiled wanly.

"Nereus discovered your background and demanded your former employer intercede?"

Xanthe drew herself up proudly. "Not at all. I left Triton and returned to Prudentius' service by my own choice. Afterwards, Nereus came here, asking Prudentius to keep me away from Triton. Then Triton showed up at the house door demanding Prudentius return what he had stolen. He thought he owned me because I'd married him, you see."

"And you bore his child."

"The marriage was a mistake."

"Was it? Considering he was the only son of an extremely wealthy man?"

Xanthe made no reply.

"On my first visit here, one of the beggars remarked that you are Prudentius' favorite," John finally said. "I couldn't help noticing Prudentius has a special fondness for you, and such conversations between you as I witnessed tended to support the notion. Is it possible Prudentius wishes to marry you?"

Xanthe's mouth trembled. "Prudentius is dying."

***

John followed Xanthe through the garden. Above them, Ezra the stylite mumbled a mournful hymn. John could distinguish occasional phrases. Christ the physician, come to treat ailing mankind. A spear and nails for surgical instruments, vinegar to treat its wounds. His robe for a dressing. By suffering He will end all suffering.

John thought that if suffering could really end suffering there would have long since been no pain left in the world.

"Here he is." Xanthe stopped beside Prudentius' door, which faced into the garden peristyle.

Yet another door, John thought.

The last door.

"The sickness came upon him suddenly. It is the worst sort." Tears rolled down her face.

John stepped alone into Prudentius' darkened room.

Its smell overwhelmed the senses, a heavy sweetness overlaid with the ripe odor of decay.

Prudentius lay propped up on his narrow pallet. The elongated rectangle of bright light falling through the open door lay across a figure which appeared to have already collapsed in on itself. The lawyer's hands lay motionless at his sides. Only glittering eyes under bristling brows gave any hint of life.

Prudentius blinked, dazzled, at the tall, elegant figure silhouetted in the nimbus of light streaming in from outside.

When John shut the door, the only illumination was from bars of light filtering in through cracks in the closed shutters.

"I knew you would come for me," Prudentius gasped, his voice as distant as a whisper from the grave. "I am ready."

John stepped forward until he stood by the dying man's bedside. "You murdered Triton."

Prudentius released a long whistling breath that carried a faint denial.

"Why wasn't Triton suspicious of the smoked cheese you gave him, considering the enmity he'd shown you? Was it presented as being a gift of reconciliation from his father? Its unusual taste would have masked whatever poison you used," John continued. "Naturally people took the cause of his death to be the plague. When Cador delivered Nereus' letter and with it the news that Nereus had died, you questioned him closely."

The dying man stared wordlessly at him.

"You asked Cador the things a lawyer would need to know, and so discovered he was among the witnesses to Nereus' final will," John went on. "He didn't need to tell you he could not hear since it became obvious during your conversation, at which point you realized at once Nereus' oral will was invalid. Since his intent was to disinherit Triton, obviously this meant under the original will the estate would pass to Triton, or through him to his heir, Nereus' grandson. Who just happened to be living here with his mother under your protection."

Prudentius remained silent.

"So simple, isn't it?" John went on. "Even if Cador died, any of the other servants, Sylvanus for example, would testify to the fact the man was deaf."

"It was Nereus' wish to disinherit his son…" Prudentius protested feebly. "I exerted no influence on him regarding the matter.…Nereus agreed to assist me with my philanthropy.… The letter Cador brought concerned certain…financial arrangements to this end.…"

"Whatever you choose to call them, those payments were to ensure you kept Xanthe well away from Triton. However, once you realized the will under which Triton inherited his father's wealth was still valid, you murdered Triton so that his son, his legitimate and only child, would inherit instead. In the end, the real key to this final door was Triton's murder, which was not directly connected with the witnesses I sought so hard to find, and yet everything to do with the will."

John paused for an instant. "Tell me, would Xanthe and the boy have long survived her marriage to you, Prudentius?"

Prudentius made a sound that was a sigh or a murmured prayer. One of his hands twitched weakly, unable to rise from the coverlet.

"I care deeply about them both…but surely you have come to take me to heaven, holy one? I have given all I can in charity. I could have done so much more with Nereus' wealth.…You understand, I am certain.…Hurry! The others are coming. Don't you hear them scratching? Their wings beating? Don't let them drag me away!"

The frail body trembled.

Understanding dawned on John.

"Who do you suppose I am, Prudentius?"

"Why, you are an angel, of course, a messenger from heaven… which ordained Cador should serve as a witness and then sent him to me....The Lord knew how difficult it has been for me to continue my good works, to care for all my charges....It was a miracle."

The rasping, fading voice trailed away. The lawyer's lips continued to form words without enough breath to animate them.

John bent and put his face next to the dying man's.

"...deserved to die," Prudentius was whispering. "The plague might have taken him soon enough anyway. He would have squandered everything and what would my poor family have done then? I was heaven's tool, nothing more."

His head jerked to one side and he stared into the shadows. "They're here...please, holy one...they're here! No! Let go!"

Prudentius let out a strangled shriek.

John took a step away.

Prudentius' hand shot out and clutched John's garment.

"Don't go! Take me with you! I had to kill him, don't you see? To help my family....I was merely serving the Lord as best I could."

The hand on John's robe lost its grip and fell away.

Prudentius stared fixedly at John. "I beg you, holy one. Tell me whether or not heaven has forgiven me...."

John looked down at the tormented face.

He did not reply.

Epilogue

John stood in his atrium and gazed out into the brightly illuminated garden.

He imagined its green expanse as a pool of brightness set amid largely darkened city streets beneath a sky veiled by acrid smoke. At this hour lamplight would be spilling from the windows of the Great Church to join with the lurid glow of burning vessels, silhouetting the roofs of dwellings under which no living person lay. Few were abroad now except carters transporting the departed to their final earthly destinations or the faithful attending church services, adding their pleas to those praying for the plague to pass.

There was a matter that would not wait for the plague to leave, if indeed it intended to depart at all.

Singing tunelessly to himself, Peter bustled past bearing a large platter of fruit. Hypatia followed, carrying an enormous silver wine jug. Rarely used, it was engraved with bunches of grapes and vine tendrils, appropriate decorations for the forthcoming celebration.

John could not smell smoke tonight. Rather he was aware of the sweet scents from garlands of flowers decorating the atrium, mixed with the odor of rich sauces wafting down from the kitchen.

Anatolius arrived, wringing his hands.

No, John realized as they exchanged greetings, not wringing his hands, but rather absently rubbing badly swollen knuckles. He gave him a questioning look.

"I've had a disagreement with Crinagoras," Anatolius spat out angrily. "I don't expect to see him again. He came around this evening and started to recite an ode to Lucretia. He claimed it was what I needed to comfort me, not to mention it would keep her memory alive at court. Needless to say, I knocked him down immediately and kicked him out of my house. Then I gathered up all my poems and fed them to the kitchen brazier. My servants must have thought I'd lost my senses. Lucretia…Lucretia I will mourn in private. There are no words…the world is very empty now."

"I understand. I had to tell Europa her mother was gone, yet tonight how can I not be happy? My daughter is to be married in less than an hour."

"Of course. We must try not to let our sorrows mar the joys of others, it's just that…well…."

"Yes, indeed."

They strolled out into the garden.

There they found Thomas fidgeting beside the pool. He barely acknowledged their arrival.

"Have you solved the knotty problem of the form of the ceremony, John?" Anatolius asked. "I gather the Patriarch was otherwise engaged tonight."

John smiled. "Don't worry about that. Peter was bold enough to observe to me earlier this evening that while this would not be a traditional wedding in any sense of the word, what mattered was it was being entered into with sincere intent and that being so, surely heaven would bless it."

Thomas nodded solemnly. "A wise man, that servant of yours." He took a few nervous steps away and back again and then glanced at the sky. "Mithra, it's worse than waiting to go into battle."

"Hours drag like chains while we wait and fly away like eagles when we wish them to stay," Anatolius agreed. "However, few go into combat dressed in such fine garments. Silk, I see."

"Borrowed," Thomas muttered, looking uncomfortable. "In honor of the occasion."

"Don't worry, you'll soon be back in that barbaric clothing you prefer, and I see you kept your own boots," Anatolius observed.

Thomas turned to John. "About Nereus' bull, John, the one you told me about. I've obtained a loan from Isis and purchased it as a wedding gift for Europa. She doesn't know yet."

"What strange notions barbarians harbor about suitable gifts," Anatolius commented with a grin. "Though I suspect you could scarcely have chosen a better one."

Thomas looked gratified.

"It appears Anatolius' metaphorical chains have begun to change into birds," John observed, glancing over his shoulder.

Europa, crowned with a chaplet of spring flowers and dressed in a simple, white tunic, had just emerged from the house and was now making her way down the neatly graveled path toward them, accompanied by Hypatia and Peter.

The small group took up their places beside the pool.

Thomas and Europa stepped forward to stand in front of John.

John looked down at his daughter's sunburnt face. How much she resembled her mother, he thought.

A mosaic of memories passed rapidly through his mind's eye. The torchlit garden fell away as he recalled the bright and open skies of Crete and Egypt, Cornelia's saucy smile and sharp-tongued response the day he, then still a young mercenary, had first dared to ask for her companionship, the clay cup broken one amorous night, the cup whose twin he had ordered made and from which he had habitually drunk the raw Egyptian wine he favored until he had deliberately destroyed it, the years of slavery and then regaining his freedom, the even longer period he had spent living in the palace, rising to his present high office....

All those years had disappeared as swiftly as water passing along an aqueduct, babbling swiftly past never to return, flowing ceaselessly along the channel of time, bearing with it all who lived.

And those who had died.

Cornelia, if you can, be here tonight, he silently prayed.

Holding Thomas and Europa's clasped hands between his, he addressed the couple. His voice was low, but clearly audible in the strangely quiet night air.

"Europa and Thomas, you have stated your intentions to me in private. You will now declare them openly before those assembled here. Europa, do you freely confirm it is your desire to be wife to this man, Thomas?"

"It is," Europa responded in a determined tone that drew smiles from those present.

"Thomas, do you freely confirm it is your desire to be husband to this woman, Europa?"

"That is what I wish," Thomas replied.

"Very well. Thomas, do you swear by Lord Mithra and all you hold sacred that you will treat Europa honorably and be true to her always?" John continued.

"I swear by Lord Mithra and by the Sacred Bull it will be so!" Thomas stated firmly, smiling at Europa.

Europa made the same affirmation, making her oath by the Mother Goddess and all that she held holy.

"Then I formally ask Lord Mithra and the Mother Goddess for their blessings upon this marriage," John concluded, "for by freely confirming your intent and giving oaths below heaven and before witnesses you have taken each other as man and wife. Thus I declare you to be so joined."

Thomas turned to Europa and kissed her.

As the women hugged each other and Peter, Anatolius offered awkward congratulations to Thomas. "And you had better treat her well, Thomas," he added, "because if I should hear anything different...."

"Oh, she'll keep me in line, don't you worry about that," Thomas remarked as Peter bustled forward to announce the wedding feast was waiting.

"And what culinary delights have you concocted for us, Peter?" Anatolius asked the elderly servant.

"The master felt it would be inappropriate to offer anything too lavish given the circumstances, but since he agreed a small repast would be suitable to mark this joyous occasion, Hypatia and I have baked honey cakes and there is also roast fowl with a special sauce I invented this very day, and fruit, not to mention plenty of the master's best wine, and I don't mean the Egyptian vintage either," Peter replied in a rush of words.

"Excellent!" Thomas grinned. "Shall we go and sample this excellent wine, Anatolius?"

The party made its way back indoors and went noisily upstairs.

Last to cross the atrium, Peter and John had just arrived at the foot of the stairway when there came a loud rap at the house door.

Peter opened it warily and stepped quickly back, away from a shape swathed in a dark cloak.

"It's the demon I saw in the alleyway just before I fell ill!" he cried in panic. "Don't allow it in the house, master, it'll bring the pestilence!"

The shape let out a croaking laugh. "Not so! I merely saved you from a thief and your own hallucinations, Peter."

It was Ahaseurus, the holy fool, still dressed in rags yet now festooned with gold necklaces and sporting gem-encrusted rings on every finger.

"What sort of greeting is this, Lord Chamberlain?" the nocturnal visitor went on severely. "No matter. I am here because you saved my life and I always pay my debt. However, while there are rich pickings to be had in every alley in the city right now and I've certainly gathered my share, to settle this particular debt I had to travel a very long way, so I'm arriving somewhat later than I'd anticipated."

Before John could reply, a brief gust of wind swirled into the atrium. Torches guttered, sending dark shapes spinning around its walls.

When the shadows stopped dancing, the fool was gone.

Another figure had appeared from the blackness beyond the doorstep.

A woman holding a pomegranate.

"Cornelia!" John's voice cracked.

She must be a hallucination, he thought, a sign he had been stricken with the plague.

Strangely, the thought made him thankful.

Or might she be a shade?

Without hesitation she stepped forward into the torchlight, into his embrace.

Glossary

All dates are CE unless otherwise noted.

AESCHINES (?c 390-?314 BC)

Athenian orator, said to have been a sausage-maker's son. His perfume business failed. A bitter rival of DEMOSTHENES, Aeschines was fined after losing a law suit he brought against him, and subsequently retired to Asia Minor.

AESCHYLUS (c 525-456 BC)

Athenian playwright regarded as the father of Greek tragedy. He wrote dozens of plays, of which only a handful are extant. Of these, *Agamemnon* (458 BC) is considered by many to be the greatest surviving Greek drama. Aeschylus is said to have been killed when an eagle dropped a tortoise on his head.

ALCIBIADES (c 450-404 BC)

Athenian statesman and general, reportedly extremely handsome. Condemned to death for sacrilege, he escaped to Sparta, whose leaders he subsequently advised in their war against Athens. Eventually he returned to duty, leading the Athenians to several victories over the Spartans. This resulted in personal popularity and the quashing of his sentence. However, Alcibiades' political fortunes declined and he was again banished. A year or so later he was assassinated in Phrygia at Spartan instigation.

ANASTASIUS I (c 430-518; r 491-518)

Minor functionary who became emperor upon the death of Zeno (d 491, r 474-491) whose widow, Ariadne, Anastasius married after his elevation to the purple. Zeno was an ISAURIAN and his brother expected to rule after him. His loss of the throne led to an ISAURIAN rebellion. Anastasius I and Ariadne were buried in the CHURCH OF THE HOLY APOSTLES.

ARGUS-EYED

Watchful. According to Greek mythology, Argus possessed a hundred eyes. The "eyes" in the pattern on a peacock's tail are said to be his, having been placed there by the goddess Hera after his death.

ATRIUM
Central area of a Roman house. It held the household's IMPLUVIUM.

AUGUSTAION
Square between the GREAT PALACE and the GREAT CHURCH.

BACCHUS
Roman god of wine. His Greek equivalent was Dionysus.

BATHS OF ZEUXIPPOS
Public baths in Constantinople, named after ZEUXIPPOS. Erected by order of Septimius Severus (146-211, r 193-211), the baths were a casualty of the Nika riots (532). They were rebuilt by JUSTINIAN I. Situated near the HIPPODROME, they were generally considered the most luxurious of the city's baths and were famous for their statues of mythological figures and Greek and Roman notables.

BLUES
Followers of the Blue chariot racing faction. Great rivalry existed between the Blues and the GREENS and each had their own seating sections in the HIPPODROME. Brawls between the two sets of supporters were not uncommon and occasionally escalated into city-wide riots.

CALLIOPE
One of the nine Muses, Zeus' daughters by Mnemosyne (Memory). Calliope is the muse of eloquence and epic poetry.

CAPITOLIUM
Little is known about this building, reportedly constructed by order of Constantine I (c 288-337, r 306-337). Three sides of the Capitolium featured exedras, a number of monuments made of porphyry stood before it, and the building itself displayed a cross.

CERATE
Thick ointment made from wax, lard, and medicinal components, applied to the skin or to dressings and bandages.

CHARON
In Greek mythology Charon ferried the souls of the departed across the River Styx to the underworld. His payment was the coin placed under the tongues of the dead.

CHRIST THE PHYSICIAN
See ROMANOS MELODOS.

CHURCH OF THE HOLY APOSTLES
Constructed by Constantine I (c 288-337, r 306-337) as his place of burial. In addition to its portion of the COLUMN OF FLAGELLATION, the church owned relics of SS Andrew, LUKE, Timothy, JOHN CHRYSOSTOM, and a number of other saints and martyrs.

CITY PREFECT
High-ranking urban official whose principal duty was to maintain public order.

COLUMN OF FLAGELLATION
Pillar to which Christ was bound for scourging before crucifixion. Made of marble with green, white, and black veining, a tapering portion measuring approximately two feet long is presently displayed in St Praxedis Church in Rome. See CHURCH OF THE HOLY APOSTLES.

COMPLUVIUM
Oblong or square opening in the roof of an ATRIUM. It permitted rain to fall into the IMPLUVIUM.

CONCRETE
Roman concrete, consisting of wet lime, volcanic ash, and pieces of rock, was used in a wide range of structures from cisterns to the Pantheon in Rome, which has survived for nearly 2,000 years without the steel reinforcing rods commonly used in modern concrete buildings. One of the oldest Roman concrete buildings still standing is the Temple of Vesta at Tivoli, Italy, built during the first century BC.

CROCUSES TO CILICIA
Equivalent to carrying coals to Newcastle, Cilicia being famous for its saffron.

DEMOSTHENES (?384-322 BC)
Considered by many to be the foremost Greek orator. Having spoken out against the growing danger posed by the Macedonians, after the triumph of their general Antipater (?398-319 BC) he committed suicide rather than fall into enemy hands.

DERBE
Lycaonian town through which St Paul passed during his missionary journeys.

DIOGENES (c 412-323 BC)
Ascetic philosopher born in Sinope. He taught the virtue of a simple life. Said to have given away all his possessions and thereafter taken up residence in a tub. He reputedly once carried a lantern during a daylight search for an honest man.

DODONA
Shrine in northwestern Greece. Its oracular pronouncements were interpreted from sounds made by leather thongs slapping against a brass plate hanging on the sanctuary's sacred tree or alternatively from the rustling of its leaves.

EPIGRAMMIST
Author of pithy poems dealing pointedly with a single subject and written in the manner of a memorial inscription. In Greek literature, the term includes a wide variety of short verse, sometimes of a satiric nature.

ERINNA OF RHODES (fl 600)
Greek poetess. She died at a young age and little of her work has survived.

EUNUCH
Eunuchs played an important role in the military, ecclesiastical, and civil administrations of the Byzantine Empire. Many high offices in the GREAT PALACE were typically held by eunuchs.

EXCUBITORS
GREAT PALACE guard.

FLAVIAN (d 449)
PATRIARCH of Constantinople who was falsely condemned, deposed, and banished. He died in exile as the result of a savage beating.

GORGONIUS (d 304)
Although he held high office in the imperial household, Gorgonius was martyred in 304 during the persecution of Christians ordered by Diocletian (245-313, r 284-305).

GREAT BULL
See MITHRA.

GREAT CHURCH
Colloquial name for the Church of the Holy Wisdom (Hagia Sophia). One of the world's great architectural achievements, the Hagia Sophia was completed in 537, replacing the church burnt down during the Nika riots (532).

GREAT PALACE
Situated in the southeastern part of Constantinople, it was not one building but rather many, set amidst trees and gardens. Its grounds included barracks for the EXCUBITORS, ceremonial rooms, meeting halls, the imperial family's living quarters, churches, and housing provided for court officials, ambassadors, and various other dignitaries.

GREENS
Followers of the Green chariot racing faction. Great rivalry existed between the BLUES and the Greens and each had their own seating sections in the HIPPODROME. Brawls between the two sets of supporters were not uncommon and occasionally escalated into city-wide riots.

HERODOTUS (c 484-425 BC)
Greek author of *The Histories*, a lively and informative narrative of the wars between Greece and Persia covering the histories of both countries as well as those of Egypt and Babylon. Herodotus traveled extensively and his work is largely based on personal observation and contains comments on archaeology, architecture, geography, unusual customs, and beliefs, among other things. Now known as the Father of History, in antiquity he was dubbed the Father of Lies because of the incredible and extremely unlikely stories he included in his work.

HIPPODROME

U-shaped race track near the GREAT PALACE. The Hippodrome had tiered seating accommodating up to a hundred thousand spectators. It was also used for public celebrations and other civic events.

HOLY FOOL

Holy Fools engaged in extremely unconventional and sometimes obscene behavior as a method of demonstrating spiritual lessons, as well as pointing up onlookers' sinful ways. Their antics included dancing with prostitutes, relieving themselves in the street, over-eating during periods of fasting, disrupting church services, going about naked, and so on.

INSTITUTES

Part of the definitive codification of Roman law ordered by JUSTINIAN I. The Corpus Juris Civilis (Body of the Law) as it is now known was issued between 529 and 535 and consisted of The Institutes, a basic introduction to the law; the Digest, which included selections from classical jurists; and the Codex, dealing with legislation dating from the reign of Hadrian (76-138, r 117-138) onward. The Novels, a collection of legislation issued by JUSTINIAN I, was added between 535 and 565. This codification served as the foundation for present day civil law in most European countries and those whose legal systems are based thereon.

IMPLUVIUM

Shallow pool in the center of an ATRIUM. Situated under the COMPLUVIUM, it caught rain for household use and also served a decorative purpose.

ISAURIA

Province in Asia Minor, occupied by a notoriously rebellious people. ANASTASIUS I quelled a revolt, but although the Isaurians were soundly defeated at the battle of Cotyaeum (491) it took several years to finally subdue them. JUSTIN I, adoptive father of JUSTINIAN I, was a commander in the army during this campaign.

ISOCRATES (436-338 BC)

Attic orator and teacher. His slaves famously included a number of skilled flute-makers. He is said to have committed suicide upon hearing of the defeat of the Athenians at Chaeroneia by Philip II of Macedonia (382-336 BC, r 359-336 BC). However, given Isocrates' advanced age at the time, his death may well have been due to natural causes. His tomb was distinguished by a tall pillar topped by a statue of a siren.

JOHN CHRYSOSTOM (c 347-407)

Born in Antioch, St John Chrysostom (Golden Mouthed, a tribute to his eloquent preaching and writings) became PATRIARCH of Constantinople in 398. His piety, condemnation of the immorality of those in positions of power, and numerous charitable works made him well loved by the populace. Enemies in the imperial court, civil administration, and the church itself brought false accusations against him and he was exiled. After severe riots in Constantinople he was recalled to the city, but was soon again banished. Eventually ordered moved to an even more isolated location, he died during the journey. In 438 his remains were brought to Constantinople and buried in the CHURCH OF THE HOLY APOSTLES.

JUSTIN I (c 450-527, r 518-527)

Born in present day Macedonia, Justin and two friends journeyed to Constantinople to seek their fortunes. All three joined the EXCUBITORS and Justin eventually rose to hold the rank of commander. He was declared emperor upon the death of ANASTASIUS I. Justin's nephew JUSTINIAN I was crowned co-emperor in April 527, four months before Justin died.

JUSTINIAN I (483-565, r 527-565)

Adopted nephew of JUSTIN I. His ambition was to restore the Roman Empire to its former glory and he succeeded in regaining North Africa, Italy and southeastern Spain. His accomplishments included codifying Roman law (see INSTITUTES) and an extensive building program in Constantinople. He was married to THEODORA.

KALAMOS

Reed pen.

KOLLYBA

Small cakes made of boiled wheat, nuts, and dried fruit, eaten when prayers for a departed person were made at the gravesite at set intervals during the month after the death, and again a year later. In today's Greek Orthodox Church similar cakes are distributed at memorial services.

LEANDER'S TOWER

According to Greek mythology, Leander was a young man who lived on the Asian side of the Hellespont. He fell in love with Hero, a priestess of Aphrodite who lived on the European shore. Every night Leander swam across the Hellespont to visit her, guided by a torch placed on a tower by his beloved. One night, however, he was drowned in a sudden storm. When his body washed ashore, Hero committed suicide by throwing herself from the tower into the sea. Subsequent versions of the legend occasionally mistakenly placed Leander's nightly swim in waters other than those of the Hellespont.

LEX FALCIDIA

Law guaranteeing heirs would receive a certain portion of the estate.

LORD CHAMBERLAIN

Typically a EUNUCH, the Lord (or Grand) Chamberlain was the chief attendant to the emperor and supervised most of those serving at the GREAT PALACE. He also took a leading role in court ceremonial, but his real power arose from his close working relationship with the emperor, which allowed him to wield great influence.

LUKE

Accompanied St Paul on some of his missionary journeys. Luke, a physician by profession, is the patron saint of doctors and surgeons. Certain of Luke's relics were owned by the CHURCH OF THE HOLY APOSTLES.

MARCUS AURELIUS (121-180; r 161-180)

Adopted by his uncle by marriage, Antoninus Pius (86-161, r 138-161), and succeeding him, Marcus Aurelius sought to improve conditions for slaves, criminals, and the poorer classes. However, he also persecuted Christians, viewing them as a threat to the empire. His MEDITATIONS (167) expound upon his Stoic philosophy and sense of moral duty.

MASTER OF THE OFFICES

Official who oversaw the civil side of imperial administration within the GREAT PALACE.

MEDITATIONS

See MARCUS AURELIUS.

MESE

Main thoroughfare of Constantinople. Its entire length was rich with columns, arches, and statuary depicting secular, military, imperial, and religious subjects as well as fountains, churches, workshops, monuments, public baths, and private dwellings, making it a perfect mirror of the heavily populated and densely built city it traversed.

MIMES

After the second century CE mime supplanted classical Roman pantomime in popularity. Unlike performers of pantomime, mimes spoke and did not wear masks. Their presentations featured extreme violence and graphic licentiousness and were strongly condemned by the Christian church.

MITHRA

Persian sun god. Born in a cave or from a rock, he slew the GREAT BULL, from whose blood all animal and vegetable life sprang. Mithra is usually depicted wearing a tunic and Phrygian cap, his cloak flying out behind him, and in the act of slaying the GREAT BULL. He was also known as Mithras.

MITHRAEUM

Underground place of worship dedicated to MITHRA. They have been found on sites as far apart as northern England and what is now the Holy Land.

MITHRAISM

Of Persian origin, Mithraism spread throughout the Roman empire via its follow-ers in various branches of the military. It became one of the most popular religions before being superseded by Christianity. Mithrans were required to practice chastity, obedience, and loyalty. Women were excluded from Mithraism. Some parallels have been drawn between this religion and Christianity because of shared practices such as baptism and a belief in resurrection as well as the fact that Mithra, in common with many sun gods, was said to have been born on December 25th. Mithrans advanced within their religion through seven degrees. In ascending order, these were Corax (Raven), Nymphus (Male Bride), Miles (Soldier), Leo (Lion), Peres (Persian), Heliodromus (Runner of the Sun), and Pater (Father).

NICARCHUS (known 1st century)
Greek EPIGRAMMIST. Over 40 of his epigrams are extant, many of them lampooning physicians.

NOMISMATA (singular: NOMISMA)
Gold coin at time of JUSTINIAN I.

NUMMI (singular: NUMMUS)
See NUMMUS.

NUMMUS (plural: NUMMI)
Smallest copper coin during the early Byzantine period.

PATRIARCH
Head of a diocese or patriarchate. The ancient patriarchates were those of Rome, Constantinople, Alexandria, Antioch, and Jerusalem.

PLAGUE
Writings by Procopius (known 6th century) and John of Ephesus (c 505–c 585) provide vivid eyewitness accounts of the Justinianic plague. It appears to have broken out in Egypt or central Africa and, spreading along trade routes, arrived in Constantinople in the spring of 542. Sufferers generally died within three days of the onset of symptoms, which included hallucinations, fever, anxiety, chills, and swellings in the armpits, groin, or beside the ears. Some patients lived only a few hours after infection. In many cases, victims' bodies became covered with black blisters. In Constantinople up to 10,000 people died each day, so that by the time the plague departed the population of the city had been reduced by 40 per cent.

ROMANOS MELODOS (known 6th century)
Hymn-writer and saint, Romanos Melodos (The Melodist) composed over a thousand works, whose subjects included sacred festivals and saints' lives. About 60 have survived, including Today the Virgin Gives Birth and THOUGH THOU DIDST DESCEND INTO THE TOMB. Medical metaphors used by CHRIST THE PHYSICIAN appear in Romanos' composition on the Passion. Born in Syria, Romanos Melodos is thought to have lived in Constantinople from 515 to 556.

SAMSUN'S HOSPICE
Founded by St Samsun (d 530), a physician and priest. Also known as Sampson or Samson the Hospitable, he is referred to as the Father of the Poor because of his work among the destitute. His hospice was near the GREAT CHURCH.

STRATEGION
Forum in north Constantinople, close to the Golden Horn.

STYLITES
Holy men who often spent years living atop columns. Also known as pillar saints, from *stylos*, pillar.

TESSERAE (Singular: tessera)
Small cubes of stone or glass used in the creation of mosaics.

THANATOS
Personification of death in Greek mythology.

THEODORA (c 497-548)
Influential and powerful wife of JUSTINIAN I. It has been alleged she had formerly been an actress and a prostitute. When the Nika riots broke out in Constantinople in 532, she is said to have urged her husband to remain in the city, thus saving his throne.

THOUGH THOU DIDST DESCEND INTO THE TOMB
See ROMANOS MELODOS.

ZEUS APOMYIOS
According to Greek mythology, Hercules was tormented by flies while performing a religious rite. He therefore sacrificed to Zeus Apomyios (loosely, averter of, or protector from, flies) and the swarm immediately departed.

ZEUXIPPOS
Thracian deity whose name combined Zeus and Hippos (horse).